"I can call my driver to come pick you up."

"You have a driver?" Who has a driver? No one in my university world. Even the university president drives himself. A little sports car, but he still drives.

"I do."

"And you work with Trey?"

"I know," he says. "It's hard to believe."

I look down at my phone again.

No Ubers available.

I glance over at Trey.

He's talking to the hostess.

Seriously? Does the man have no shame?

It was too much.

"Okay," I say, looking into Grayson's smoldering blue eyes waiting patiently. "Let's take your car."

VOW TO PROTECT

Vows of Inheritance Series

(Reading Order)

Vow to Protect

Vow to Redeem

All of the books in the Vows of Inheritance Series are standalone and can be read out of order. However, some books have characters from the previous stories in them.

Contemporary

(ALPINE FALLS)

Secrets and Second Chances

Honeymoon with a Stranger

Not Our Wedding

Stranded in Alpine Falls

Belonging in Alpine Falls

The Spirit of Christmas in Alpine Falls

Christmas Wishes in Alpine Falls

Finding True North in Alpine Falls

A Ghost of Christmas Magic in Alpine Falls

(SILVER PINES)

The Way Back to You

Back to Where We Began

When We Were Us

(ONCE UPON FOREVER)

My Forever Guy

Our Forever Love

Forever Vows

Finding Forever

Just Pretend

Just Because

(MAGNETIC NORTH)

Second Chance Kisses

Second Chance Secrets

First Time Charm

Three Broken Rules

Second Chance Destiny

Unexpected Vows

(FALLING FOR CHRISTMAS)

The Heart of Christmas

The Magic of Christmas

In a One Horse Open Sleigh

A Secret Royal Christmas

An Old Fashioned Christmas

(CITY SKYLINE BILLIONAIRES)

Billionaire's Unexpected Landing

Billionaire's Accidental Girlfriend

Billionaire's Fallen Angel

Billionaire's Secret Crush

Billionaire's Barefoot Bride

(TRULY, MADLY, DEEPLY)

The Lady in the Red Dress

On the Edge of Chance

Sealed with a Kiss

Kiss Me at Midnight

The Heart Knows

(STOLEN ECHOES)

When Cupid's Arrow Strikes

Chasing Fireflies

A Chance Encounter

(EDGE OF THE HORIZON)

The Forever Equation

Pretend Boyfriend

All our Tomorrows

Kissing for Keeps

Out of the Blue

The Princess and the Playboy

(RED LIPSTICK KISSES)

Red Lipstick Kisses and Small Town Wishes

Stolen Dances and Big City Chances

Chance Connections and Upside Down Plans

A Christmas Kiss on the Twenty-Fifth

Believe in the Magic of Christmas

All of the books in each Series are standalone and can be read out of order. However, some books have characters from the previous stories in them.

ROMANTASY

(IN THE SPIRIT OF LOVE)

Spirits of the Heart

Out of Dreams and Ashes

Etched Upon the Heart

WESTERN ROMANCE

(LONE STAR HEARTS)

Wanted by a Texas Ranger

Saved by a Texas Ranger

(WHISKEY SPRINGS)

Finding Natalie

Promising Samantha

Falling for Allyson

Saving Savannah

Claiming Charlie

Rescuing Keira

Protecting Gabriella

Courting Isabella

TIME TRAVEL

(INTO THE MIST)

Written in the Wind

Scripted in the Stars

Destined in the Twilight

Promised in the Mist

Trapped in the Melody

(DRAGON'S BLOOD)

Dragon's Blood

Lavender Blue

Champagne Silver

Twilight Frost

Mountbatten Pink

(WHEN HEARTSTRINGS BECKON)

Rescued in Time

Meet me in 1879

(WHEN HEARTSTRINGS ECHO)

Messages Across Time

Falling Through to Forever

Once Upon a Winter's Spell

(BECKONED)

Before the Storm

Twist of Fate

When the Stars Align

Once Upon a Christmas

Once in a Blue Moon

A Wish Upon a Star

(BEGUILED)

When Lightning Strikes

Storm of Time

Midnight Storm

When the Moon Falls

Stormborn Angel

(SPELLED)

Time Tempest

The Heart Remembers

A Moment in Time

Moonlight Shadows

HISTORICAL

(TAPESTRY OF BLUE AND GRAY)

Shadows Beneath Magnolia Blooms

Secrets Among Southern Roses

(IT HAPPENED BY ACCIDENT)

Accidentally Alluring

Accidentally Married

(SOUTHERN BELLE CIVIL WAR)

Beyond Enemy Lines

Love Always

Hearts Under Siege

Hearts Under Fire

Away Down South in Dixie

The Reluctant Bride

Stay with Me

Jasmine Kisses

Magnolia Kisses

Gardenia Kisses

(THE QUINNS)

Wait for Me

Take Me Home

Keep Me Safe

FATED MATES

Riley's Mate

Aiden's Mate

Brayden's Mate

STANDALONE SUSPENSE

VOW TO PROTECT
THE VOWS OF INHERITANCE

KELLA KALEIGH

CHAPTER
ONE

Emma White

I STAND in front of the old-world gilded oval mirror over the sink in the restroom of the Uptown Speakeasy and examine my face.

I am a mess. A hot mess.

Note to self. Always buy waterproof mascara.

The girl behind the makeup counter had assured me that all their mascara was waterproof. Maybe tears are not considered water due to their high salt content.

A technicality. One that salespeople would certainly use to their advantage. Obviously.

But how was I supposed to know that I'd catch my

boyfriend dry humping the hostess outside on the patio behind one of the potted Japanese maple trees? I almost hadn't seen them behind the vibrant scarlet leaves, but then I'd heard his voice.

Trey Martin had never been known to be quiet in the throes of passion.

He hadn't seen me. Thank. God. But I think the hostess might have. I didn't stay long enough to find out.

"Would you like a cloth?" the lavatory attendant asks, holding out a white washcloth to me.

I glance over at her impassive face. I suppose she's seen everything.

"Okay," I say, taking the cloth from her and just holding it.

"You might dampen it," she says with a little shrug. "Sometimes it helps."

I glance over at the attendant, but she had already walked off, going back to her station in the back corner.

I scowl at the washcloth, then dampen one corner.

Unfortunately the mascara lives up to its name. Waterproof.

Amended note to self. Always bring concealer when showing up early for drinks with boyfriend.

Not that I will be showing up early for anything with this particular boyfriend.

As I stand there contemplating what to do about the mascara on my skin where it doesn't belong, two other young ladies come into the restroom and stand behind me, arms crossed, toes tapping, shooting me impatient glances.

Well. Maybe not really, but that's what I imagine they're doing.

It doesn't matter. I'm not staying here anyway.

All I have to do is walk through the crowded bar and get into an Uber. Should probably schedule that Uber first.

Stepping away from the mirror, I unlock my phone and concentrate on scheduling an Uber.

Apparently this is not a good time of night for Uber availability.

The attendant opens the restroom door for me, letting the loud music from the bar spill in. Big band music to go along with the Speakeasy theme.

And to think this use to be my favorite watering hole.

"He's not worth it," the attendant says, but when I glance over at her, her face is stoic.

Imagining things. Never a good sign.

Turning my attention back to my phone, I find an Uber, but it's not available when I go to book it.

I stop halfway across the bar to the front door and scowl at my phone.

All I need is a way back to my apartment. Trey was supposed to give me a ride home, but there's no way I'll ever see the inside of his Mercedes again.

No available Ubers.

I drop my phone to my side and silently curse Trey in a very unladylike fashion.

"Emma!" Without even turning my head, I know it's Trey, motioning for me to come over to his table.

I ignore him. No Emma here as far as he's concerned.

I take three more steps, while going back to my task of booking an Uber.

"Emma?"

I'm just about to finalize my reservation when I find myself inches from someone else's chest.

Hesitating, I look up right into that broad chest in a white shirt.

I have to tilt my head up to see his face.

His very handsome face.

Strong jaw. Five o'clock shadow.

Kissable lips. And smoldering blue eyes.

I don't know him.

I look back down at my phone.

The Uber I was seconds away from booking is now no longer available.

"Oh no," I say.

"Where are you trying to go?" the handsome man looking down at my phone screen asks.

"Home," I say, finally flicking a glance over at Trey.

Still next to his table, he's standing up now, his arms crossed. A scowl on his face.

Good. Asshole.

"I don't know you," I say, looking back at the handsome stranger still standing inches in front of me. If either one of us swayed an inch, he would be pressed against me.

"I'm Grayson. I work with Trey."

"His friend," I say, distaste in my mouth, moving to step past him. Just what I need. Another asshole. Don't assholes flock together?

He, too, steps aside, blocking me.

"Wouldn't go that far," he says. "We work together. Wouldn't say we're friends."

"How do you know me?" I ask. Maybe he's not an asshole after all.

"He has your picture on the desk we share. I've spent quite a bit of time looking at you."

I find that thought decidedly unsettling. And yet... there's something rather naughtily delicious about it.

"What picture does he have on his desk?"

"You don't know." Grayson seems genuinely surprised by that.

I just shrug. Trey never took me to his office. Never even told me, in fact, that he had a desk.

"You're wearing a black leather jacket and a red scarf around your neck."

I remember that photograph. Trey had taken it last year on Christmas Eve. Right before he took off for a flight. He'd never told me he printed it out and put it on his desk.

I suddenly remember the mascara smudged beneath my eyes.

"I must look quite a bit different," I say, putting a hand to my face.

"I hadn't noticed."

Charming. Too charming.

"Like a raccoon," I say. I press my fingers against the mascara that isn't coming off without using the special mascara removing formula the saleslady had so generously suggested I add to my purchase. It's a good thing. Otherwise I can only guess it would have to wear off.

"I like raccoons."

He says it with such a charming little smile that I actually believe that maybe I don't look quite so bad as I had thought.

Perhaps it's the dim light of the bar. Maybe he can't really see the smudged mascara. Perhaps he only sees shadows on my skin.

I bite my bottom lip as I look at him.

"So," he says. "What about Trey?"

"What about him?" I ask crossly. As far as I'm concerned, Trey no longer exists.

"Do you want me to say something to him?"

The lavatory attendant's words come back to me.

"He's not worth it," I say, repeating what I think she might have said to me. "I need to schedule an Uber."

"You don't need an Uber," he says. "I can take you home."

"Why haven't I met you?" I ask, narrowing my eyes at him.

"Why haven't you been to the office?"

Good point.

"Still. I don't know you."

"Hmm," he says thoughtfully. "Trey could introduce us."

"I think not."

"Or... I can call my driver to come pick you up."

"You have a driver?" Who has a driver? No one in my university world. Even the university president drives himself. A little sports car, but he still drives.

"I do."

"And you work with Trey?"

"I know," he says. "It's hard to believe."

I look down at my phone again.

No Ubers available.

I glance over at Trey.

He's talking to the hostess.

Seriously? Does the man have no shame?

It was too much.

"Okay," I say, looking into Grayson's smoldering blue eyes waiting patiently. "Let's take your car."

CHAPTER
TWO

Emma

I'M NOT in the habit of getting into cars with men I don't know, but the satisfaction of knowing that Trey sees me leave with Grayson overrides any sense of caution.

Besides, Grayson obviously really does know me. He shares a desk with Trey. It's plausible enough to be believable.

The only thing that throws me off about the whole thing is that Trey actually has a photo of me on his desk. Very unexpected. All but unbelievable.

We stand outside the bar, the music pounding against the closed door as though it's trying to get out.

When a luxurious black SUV rolls up and stops in front of us, Grayson opens the back passenger door. "After you," he says.

At least if I'm going to be kidnapped, I'm being kidnapped in style.

I climb into the backseat of the car, sliding across the buttery soft black leather seat.

Grayson climbs in behind me and sits close enough that our thighs touch.

I move away, but he only shifts closer. I can't keep moving away without being obvious and ending up squished against the door on my left.

"What's your address?" he asks.

I rattle it off.

Grayson repeats it to the driver, a man he addresses as James.

"Got it, Sir," James says, then presses a button that raises a panel separating us from the front of the car.

I turn and with a raised eyebrow, look at Grayson.

He shrugs.

"So you just pick up strange girls all the time?"

"Every chance I get," he says with a frighteningly straight face. "But you're my first raccoon girl."

I choke back a laugh. "You're funny."

"Just be glad you're Trey's girlfriend."

"Ex-girlfriend," I say, wondering what he means by that, but not daring to ask.

"Does he know that?"

The driver turns right and with nothing to hold onto, I find myself pressed against Grayson's shoulder.

"I think he's known it longer than I have," I say.

"The hostess?" he asks.

"You saw them, too?" I ask.

"I have seen them," he says carefully.

"Oh. My. God." I press my fingers against my brow. "How could I be that stupid?"

"If I had known you," he says. "I would have told you."

"Right."

"You don't believe me," he says.

"Why wouldn't I believe you? Are you not trustworthy?"

"I'm very trustworthy. Exceptionally so."

"Are you now?"

The driver merges us onto the freeway and I'm stupidly happy to see that there's a traffic jam bringing us to a stop.

"I am."

I turn and look out the window at the cars lined up impatiently waiting for the traffic to move.

"Would you like some champagne?" Grayson asks.

"You have champagne?"

"Have you never been in a chauffeured car?"

"Not like this," I say with a glance around the back seat, the only light coming from the moonroof and the side windows.

He shifts away from me and lets down a little door between us revealing two glasses and a bottle of chilled champagne.

After twisting out the cork, he pours bubbly wine into two glasses and hands one to me before closing the little wine door and sitting back again.

"To Houston traffic," he says, then taps his glass against mine.

As a blush slowly creeps up my mascara laden cheeks, I wonder how he had read my mind about being happy about the traffic.

The champagne is sweet and bubbly on my tongue.

The car moves forward a little, then stops again.

"So... did you get stood up by a date or something?" I ask.

He looks confused a moment.

"I didn't have a date tonight."

"Then you always travel in a chauffeured car?" I run my left hand along the buttery soft seat.

"Yes."

"Yes? You don't like to drive?"

"I like to drive on occasion," he says. "but I much prefer flying."

Of course he does. If he shares a desk with Trey, he's a pilot. Like Trey.

"You're very evasive," I say.

"I prefer to think of myself as mysterious."

The car is moving again now. I mentally calculate that we have approximately twenty minutes before we arrive at my apartment near the university, barring any further traffic.

Grayson puts an arm behind me on the back of the seat, drawing my attention to his broad chest.

"How long have you been a pilot?" I ask, mostly to distract myself from looking at him.

"About ten years."

And now I'm looking at him again.

"You don't look that old."

"I'll take that as a compliment," he says. "I got my license when I was nineteen."

He's twenty-nine. I might be a psychology professor but I can do basic math in my head. He's three years older than Trey.

Right now those three years seem to make a huge difference.

"How did you do that?"

"I had access to airplanes and helicopters at a young age."

"Evasive," I say again, taking another sip of my champagne.

"What's a girl like you doing with a guy like Trey?"

I breathe out slowly. "Not with him."

"Sorry. What *were* you doing with him?"

"He seemed nice," I say, thinking back to the day I'd met him. "And he was very persistent."

"Persistence works with you?" he asks with a little smile.

I cut my eyes at him.

"What? I'm just taking notes."

"Not always. I needed a date to a university thing and he offered."

"I remember that," Grayson says. "It was about this time last year."

"You have a frighteningly good memory."

"I rather have to. Being a pilot and all."

"I see."

He's sitting even closer to me now and I hadn't noticed that he'd moved.

Grayson not only has a very good memory, he has some very smooth moves.

"Do you have a car?" I ask, grasping at the first thing that comes to mind.

"It bothers you that I have a chauffeur."

"It's... unusual. You have to admit. Right?"

"Is it? I hadn't realized."

"You're strange."

He smiles. "Probably."

I cut my eyes at him and take a sip of champagne.

"What are you doing tomorrow? Now that you're single?"

Good question. Tomorrow is Saturday. The day I usually use to catch up on errands and lecture prep.

"I don't have any plans." At least nothing exciting that I can share with a man who travels in a chauffeured SUV.

In fact, I can't even think up anything that might impress such a man. Perhaps if were having lunch at a country club with the ladies. Or...

"Have lunch with me."

I shake my head. "It's Saturday."

"And I'm confused."

"Saturday is the day I catch up on lecture preps and do errands." There. I'm boring. What can I say?

"Okay. Do your lectures in the morning and after lunch I'll help you do your errands."

"I'm pretty sure you don't want to go grocery shopping." A little bubble of panic is in my throat. Does he really want to go with me to do errands?

"Then give me a list and I'll send someone to do your errands."

"I don't think so," I say.

"Okay. Then grocery shopping it is."

I stare at him as we exit off the freeway. Twelve minutes out now.

I glance down at my glass to see just how much champagne I had, but I've barely touched it.

It's not the alcohol that has my brain all fuzzy.

It's Grayson.

CHAPTER

THREE

Grayson

I HADN'T BEEN PLANNING on going to the Uptown Speakeasy tonight.

I had, in fact, been planning NOT to go simply because I'd known that Trey was meeting Emma here.

Maybe that was unconsciously the reason behind my last minute decision to head in that direction.

The Speakeasy is a place where mostly couples hang out. That's probably the thing I like least about it. Otherwise, I like the music and I like the vibe. 1920s.

But on the other hand, since mostly couples hang out here, there aren't so many women hitting on me. That's definitely a plus. And, besides, it helps that no one knows who I am there. Can't say the same for some of the other places I frequent.

I knew that Trey had been seeing the hostess, the tall leggy blonde one, on the side. I'd seen them talking the last time he and I were there. Talking with those looks that reveal something naughty is definitely happening.

Watching them talk, it had been hard not to think about Emma's meadow green eyes and pretty smile. I hadn't been lying when I'd admitted to spending a lot of time looking at her photo.

Her hair is longer now. It just skims her shoulders in the photo, but now curls over her shoulders.

The thing that really hits me in the gut is the smudge of mascara beneath her eyes.

I know a girl who's been crying when I see one.

Since I hadn't known Emma personally until now, I hadn't seen it as my place to tell her about Trey and his tendency to wander. Trust me. The leggy blonde hostess is definitely not the first or only.

It might have been a little creepy if I'd gone to the trouble to look her up to tell her that Trey is a cad.

Unfortunately, Emma had to discover it for herself. Perhaps it was better that way. This way she can't question the source.

She had caught Trey red-handed.

I do find it rather interesting, however, that she didn't confront him.

Intriguing actually.

Most women would have been in his face. If not for the mascara smudges beneath her eyes, I'd think that there was something wrong with her.

Emma chose to simply walk out without speaking to him. I suppose there is some satisfaction for her in letting him see her leave with another man.

Me being the other man. With most situations like this, I would expect an impending fist fight, but Trey has no ground to stand on. He'd been wrong and he knows it.

A real man would have let Emma go before toying with the next girl. It's men like Trey who give pilots a bad name and unfortunately I'd flown with him enough to know that he dallies with ladies every chance he gets where he can get it.

It takes a lot of boldness to do what Trey had done. To make out with the hostess when he knew good and well that his girlfriend was on her way.

Shouldn't be surprised. Trey has always struck me as one those entitled pricks who don't care what they do to others as long they get what they want.

By the time I'd gotten to the speakeasy, Trey was already with the hostess on the back patio behind the potted Japanese maple trees.

I had simply rolled my eyes and walked off, finding myself a stool at the bar and ordering a martini.

I'd abandoned the untouched martini when I'd seen

Emma come out of the restroom, her face a mess from crying.

I'd been prepared to intervene between her and Trey, but that hadn't been necessary.

Never one to leave a damsel in distress, I intercepted her before she could vanish into the night.

She was a whole lot prettier than she was in the photograph and that was saying something.

The little pout she wore now was a whole lot sexier than the pretty wholesome smile she'd worn in the photograph.

Not that I was complaining about her either way.

I'm making an impromptu game plan as I go.

So far my game plan is to see how quickly I can make her forget about Trey.

Trey isn't fit to wipe her boots. Or in this case, her heels.

James drove us toward the university, reminding me that Emma is a university professor. It's hard to remember. She looks nothing like any professor I ever had.

If I'd had a professor who looked like her, I'd probably still be in college.

"Are you going to be okay?" I ask her as we turn into a gated community.

"Of course," she says.

"Anything I can do?" I ask, pressing my knee a little closer to hers.

"You got me home," she says, not seeming to notice that our knees are touching. "That was all I needed. Thank you."

James pulls up in front of a duplex and parks.

"Is this it?" I ask her.

She glances out the window. "Yes."

I make no move to open the door and James knows to stay in the car. Something he and I worked out years ago.

She looks at me questioningly.

"We have time to finish our champagne," I say.

"I should probably go inside."

"Suit yourself," I say, still not moving.

She takes another little sip of champagne, then hands her glass to me.

"I'll pick up you tomorrow at eleven thirty," I say, fully expecting her to come up with an excuse to get out of our lunch date any minute.

"Okay," she says. "but don't say I didn't warn you."

"Warn me?"

"We have lots of errands, so wear comfortable shoes."

I grin. She's obviously telling me that she'll be wearing comfortable shoes.

"I'll walk you to the door," I say, sliding over a bit toward my door.

"That's not necessary."

I stop and look at her. "Are you telling me that your other boyfriends don't walk you to the door?"

"Sometimes," she says.

I make a clicking sound with my tongue.

"I'll never understand why ladies settle these days."

Holding both almost full glasses in one hand, not sure

what to do with them, I open the door and step out of the car. After setting the glasses on the ground next to the car, I turn back to help her out, but she's already sliding her feet out of the car.

With a challenging glance at me, she holds out a hand for me to help her out of the car and puts her hand in mine.

As a pilot, I've assisted hundreds of ladies in and out of airplanes. Extending a hand to help is not only polite, it's expected.

But I've never felt such a rush through such a common hand to hand connection.

I don't release her delicate fingers as we walk down the sidewalk and through the cast iron gate leading to her front door.

I notice her fingers trembling a little as she presses her finger on the sensor pad.

"Well," she says, turning the doorknob, but not opening the door. "Goodnight."

"Goodnight," I say with a mischievous grin. "Sleep well."

She pushes the door open and steps inside.

I stand there until I hear her turn the deadbolt.

Things just got a whole lot more interesting.

CHAPTER
FOUR

Emma

I THROW THE DEADBOLT, then turn around to see Oscar bounding happily toward me.

"Hey, sweetie," I say, picking up my white flame-point Himalayan cat. Oscar must weigh twenty pounds, but he snuggles and purrs in my arms like a kitten.

I carry him to the kitchen and open up a can of cat food. Oscar jumps on the island counter and rubs his face against my hand as I dump his food onto a plate.

While he eats, I check my cell phone for messages.

None.

I lean my elbows on the counter and scowl at my phone.

Trey could have at least asked if I was okay.

But nothing. Not a word.

Asshole.

I set my phone down and watch Oscar gobble up his food.

I'd dated Trey for just about a year to the day.

And all this time, I'd thought he was a decent guy.

Or maybe I'd wanted him to be a decent guy.

Truth is, he'd suited my lifestyle.

He didn't bother me at work. He didn't bother me when I was working at home which was pretty much all the time.

We met for drinks about once a week and had dinner about every other week.

It had been enough.

We'd never talked about taking our relationship to the next level.

It crossed my mind on occasion. I'm not getting any younger, after all, but chasing tenure is a full-time job that takes all my focus.

And now there is Grayson.

I'm not sure how Grayson slid into my life so seamlessly as he had, but I have the distinct feeling that Grayson requires more energy and attention than Trey ever had.

Grayson does not seem to be the kind of guy who just shows up occasionally for dinner or maybe just drinks.

Maybe he'd been kidding about doing errands with me tomorrow.

Surely he'd been kidding.

A guy who travels around town in a chauffeured car isn't the kind of guy who would walk around in the supermarket buying apples and bottles of water.

If he has a chauffeur, he probably has everything delivered.

After filling Oscar's' dry cat food bowl and putting fresh water in his bowl, I head upstairs to my bathroom.

With a groan at how bad my face looks, I turn on the hot water.

It takes special mascara remover and four cotton balls to clean up my eyes before I even have a need for the hot water.

More trouble than Trey was worth, I decide as I change into my pajamas and go back downstairs to sit on my sofa and read. Nothing fun tonight. I've got to get ahead on reviewing my abnormal psychology textbook.

I've taught abnormal before, but a new textbook requires reading and new PowerPoint presentations.

After about an hour of reading with Oscar curled up next to me, his head nestled beneath the book, I decide that the current chapter on anxiety is close enough to the one in my previous textbook that I don't have to redo my notes.

Just a few updates and I'll be good.

Setting my book aside, I pull Oscar into my lap.

"I hope you don't mind," I tell him. "Trey won't be coming around anymore."

Oscar makes a noise that sounds suspiciously like an impending hairball.

"You get to meet someone new tomorrow," I say. "His name is Grayson."

Oscar purrs.

"My thoughts exactly," I say.

CHAPTER
FIVE

Grayson

I'm having coffee the next morning when James comes in the back door of my high rise condo.

"Good morning, Sir," he says.

"Good morning James. Coffee?"

"Sounds good," James walks over to the coffee machine and proceeds to make himself a cup of coffee.

"How would you like to have the day off?" I ask.

"Wouldn't complain," he says. "Need me to do anything first?"

"No. Just take the day off. I think me having a driver makes Emma uncomfortable."

"Emma. The young lady from last night."

"That's right."

James grins. "I'll be around if you change your mind." He taps his hand on the counter then picks up his coffee mug. "And I'll go ahead and run the car through the car wash."

"You're a good man," I say.

"She seems like a nice girl."

"I think so, too."

James has a super power about girls. He can tell whether a girl is a keeper when she so much as sits in the back seat. He's never been wrong yet.

James wanders back down the hallway to what I had designated as the staff room.

My condo is on the thirty-first floor of the Arabella High Rise building. It actually IS the thirty-first floor. Three elevator entrances. One of them my private elevator.

The staff have their own entrance and their own room where they can sleep overnight if they need to. My assistant coordinates all that, but mostly they work it out themselves.

I got lucky and have some good people on my staff.

I open up my iPad and go about my daily routine of checking the news. The stocks. Everything related to my business.

But my attention wanders.

I'm rather looking forward to my day with Emma.

She thinks I won't enjoy doing errands with her, but the truth is, I find the idea refreshing.

I can't remember the last time I spent time with someone who does their own errands.

It'll be fun.

But then I'm biased. I'm pretty sure that anything that allows me to look at the real life version of Emma will be enjoyable.

I'm not going in to the office today and I don't have any flights scheduled, so my day is clear. Even if it hadn't been clear, I would have cleared it.

I halfway expected a message from Trey, but the other half of me isn't the least bit surprised that I haven't heard from him.

Trey is one of those guys who just doesn't care. He's what my mother calls a cad.

I call him a player.

Emma deserves so much more than Trey.

I just hope she realizes that and her tears were more from shock at seeing her boyfriend make a spectacle of himself than any lingering love lost.

A college professor, she should understand that.

I realize I don't know what she teaches.

How could I not know that?

Because Trey hadn't told me, that's how.

He put her photograph on his desk for display, but it's just that. For display.

Marking his territory. Making himself look good and all that.

Not from any sense of loyalty.

Closing my iPad, I walk down to my bedroom toward the shower, stopping to admire the view from up here.

With a pilot's heart, for me there is no better place to live than in the sky. Floor to ceiling windows. I can look over the whole city from up here.

Uptown with all its retail traffic on the west. Downtown, a cluster of buildings that look like toys. And everything in between.

A jet plane silently drifts through the sky as I stand there. I watch it until it vanishes over the horizon.

Not a cloud in the sky. It's going to be a beautiful day.

Or it was until my cell phone vibrates in my hand.

My father. Summoning me in for a meeting. By text.

That's my father. Never just inviting me over for a visit. Always a summons.

As such my shower is a quick one.

My father lives in a mansion in River Oaks guarded behind a stone wall and a gated entrance.

Since I'd given James the day off, I drive up to the gate, wave at the guard, and drive around the circle drive of what can only be called a courtyard.

I hadn't grown up here. Not exactly. I'd grown up in a boarding school and visited my family here during the holidays.

At the boarding school for the affluent, no one had cared how my parents lived. They had actually assumed that we were all from similar backgrounds. And since we were, no one cared and no one was impressed by anyone else.

I suppose I wasn't so much different. Buying my own floor in a luxury high rise. That was different, though. It *feels* different from this ridiculously huge mansion.

My mother meets me at the door. She is light whereas my father is darkness.

"There's my favorite son," she says, giving me a fierce hug.

Everyone knows she says that to all of us and everyone knows that our youngest brother is her favorite, but we indulge her. She is our mother, after all.

If we learned nothing else at boarding school, it was to respect and cherish our family.

"Don't let my brothers hear you say that," I say, hugging her back.

"Well. They aren't here, are they?"

So it's not a family meeting.

"Do you know what Father wants?" I ask.

She waves a hand in dismissal and I follow her back to the kitchen.

"You know how your father is. It's always something with him."

That means he didn't tell her.

I honestly believe that my parents love each other. Or

that my father loves her at any rate. How could he not? Mother is everything lovely and bright.

As for what draws her to him, I'm not so sure. What I do know is that Mother would not stay with him if she didn't want to. My mother is one of the strongest women I've ever met.

She has a business of her own and doesn't need him financially, especially now that the kids are all grown.

"I'll make you a coffee, then he can have you."

I wince. Despite her denial I have a feeling she has an inkling what this meeting is about.

In fact, I'm certain she does. Mother knows everything Father does in both his business and his personal life. It's her super power.

And if my father has any sense, he knows how fortunate he is. My mother has a better head for business than most men, including my father.

I take the mug of coffee and head down the hallway toward my father's study. My feelings of dread increase with every step.

As usual, my father's study smells like tobacco smoke, even though I know for a fact that Mother doesn't let him smoke in the house.

He sits behind a mammoth polished executive desk. He looks up when I walk in.

"Close the door," he says, not even breaking a smile.

I close the door and take a seat in one of two leather seats positioned in front of his desk.

Not how have you been or it's good to see you.

Like always, he's wearing a business suit, but his tie is loosened a bit.

He pulls off his glasses and looks at me. That's his tell. He has something important to tell me.

I hold his gaze. I'm not afraid of my father. His bark is worse than his bite and I know it.

What I am afraid of is his power. The man has more power than any one man should have.

I also know that he doesn't take no for an answer.

As is his way, he foregoes the small talk. Accustomed to being in charge.

"You're going to be thirty next month," he says.

I give him a nod of agreement.

Father leans back in his chair, looking comfortable. That's also part of his tell. Whenever he leans back and gets comfortable, he's about to throw a curveball. A lion about to pounce.

I force myself to remain calm on the outside, but I reflexively tense on the inside.

"I probably should have already talked to you about your grandfather's will."

That's as close to an admission of making a mistake that I can remember my father ever saying out loud.

"Grandfather has been gone for five years," I say, not giving him a break. Whatever it is, I have absolutely no doubt that he should indeed have already brought it up.

"I know. I thought things would naturally... work themselves out, but... apparently that's not the case."

"What kinds of things?"

"In order for you to continue to receive your trust fund, you have to be married by the time you're thirty-years-old."

I press back against the chair, not believing what I'm hearing. He may as well have slammed a fist into my face.

"Grandpa would never do that."

"Grandpa did that."

"Why?"

My thoughts fly. I don't need the trust fund. I have my own business.

"He believed that a responsible man would settle down and start a family before getting into his third decade on this earth."

I gape at him. Not saying anything.

"After talking with the attorneys, they've agreed to use the loophole that gives you an extra six months to actually have a wedding under the condition that you're engaged by your birthday."

"This is ridiculous," I say. "You can keep the trust fund. I don't need it. You know I have my own company."

"And you know who cosigned for the funding of your company," he says.

Father did. Father cosigned for everything.

"I'm solvent in my own right."

"Not disputing that," Father says, sounding suddenly weary.

"Then what?"

"You forfeit your inheritance if you don't meet the terms."

The terms. He was talking about taking a wife as though it was a business transaction.

I open my mouth to tell him I don't need my inheritance. I can make it just fine on my own.

But no words come out. I think about my mother. She was Grandpa's daughter and she's counting on her children to carry on her father's legacy.

"I need to think about it," I say.

He wanted to treat this like a business meeting, I could do the same.

My grandfather had actually been the one to teach me not to make hasty decisions.

Always think about it before you agree to anything. Sleep on it. One night minimum. A week is better. Don't do anything in haste.

"Of course," Father says, also trained by Grandpa. "I would expect no less. But know that I have two business associates with daughters suitable for you to marry."

Good God. I've met enough daughters of my father's business associates. No way in hell will I shackle myself to one of them. Business associates or not, they're social climbers, one and all.

"I don't need you to find me a wife," I say. "I already have a girlfriend." The words, as untrue as they are just spill out of my mouth. An unreasonable response to an unreasonable demand.

"She has to be suitable," he says with something far too close to disdain in his voice. "To come from a good family."

"If she didn't come from a good family," I say. "I wouldn't be dating her."

Father studies me a moment.

"Very well," he says. "You have two weeks."

"My birthday is in three."

"No sense in waiting to the last minute." His tone is laced with irony.

"I'll think about it," I say again.

"It's for your own good.'"

"I have no doubt." Now my tone is full of irony I don't even try to disguise.

CHAPTER
SIX

Emma

"Can you come over?" My grandmother's voice comes through the line, sounding frantic enough that I sit up in bed.

I shove the eye mask off my eyes and glance at the time. "It's not even seven o'clock in the morning."

"I know," she says, resorting to tears. "But our parakeet got out."

Groaning, I put a hand over my eyes.

And what am I supposed to do about a parakeet getting out? But I don't ask it out loud. I don't even ask when she got a parakeet. It seems too much like a conversation for later. Or maybe never.

"How did that happen?" I ask, mustering as much empathy as I can after having been so rudely awakened at six forty-five in the morning.

"Franny left the door open," she says.

Franny is my grandmother's older sister. Franny has a light case of early dementia. At least that's what the doctors call it.

Franny's in her mid-seventies, so it's not all that early and sometimes it's not all that light.

Like this morning.

"Parakeets get out when the door is left open," I say.

"I know. But can you come find it?"

"Of course," I say, already resigned. Being a good grand-daughter most definitely comes with a cost. And I had promised my mother I'd look after them. "I have to get dressed."

"Just throw on something and get here as soon as you can. Franny is beside herself." She whimpers. My grand-mother always resorts to hysterical tears when she wants me to do something crazy.

"She's *your* sister," I mumble.

"What's that?"

"I said I'll be right there. Just try to stay calm."

Grandmom hangs up the phone. No goodbye. Just hangs up.

Sometimes I wonder if maybe I was switched at birth.

Sometimes I hope I was switched at birth.

But I get up, throw on some sweatpants and shoes, brush my teeth, and feed Oscar before I head out.

"I won't be long," I tell my cat as I throw my purse over my shoulder. "Just however long it takes to find your aunt's bird."

Oscar stops eating long enough to glance up at me, then goes right on back to eating.

"Exactly," I say and lock the door behind me.

There's no traffic this time of day on a Saturday morning and I make it to my grandmother's house in twenty minutes. It's a small one story house in an older neighborhood. Safe enough. Everyone watches out for everyone else, meaning everyone knows everyone else's business.

The front yard looks normal enough. Freshly mown lawn. Sidewalk with a couple of cracks. A black mailbox on a post that leans a little to the left.

The house could use a coat of paint, but it's not noticeable from the street.

Any normalcy ends at the door.

Inside, the furniture is old and doesn't match. Grandmom and Aunt Franny had combined their belongings when they moved in together and there taste is completely different.

There's a dark brown leather sofa and a green plaid couch that looks like it came from the last century.

Aunt Franny is pacing the floor. Grandmom is trying to

calm her down by trying to get her to drink water from a bottle. Aunt Franny is having nothing of it.

The parakeet's cage is wide open. I don't even want to know how the cage just happened to get left open at the same time as the back door.

"He just flew," Franny says, flapping her arms wide like a bird. "I couldn't stop him."

This is one of those times when I really, really hope I was swapped at birth. Or at least adopted.

"Did you look outside?" I ask Grandmom.

"A little," she says. "but I can't leave Franny alone like this.

"Of course not," I say. "I'll go outside and look."

I walk out the back door of my grandmother's house where her sister lives with her.

The back yard is littered with vegetable plants scattered about. It doesn't look like a lawn at all. It looks like some kind of randomly planted vegetable garden.

A tomato plant next to a carrot plant next to a stalk of corn.

It's all as very strange as it sounds.

My grandmother indulges her sister's strange ideas almost to a fault.

But it's not my business.

Standing outside in the backyard/garden, I take a quick survey.

I don't see the bright blue parakeet anywhere.

I don't even know how much parakeets can fly.

A quick google search tells me that parakeets can indeed fly with some exceptions.

Aunt Franny comes to the back door with Grandmom right behind her.

"Can he fly?" I ask looking over my shoulder.

"Franny had his wings clipped so he can't fly more than a little," Grandmom says.

"Then he can't have gone far," I say as though I'm an authority on parakeets which I most certainly am not.

"Where did he go?" Aunt Franny wrings her hands. "I'm so worried."

I slowly walk around the yard, avoiding stepping on any kind of plant sprouting out of the ground. Stepping over anything that could be a weed that doesn't look like a weed.

I look behind the tool shed. I search the limbs of the maple tree in the back corner by the fence. I look *in* the tool shed.

"I'll have to check with the neighbors," I say, deciding the little parakeet is most certainly not in the back yard.

"We'll make flyers," Grandmom announces.

By *we* I know she means *me*.

"I need coffee," I say. "Then I'll go check with the neighbors."

"I'll make us coffee," Aunt Franny says.

"Thank you, Aunt Franny."

I check the time on my phone.

I'm supposed to be working.

Less than four hours before my date with Grayson.

I can't cancel. I don't have his phone number.

This day is most certainly not going as planned.

I sit at the kitchen table and google missing parakeets. What to do. How to lure them home.

Franny hands me a mug of hot, but instant coffee.

I look over at Grandmom, but she's busy cleaning out the parakeet's cage.

"Do you have any milk?" I ask Aunt Franny. "For the coffee?"

Aunt Franny pulls a carton of milk out of the refrigerator and hands it to me.

I sigh. There's going to be a stop at Starbuck's on my way home.

I pour a dash of milk into my coffee and after stirring it into a light mocha color, I look around for some kind of sweetener.

Just as I'm scowling with my first bitter sip, a commotion ensues in the laundry room.

Grandmom and Franny dash toward the laundry room and I follow at a slower pace.

"Enzo," Aunt Franny says, holding up her hand.

The little blue parakeet lands on her shoulder.

"I didn't think I'd ever see you again," Aunt Franny coos.

"I have to go," I say.

"Don't be a stranger," Aunt Franny says, still cooing at Enzo, the purportedly missing little blue parakeet.

CHAPTER
SEVEN

Grayson

At eleven o'clock, I ride down the private elevator taking me to the valet where my car will be waiting.

I'd taken a shower, my second one of the day and it's not even noon, to wash off the distaste left behind from my meeting with my father and at the same time tucked the new information into the back of my mind.

After my meeting, my mother had been nowhere to be found. That told me one thing. She knew.

She knew what her father had done to me.

Had he done this to my brothers as well? My educated

guess was yes. He had absolutely done the same thing to my brothers.

I have to stew on it before I decide to tell them. It's a matter of when not if.

As the oldest son, I'm not going to put my younger brothers through the hell of finding out at the last minute that they have to marry by thirty or else be cut out of their inheritance.

I'm the only one of us four brothers who has the luxury of only halfway caring. I'm the only one of us who has been successful in establishing a seven figure business.

Without our inheritance none of us will hit ten figures. Not even me.

True to his word, James has my Lamborghini SUV clean and shiny inside and out.

The valet opens my door and I climb into the driver's seat. Nothing like that new car smell.

As I drive off, I decide I need to take Emma flowers. By the time I reach the flower shop and park, I've changed my mind.

It's just lunch and errands. Lunch and errands don't call for flowers.

I sit in the car, tapping my fingers on the steering wheel while music blares from the stereo.

Three weeks.

I have three weeks to get engaged.

But that is not my plan.

Emma is not part of my plan even if I do entertain my father's... what was it... ultimatum.

Technically my grandfather's ultimatum.

My father simply got caught being the one to deliver it. Still. I blame him.

He could have told me five years ago.

Cursing under my breath, I get out of the car and storm into the flower shop.

Ten minutes later I walk out with a bouquet of six pink tulips along with a much better mood than I had walked in with. Something about picking out flowers for a pretty girl will do that to a man.

I determine to shove my conversation with my father into the back of my mind.

I jump on the freeway heading to Emma's apartment.

Today is going to be a good day.

I'm going to just enjoy it. To enjoy being with her. Going to lunch. Doing whatever errands she has to do.

Tomorrow I'll worry about my conversation with my father.

Today I will be at Emma's beck and call.

I can truly think of nothing I'd rather do today.

CHAPTER
EIGHT

Emma

I can't remember getting dressed for lunch ever being so hard.

By the time I decide on a pair of black jeans and a long shirt-tailed button-down topped with a black leather jacket, I have clothes scattered all across my bed and no time to hang them back up.

After debating between my little black leather ankle boots and my white sneakers, I go with the white sneakers. I'm the one who suggested walking shoes.

I still have to do my hair.

If not for the unplanned parakeet incident, I might have splurged for a blow out, but there was no time.

So I heat up my hair straightener and get to work on my hair. It's not a professional blow out, but it'll have to do.

I hesitate before applying mascara to my lashes, but today is a day for fun. No mascara smudges in the forecast.

A little lip gloss and I declare myself ready.

I tuck my little shopping list in my purse. I rewrote it three times, taking off things I can pick up later. By myself.

Today I'm just doing the basics. Like cat food and bottled water.

Oscar follows me down the stairs, his tail high, knowing he's going to get lunch before I leave the house.

I fill his dry food bowl, then open up a can of cat food for him. He rubs his face against my hand while I rake it out with a spoon and stir it up.

I wash my hands and look around while I dry them.

I'm nervous now.

Grayson will be here any minute.

Fortunately, I keep a clean house. Tidy. Uncluttered.

I haven't lived here long enough to accumulate any clutter. Besides, I like to keep things simple.

Most of my time is spent at my computer desk tucked beneath the staircase where I prepare my lectures or sitting on my sofa where I read textbooks with Oscar as my constant companion.

He tolerates me being gone three days a week to teach

at the university and he's always happy to see me when I get home.

I sit on the sofa to wait, pick up my iPad, and read about two words of a new article about major depressive disorder, then give up and close the iPad.

Pacing back to where Oscar is still eating, I stop and tap my fingers on the counter and realize I should have painted my fingernails.

I am most definitely overthinking this date with Grayson.

I check the time. It's eleven twenty-five.

He might not even show up. Maybe something came up or he changed his mind. He doesn't have my number so he can't call me.

Surely he wouldn't be bold enough to ask Trey for my phone number.

When a car pulls up in my driveway, I give Oscar a quick hug.

"I won't be long," I tell him. "Just take a nap or watch the birds outside."

I take a deep breath.

No reason to be nervous.

Grayson has already seen me at my worst with mascara smeared beneath my eyes.

And yet he still came back.

No reason to be nervous.

Maybe if I keep telling myself that, I'll start to believe it.

Although he's outside, I count to ten after he knocks on the door to open it.

"Hi," I say with a smile.

"Hi." He smiles back.

Oh my. He looks even more handsome than I remembered. Maybe it's the light. I'd only seen him in the darkness after all.

He's wearing dark blue jeans, a white button down shirt, and like me, white sneakers.

Before I can comment on his good choice of shoes, he sweeps a bouquet of pink tulips from behind his back and holds them out to me.

"Oh," I say. "They're beautiful." Six pink tulips wrapped in florist's paper.

I hadn't decided if I was going to invite him in, but now I have to. Now I have to put the flowers in water.

"Come in," I say. "I'll put these in some water."

He steps inside and I close the door behind him.

"Nice place," he says.

I leave him standing in the living room and walk over to the kitchen for a vase. I only have one and it's a little dusty which says a lot for the state of my love life. Trey had never brought me flowers. Not in the year we had dated. Hadn't sent any either.

After I fill the vase with water, I notice that Oscar is still sitting on the kitchen island. His food bowl empty.

He's washing his front paws, but he's watching Grayson.

"This is Oscar," I say, putting the vase of flowers on the island.

"Hello Oscar," Grayson says, holding out a hand in Oscar's general direction.

Oscar walks over and rubs his face on Grayson's hand.

"I hope you don't mind cats."

"I like cats."

"He likes you," I say, surprised. "A little unusual. Do you have cats?"

"Nah. I'm gone too much to have a pet."

"Right. Of course." A pilot.

Like Trey.

As far as I can tell, that's where the resemblance stops.

Oscar always ignored Trey. It was something of a mutual disdain between the two of them.

"Can I borrow your mom for a few hours?" Grayson asks Oscar.

Oscar rolls onto his back and purrs.

"I guess that means yes," he says.

"I guess it does. Little traitor."

We walk to the door and step outside into the pleasantly cool air.

"Don't you love autumn?" Grayson asks.

"I do, actually. Sometimes I wonder why I live in a place that only has a few weeks of it."

He opens the passenger door. So he's driving today.

"Are you from Houston?"

"Born and raised," I say, climbing up into the SUV.

"Me too," he says, then closes the door and walks around to the driver's side.

Nice car. Clean. New.

"No driver today?" I ask as he slides into the driver's seat.

"I gave him the day off. Thought we could have some alone time."

"Okay," I say.

"Any preference for lunch?" he asks, backing out of my driveway.

"Surprise me," I say.

"Okay," he says, glancing over at me with an approving glance. "I'll take you to my favorite French café."

"You aren't good at keeping secrets, are you?" I ask.

He laughs.

"Busted. No. I'm not."

But something seems to be bothering him as he drives, heading toward the freeway.

Apparently we're heading toward Uptown away from the university district.

"I don't even know what you teach," he says, finally breaking the silence.

"Psychology."

"Oh no. I guess I have to be on my good behavior."

"Trust me," I say. "You don't have to worry about that."

"You don't analyze people?"

"Of course I do, but if you knew my family, you'd understand just how much you don't have to worry."

He shoots me a concerned look, but doesn't say anything.

I don't usually mention my crazy family to anyone.

My grandmother isn't so bad, except that she's always with Aunt Franny who has her days more often than not. Then there's my uncle who no longer lives with Aunt Franny. Anyone who meets my uncle instantly understands just why I went into psychology. Unconsciously of course, but I've accepted that has to be there as one of those reasons.

We ride in silence along the freeway, then he exits onto Westheimer, pulling into a little shopping area I didn't even know was there.

He glances down at my shoes.

"It's a little bit of a walk," he says, looking over me with his smoldering blue eyes.

"I don't mind."

And I really don't. If nothing else, I need to walk off some of this energy he stirs up in my blood.

CHAPTER
NINE

Grayson

It's a pleasant walk to the little French restaurant.

As is typical on Saturdays, there are lots of people walking about. Couples. Families with strollers. Older people.

It's just a ten minute walk from my condo, so I come here about once a month or so. Sometime more if I'm working from home.

The maple trees that line the sidewalk are losing their leaves, falling to the ground like colorful confetti of golds and reds.

"Hello Mr. Grayson," the hostess says with a smile,

sliding a curious glance at Emma.

"Hi Tiff," I say. "Do you have a quiet table? Something outside on the patio would be fine." I turn to Emma. "Or would you rather sit inside?"

"Whatever is available," Emma answers with an agreeable smile.

"We have a private table on the patio," Tiff says, leading the way with two menus.

We're no more than seated when the server, someone I don't recognize, stops by to take our drink orders.

"Just water for me," I say. "Emma?"

"Water. Thank you."

She nervously clasps her hands in her lap.

"Interesting bit of trivia," I say after the server leaves us.

"What's that?"

"Pilots rarely drink alcohol during the day."

"Are you sure?" she asks.

"I'm sure, but I'm getting the impression you've had a different experience."

Her brows creased, she looks down at her menu.

"Actually, I don't think I've had lunch with a pilot."

"Wait," I say, sitting back in my chair. "I thought you dated Trey."

The server drops off our glasses of water.

"I did." She shrugs and takes a sip of water. "But I can't remember having lunch with him."

"What kind of relationship did you have exactly?" I ask.

Then holds up a hand. "Never mind. I don't think want to know."

"It's okay," she says. "We had a relationship of convenience. He wasn't in town much and when he was, he was resting."

"I see," I say. I don't tell her that Trey rarely took overnight flights.

I don't tell her that I was familiar with Trey's schedule and his evenings were mostly spent in town.

It makes me wonder again at just why he's had her photograph on our desk for months. It's a mystery I just can't quite figure out.

She sets her menu aside.

"Do you know what you want?" I ask.

"Just the salad," she says.

"Are you sure? They have some really good food here."

"I can honestly say I'm not familiar enough with French food to know what to order."

"Oh," I say. "We have to fix this."

"How?" she asks with curiosity.

"I'll break you in slowly. No right or wrong answers. Do you like chicken or fish?"

"Fish."

"Okay. I'll order you the Sole Meuniere."

She wrinkles her nose and leans forward, reaching for her menu again, but she doesn't open it. "What is it?"

"It's fish—cooked—and vegetables. It's safe. I promise."

"Okay," she says. "I'll trust you."

"That's a step in the right direction," I say, squeezing her hand.

Right now I need something to distract myself from not throttling Trey for lying to this girl.

He'd kept her on the line while he did whatever he wants. Telling her he was out of town. I hate to think it, but my gut tells me he was just stringing her along.

"Did you get your lectures finished?"

"Fortunately, they didn't require much." She slips her white cloth napkin into her lap. "It's a good thing, too, because I had to drive over to my mother's house to take care of a minor emergency."

"Is everything okay?"

"It was a false alarm," she says. "nothing to worry about."

"I had to visit my family this morning, too," I say.

"How did that go?"

Not a question I can answer with honesty in polite company.

"About as can be expected," I say. Definitely right up there with talking about Trey and his duplicitous lies to Emma.

The sun is warm on our heads, but the breeze is pleasant. Sitting outside was a good idea.

"What kind of errands do we have on our list?" I ask, quickly moving the conversation away from anything related to my family.

She looks a bit surprised as though she'd forgotten our

plan to knock out her errands.

"Just a few things," she says. "Nothing that can't wait." She takes a breath. "Except for cat food. I can't go home without cat food."

"Can't have Oscar going hungry. He seems like a good companion."

"He doesn't ask for much."

Nervous. I'm still making her nervous.

I have to figure out a way to fix that.

CHAPTER
TEN

Emma

I CAN'T FIGURE out why I'm so nervous around Grayson.

He's nice to look at and he's kind. He's much kinder than Trey and it shouldn't be hard to relax around him.

I think maybe part of it is being in an unfamiliar place. Being in this fancy French restaurant with white table-cloths, even outside, with menus written in French. I know some basic French words, but I don't know enough to keep myself from ordering something like uncooked beef.

I'm out of my element and it's disconcerting.

I'm also not sure what Grayson must think of me for going out with him the day after my public and yet unofficial breakup with Trey. Trey and I hadn't even had a conversation.

In all truthfulness, Trey doesn't deserve an official breakup conversation. I'd seen him cheating with my own eyes. And yet things feel a bit unfinished with him.

Grayson said he and Trey weren't friends and I'm getting the feeling he doesn't think much of Trey even though he hasn't come right out and said anything of the sort.

It crosses my mind that Grayson might just be having lunch with me because he's feeling sorry for me, but that doesn't make any sense either.

Grayson turns heads. I'd seen the way the hostess looked at him. The way she'd looked at me. As though she's wondering why I'm with him.

Can't say I'm too fond of hostesses right now and surely no one could possibly blame me for that.

Our food comes and Grayson was right. My fish, well cooked, and vegetables look good. Quite normal actually.

His food looks appetizing too which is a relief. If he'd ordered uncooked beef, I might not have been able to get my own food down.

"Now this," he says. "you have to try."

"What is it?"

"It's Shrimp Francese."

He puts a bite on his fork and holds it up to me. "Try it," he says.

With a glance at him, I lean forward and close my

mouth over his fork, sliding my lips over the fork as I removed the morsel.

He watches every move and smiles as he watches me chew the bite of delicious shrimp.

"It's really good," I say.

"You seem so surprised."

"I shouldn't be, right?"

"That's right. You can trust me."

I lower my gaze back to my plate as memories of last night come flooding back.

I'd trusted Trey and look where that had gotten me. Looking like an idiot.

I square my shoulders, determined not to let Trey ruin an otherwise good day.

"Now I know what to order next time," I say. "Shrimp Francese."

"Do you not like your fish and vegetables?"

"I like my fish," I say. "but now I have options. It's good to have options, right?"

"Right," he says, but that serious expression he'd had earlier crosses his features again.

The one that the psychologist in me wants to explore, but I'm not here to get into his private life. I'm just here for a pleasant afternoon with a handsome man.

A handsome man who can keep his hands off the hostess.

But the truth is. I don't even know if he has a girlfriend.

My current experience with pilots hasn't left me feeling all that confident in their sincerity.

"How was everything?" our server asks. "Can I get you dessert?"

Grayson glances over at me.

I shake my head.

"Just the check," he says.

As the server reaches for the check, Grayson hands him a credit card without even looking at the check.

"I know we have to get cat food," he says as though it's the most natural thing in the world. Buying cat food on a first date. "But do you want to walk around some? Check out some of the shops?"

"Okay."

I can always do my errands later. In fact, I'd made contingency plans for it.

Right now I'm enjoying being out in the sunshine with a handsome man.

CHAPTER
ELEVEN

Grayson

My father's timing was most definitely off.

I stand near the restrooms waiting for Emma to come out, ignoring the interested looks the hostess keeps sending in my direction. I am most definitely not interested in Tiff.

She's been coming on to me since she started working here. In fact, I stopped coming here for a couple of months, but I figured coming here with Emma would take care of her longing glances.

Unfortunately it had not.

Maybe I'll keep my distance for a while again, but I do like the food here.

It's hard to focus on just enjoying being with Emma when my father's words keep coming back to haunt me.

He has me questioning whether Emma is the right girl for me. If she comes from a good family.

It's not fair to her. Even though I've been looking at her photo for months, I've only just met her.

She's a college professor. She's pretty. She's sweet.

I'm more than just a little attracted to her.

And yet my father won't find her to be *suitable* simply because she doesn't know French foods. Probably isn't familiar with wines. Or all the other trappings that come with running in his small billionaire circle. He, of course, expects me to stay within that small circle of friends and acquaintances.

I'd dipped my toe in that pool and I'm not impressed.

Personally, I find Emma far more impressive than anyone in my father's little circle.

She's not snooty or snotty or snobby. She's smart and kind with a heartwarming smile.

I can teach her all the things she needs to know.

But three weeks isn't very long.

Then I remind myself that I have not agreed to the terms of my grandfather's will.

Since they waited to the last minute to tell me, I sense a loophole and I plan to put my attorney on it first thing Monday morning.

I prefer to think about getting married on my own time on my own terms.

Not on my father's or even my grandfather's timeline.

Most certainly not to someone my father chooses and deems appropriate.

Emma comes out of the restroom, sees me, and smiles.

I take her hand and lead her out of the restaurant.

"Thank you," she says. "for getting me out of my comfort zone."

"You can pick the lunch spot next time," I say.

"No. It's okay. I need to branch out and learn about new things. I tend to get caught up in my own little world and forget."

"Forget what?" We walk around a lamp post, then I pull her close as we past a group of teenagers taking up most of the sidewalk.

"That my university world isn't the only one out there."

"It would be my pleasure to be your guide on exploring the outside world."

She glances over at me with a look.

I just shrug and squeeze her hand.

"I don't know what to think about you," she says.

"Most people don't."

"You're not serious."

We slow down in front of a dress shop.

"My sister loves this shop," I say.

"You have a sister?"

"You sound surprised."

"I'm not. Sorry. I'm just learning one thing about you at the time."

"It's okay. Most people don't think I could possibly be part of a functional family." But as of this morning, I no longer consider my family to be functional. Dysfunctional is a much more fitting description.

She laughs, obviously not sure what to make of me.

"Come on," I say. "Let's take a look."

She lets me lead her into the store.

"We need to get you something light and airy."

"For what?" she asks.

"My family gets together every Sunday for lunch."

She stops and looks at me as though I've told her that my family lives on the moon.

Ignoring her shocked expression, I pull a light green dress off the rack. It meets the requirement of being light and airy. The perfect dress to wear to one of my family's informal gatherings.

As for her meeting my family, it suddenly seems like the most natural solution and I should have already thought about it. I'd told my father I was dating someone. He needs to see the evidence before he moves on his threat of introducing me to more of his friends' daughters.

"Try it on?" I ask, holding it up.

"No... That's okay... I..."

"It's okay." I put the dress back on the rack and we walk around a bit more, our hands still linked.

"Hello Grayson," a middle-aged woman named Hilda, the owner of the shop, walks up to us. Smiles at Emma. "Can I help you find something?"

"We're just looking," I say.

Hilda lowers her glasses and studies Emma over them.

"I have just the thing for you," she tells Emma in a heavy German accent..

"Okay," Emma says, glancing nervously at me.

"Let's see what you have," I say.

We follow Hilda over to a rack of clothes that haven't been put on display yet.

"This," she says, pulling down a solid white dress, a high neck and long sleeves. The skirt has a pale pink under-skirt that flows beneath the white. "I call it a gypsy dress."

"It looks like something a gypsy would wear," Emma says, reaching out to touch one of the vertical layers. "So soft."

"Try it on," Hilda says. "I just got it in and I'd like to see what it looks like on someone with your figure." She sweeps a hand down her ample body. "Me. Not a good model for this style."

"Okay," Emma says with a smile. "I'll try it on."

"Very good," Hilda says, clasping her hands together.

She winks at me as Emma takes the dress into the dressing room to try on.

I just shake my head. Hilda is a wily one. It's easy to see how she's so successful in her business.

CHAPTER
TWELVE

Emma

BACK IN THE little dressing room—the only dressing room, I undress and slip into the white dress.

It really does feel like a gypsy dress or at least what I imagine a gypsy dress would feel like. Definitely light and airy. And very feminine.

I check out my reflection in the mirror.

"Do we get to see?" Grayson calls out from where he's sitting on the couch just outside the dressing room.

One more check in the mirror. Why not?

I step out of the dressing room and stand in front of him.

"Nice," he says.

I make a little twirl so he can see the way the vertical layers shift between pink and white. "It feels really nice."

"I love it."

"Oh my," Hilda says with her heavy German accent. "That dress was definitely worth the investment. Very nice. I'm going to put one of them in the display window."

"It's one of your best buys," Grayson tells her then turns back to me. "You should get it."

"Maybe," I say, heading back to the dressing room.

"She should definitely get the dress," Hilda says. "It's perfect on her."

"And you have a good eye."

I slip out of the dress and as I'm getting back into my own clothes, I take a peek at the price tag.

What?

I take my glasses out of my purse and look again.

Oh no. No. No. Definitely no.

Sitting down to put on my shoes, I look longingly at the dress. It's beautiful.

I was just trying it on for Hilda. So she could see what it looked like.

Not in the market for an investment of my own.

Two month's salary for a dress? I think not.

I carefully put it back on the hanger and step out of the dressing room.

"I ring it up for you, yes?" Hilda says taking the dress from me.

"No," I say. "It's beautiful and I love it, but no. I can't."

Hilda looks at Grayson.

He just shrugs.

"It's okay," Hilda says. "You're very kind to try it on for me. When you come back by, it will be displayed in the window."

"You're going to sell them all in no time," I say with one last longing look at the dress.

"You didn't like it that much?" Grayson asks as we step out onto the sidewalk.

"Are you kidding? I love it. But it's two month's salary. I just can't."

"Ah. I understand."

We walk a few feet when he stops. Pats his pocket.

"I think I left my—. Can you wait here for one second?"

"Of course."

I don't know what he might have left, but he'd been sitting on the couch. Maybe his keys fell out.

I wander to the next store—a hat shop—and window shop hats while I wait. I don't dare go in. First thing I know, I'll be buying a hat I most definitely don't need and would probably never even wear.

My budget doesn't include hats and gypsy dresses.

Grayson comes back.

"All good?" I ask.

"All good." He takes my hand again and we wander along the sidewalk, looking into the different shops, but not going in any.

He seems preoccupied and I'm happy to just wander in silence.

We have to pass by the French restaurant on the way back to his car.

The hostess is standing outside.

She gives Grayson a look that requires no interpretation.

He seems to ignore it.

"She likes you," I say.

"I know."

Not the answer I was expecting.

Not sure what to say, I don't say anything as we keep walking.

"Not interested," he says.

"What?"

"In the hostess."

"Why not?" I don't normally push like this, but I'm truly curious.

I'm curious why Trey had made out with a hostess while Grayson just seems annoyed by the girl's attention.

"Not my type," he says.

"Oh? What's your type?"

"I like brainy brunettes," he says. "the pretty ones."

"Ha."

"You think I'm not serious."

"I don't know." It isn't that I don't necessarily think he's not serious. It's that I don't know if he's talking about me or if he has a girlfriend that meets his requirement of being a pretty, brainy brunette.

We reach his car. He opens the passenger door and I climb inside. The car is already running and cooled down with air conditioning.

Before closing the car door, he casually rests an arm over the top of it and looks at me as though he's trying to figure something out.

"What?" I look back at him and hope he doesn't notice the way my pulse is pounding, my blood racing like quicksilver, beneath his smoldering blue eyes focused completely on me.

He winks and closes the door.

Seconds later, he comes around and climbs in behind the steering wheel.

"Where are we headed first?" he asks as though he hadn't just set my senses on fire. "Any particular pet store?"

I pull out my phone and make a quick google search for pet stores between here and my place.

I pick out one that looks decent and give him an address.

"Just tell me where to turn," he says, keeping his attention on the car in front of us.

"Left on Westheimer," I say.

The traffic is terrible today. Saturday is always the busiest day to get out and do errands. Unfortunately for me, it's also the most convenient. For me and a million other people who decide to get out and do their errands or go shopping or even walk around in one of Houston's many parks.

As we drive I think back over our conversation, trying NOT to think about that smoldering, inquisitive look he'd given me before he closed my door.

Had he invited me to have lunch with his family tomorrow?

As we sit in traffic waiting to turn left, I decide that he'd actually just been making conversation. Telling me a little more about his family.

Like telling me he has a sister.

"Do you have a brother or any other sisters?" I ask.

"Only one sister. Three brothers."

"Oh. Wow. Big family."

"You're not kidding."

"Are you the oldest?" I ask.

"What makes you think that?"

"Well. You're responsible. Successful." I run a fingertip along the soft leather of the luxury car's dashboard. "You take care of people."

"So you are analyzing me," he says with a little smile as he turns left out onto Westheimer.

"Maybe just a little," I say. "It's a hazard of the profession." And it keeps me from thinking about the way his smoldering eyes peer right into my very soul.

"My family will definitely keep you busy for a while. Trying to figure them out."

"Analyzing people isn't hard." He used the word *will*, not could or would. *Will* is a definite kind of word.

"After you meet them, you might change your mind." Again. Using definite language.

I'd never met Trey's family. They live in Dallas so it was never convenient. I'd expected him to want to get together for Christmas or maybe New Years, but he always had to work. I'd been okay with that. I had my own family to spend time with, dysfunctional as they are.

"It's right up here," I say. "On the right."

It's disconcerting going on errands on what feels a lot like a first date.

I'm not sure it's a date. I'm not sure what it is.

But whatever it is, it has me feeling edgy in all sorts of different ways.

CHAPTER
THIRTEEN

Grayson

DRIVING in the congested Houston traffic is a stark reminder just how much I no longer drive myself around.

With James driving me to and from the airport, I use those couple of commuting hours to work on my own business. Whitaker Enterprises. I buy and sell real estate. It was a side hustle I started in college, but it turned out I was good at it and it became more profitable than my flying passion.

Since I'm accustomed to working in the backseat of my car, I don't play music. In fact, it only occurs to me right now as Emma and I sit in silence.

A car somewhere behind us lays on their horn. I look over at Emma. She doesn't even seem to notice. Just looking straight ahead, her hands clasped together in her lap.

I use the time sitting at a standstill in traffic to look at her.

She's wearing dark blue or maybe black jeans and a long solid white shirt-tailed button-down. Her black leather jacket reminds me of her photo on the desk I share with Trey at Skye Travels.

Her long brunette hair swirls around her shoulders in smooth loose curls.

I have a girl up in Dallas that I see when I'm up that way. It's one of those no expectations relationships that pilots are known for. She calls herself a booty call and I guess she is. Sort of. I think of her as a friend with benefits. I take her to dinner and sometimes we see a movie. Maybe it's because I never stay in a hotel when I'm in Dallas that I think of her as more than a booty call.

But I never think about her as a girlfriend either. Monique. Her name is Monique.

The more time I spend with Emma, the more I like her.

I hadn't been planning on inviting her to have lunch with my family tomorrow.

It had just sort of spilled out of my mouth as though it was the most natural thing in the world.

Doing anything with my family is most certainly not easy and sometimes doesn't even seem natural. My mother, with four sons, knows how to act and is a gracious hostess.

My father is an asshole about half the time and with this current ultimatum hanging out there, I have no idea how he'll behavior. He's just as likely to sit there and tell Emma she's not good enough as he is to say nothing at all.

As for my brothers, who the hell knows how they'll act. Young men with too many hormones raging can be unpredictable.

But then I circle back around to the problem that I had sat there and told my father I'm dating someone. I'd done it with a straight face. Without hesitation.

Now that I take the time to examine it, Emma is undoubtedly girlfriend material.

I know I just met her, but I feel like I've known her for a long time.

It's probably that photo sitting on our desk. Maybe my brain had gotten twisted up and subconsciously started thinking of her as my girlfriend, not Trey's.

Truth is. Trey doesn't deserve a minute of her time.

I pull into the parking lot and find a spot not too far from the door.

"I'll come around," I say, but she's already clicked her door open. "Get your door."

"Okay." She pulls the door back, but not really closed.

That tells me a lot about the kind of guys she's been hanging out with. Guys who don't open a girl's car door.

I might be old-fashioned, but my grandfather taught me to be a gentleman. It was all Grandpa. My father was never around and my mother had her hands full with the younger ones.

I don't hold it against either one of my parents. I'd come out on top having my grandfather.

Opening up her door, I hold out a hand to help her climb out of the SUV.

I don't let go of her hand as we walk inside the store.

It's a typical pet store. A dog section. A cat section. A section up front for fish. They put the fish up front so people buy them impulsively.

One of my friends in college had a big oversized fish tank. He truly believed that girls liked it.

Maybe. Maybe not. But I don't think so.

"You ever think about getting Oscar a fish?"

"Ugh. He's always asking for one," she says. "But I know what'll happen. I'll end up feeding it and cleaning the fish bowl."

I laugh.

We spot the cat section and head over.

"Is Oscar on a special diet?" I ask.

"Nope. Just plain old cat food."

She grabs a bag and shoves it into my hands. Then she picks up half a dozen tiny little cans of wet food and hands them to me, too.

"I might need an extra hand."

She looks over at me with amusement.

One of the girls who works there sees my predicament

and hurries over to hand me a hand cart. Helps me put everything inside.

"Can I help you find anything else?" the girl asks me.

"Do you need help finding anything?" I ask Emma.

"No. I'm good," Emma says over her shoulder, perusing cans of food with a bored expression, trying to ignore the whole interaction.

"Do you get that a lot?" Emma asks after the girl walks off.

"I don't know what you mean," I say. But I know exactly what she means. And yes. I do get that a lot. "Maybe she could tell this is my first time in a pet store."

Emma looks at me. Tilts her head to the side in what can only be disbelief.

"I feel sorry for you," she says.

"I'm a pilot. It wouldn't be fair to get a pet only to leave it alone most of the time."

"You're probably right," she says, crossing her arms and meeting my gaze. "We need cat litter."

I follow her down the aisle and wait while she picks out a big plastic pail of cat litter.

I never knew that visiting a pet store would be such a workout.

But anything for the fair Emma White.

FOURTEEN

Emma

CAT LITTER HAD NOT BEEN on my list.

It wasn't Grayson's fault that the salesgirl doted on him.

And it wasn't my fault that it annoyed me. She didn't even offer to help me and Oscar is my cat.

So in an effort to balance the invisible scales, I picked out the biggest pail of cat litter I could find. Thirty-five pounds of scented clumping cat litter.

Oddly enough, it does nothing to put a damper on Grayson's good mood.

With a pail of cat litter in one hand and a hand cart of

food in the other, he stops and looks at the cat trees. The tall ones with hiding places and a hammock.

"Does Oscar have one of these?" he asks.

"You have to remember that Oscar lives with a college professor. He has to entertain himself by sitting on the window sill and hiding in the closet."

"That's too bad," Grayson said. "I always thought these were fun."

"I'm sure they are," I say, not letting myself look at them too much. The cat trees are right up there with gypsy dresses and hats.

We get to the checkout counter and he puts everything on the counter.

While we wait for the person in front of us to check out, I pull my list out of my pocket and glance over it.

"I forgot something," I say.

"What is it?" he asks. "I'll get it."

"No. It's a water bowl filter. You wouldn't know which kind to get." I shove the list back in my pocket. "Will you stay here while I run grab it?"

"Of course."

I hurry back to the cat section and find the filters. This isn't my usual store, so even though it's a chain everything is in a different place and it takes me a few minutes to find what I need.

By the time I get back to the counter, the checker, a young man who looks bored out of his mind already has everything rung up and loaded into a shopping buggy.

I put the filter on the counter for him to scan and open up my purse to pull out my credit card.

"Thank you," the young man says, handing me a receipt.

"But I—"

The young man has moved onto the next customer.

"Ready?" Grayson asks, hands on the shopping buggy.

"I didn't pay."

"I took care of it," he says. "Come on. Unless you want to get Oscar his own fish tank."

"Let's go," I say.

Trouble. Grayson is trouble.

But he's funny. And kind. And too handsome for his own good.

He's doing things to win me over and I don't think it's even on purpose. After everything is loaded into the back of his SUV and I'm settled into the passenger seat, it occurs to me that I haven't thought about Trey in hours.

Good. Trey's an asshole.

But Grayson. He climbs into the driver's seat and puts on his sun glasses.

"Ready?" he asks, glancing over at me.

"Ready." He's so handsome it's hard for me to look away.

"Where are we going next?" he asks.

"That's all," I say. "Nothing else is important." He genuinely looks disappointed.

"I was looking forward to a trip to the supermarket."

"Okay," I say with a little shrug. "But it's nothing exciting."

"I have all the excitement I need sitting right next to me," he says as he backs out of the parking spot.

The comment he just sort of tossed out there like it's nothing has me completely thrown off guard. Between that and the way the sun glasses make him look even more handsome has me at a loss for words.

"Tell me where to turn," he says.

"Okay." I open up my phone and search for the nearest HEB.

Now all I have to do is figure out how to pay him back for the pet supplies.

"Turn right," I say.

He pulls out into traffic.

"Do you take Zelle?" I ask.

FIFTEEN

Grayson

"Don't even think about it," I say.

"But you can't—"

"I can," I say. "Besides, it already done."

She leans back in her seat, letting the air conditioning blow in her face.

The traffic seems a little lighter heading east, away from Uptown.

It's a pretty day. Not a cloud in the sky. A great day for flying.

And yet even knowing it's a great day for flying, I'm not

bothered by being on the ground today. Not when I'm with Emma.

Emma makes the mundane interesting.

I'm thinking the next time I bring her out for shopping, I'm going to have James drive us. It's impossible to pay attention to her while navigating traffic. The whole point of having a driver is to not have to focus on the traffic.

"Is this a typical Saturday for you?" I ask to distract her away from trying to reimburse me for Oscar's pet supplies.

"Usually," she says. "I like to stay focused on work during the week. Otherwise I get distracted and don't get everything done that has to be done."

"There's a lot more to being a professor than meets the eye," I say.

She blows out a breath. "You can say that again."

"You like it though?" I ask. It's important to me that people like their jobs. I'd had a counselor in college tell me something that I never forgot.

If you don't like your job, you're going to have a miserable life. The most important thing you can do for yourself is to do what you love.

I'd already known that I love flying, so I never had a problem with knowing what career I wanted.

Even my real estate company is going to help me fly more before long.

It won't be long, according to my projections before I can buy my own Phenom. Once I get my own airplane, I can branch Whitaker Enterprises' acquisitions and sales to other cities.

Again, I really don't need my grandfather's inheritance and if it wasn't so important to my mother I wouldn't even be considering meeting the requirements of the will or even finding a loophole to get out of it completely.

"I don't think there's anything I'd rather do," she says.

"What do you like best about it?"

"The best part is being in front of a classroom and watching the students engaging with the material. Turn left at the next light."

It's interesting. Emma strikes me as a quiet young lady. Not someone who would enjoy being in the spotlight. But her face lights up when she talks about teaching.

"Good," I say. "I wouldn't want you to be miserable in your job."

"I won't say it doesn't have its moments." She wrinkles her nose. "I could do without department meetings and committee meetings."

"I know what you mean," I say, thinking about the tedium of board meetings.

We pull into the parking lot of an HEB and walk inside, hand in hand.

"Do we need a cart?" I ask, not wanting a repeat of what happened at the pet store.

"Probably," she says with a little smile.

Emma is an imp. She'd known exactly what she'd been doing when she'd loaded me down at the pet store.

"I think I'm going to have to keep a better eye on you," I say.

"I don't know what you're talking about," she says with a little smile.

I narrow my eyes at her. "You know. You know exactly what you're doing."

We spend the next hour loading up the shopping cart with everything from bottled water to apples to coffee creamer.

While I unload everything out of the shopping cart onto the conveyor belt at the checkout, she makes it a point to have her credit card out and ready to scan.

She has no idea just how amusing that is.

My petty cash account would cover her whole cart of groceries a hundred times over. Minimum.

She smirks at me as she taps her card to pay. I just put my hands in my pockets and smile at her.

Emma has so much to learn.

CHAPTER

SIXTEEN

Emma

BY THE TIME we have all the bags of groceries, and cartons of water, and cat supplies in the house, I'm convinced that having a man like Grayson around has benefits I wasn't even aware existed.

None of my boyfriends, certainly not Trey, had ever gone grocery shopping with me.

I'd been dating the wrong kind of guy.

Other than Trey, my previous boyfriends had been guys in academia.

I'd taken a risk in dating Trey, not in academia, but he wasn't any better.

But Grayson. Grayson was a new experience for me.

He didn't try to take over. He just let me point and he put things where I needed them to go.

After everything is put away, Grayson stands in my kitchen with his hands in his back pockets and watches me.

Oscar leaps up onto the island and rubs his face on Grayson's elbow.

"Hey little buddy," Grayson says, petting Oscar. Oscar purrs as Grayson runs his hands down Oscar's back from his head to his toe.

My throat feels a bit dry as I watch, imagining those hands running along my body.

"Are you okay?" Grayson asks, looking over at me, his hands still on Oscar.

I mentally shake myself as I grab a can of cat food and pop the lid off. My hands are trembling as I dump it into a plate.

"Oscar," I say, my throat suddenly dry. I swallow. "Oscar." My cat ignores me. "I guess he wants you to feed him."

I hand the plate to Grayson.

He sets it down in front of Oscar who proceeds to eat.

"Traitor," I say to Oscar.

Grayson straightens. "I have to run do an errand of my own."

"Okay." I try to smile, hoping my disappointment doesn't show.

"Can I borrow your phone?" he asks.

An odd request. "Sure." I hand him my phone.

Giving me a strange look, he holds it up to my face to unlock it.

Right. Unlocking it would have been helpful. But...

"What are you doing?" I ask as he starts typing.

"Giving you my number."

As he hands my phone back, his starts to ring. He holds it up, his screen displaying my phone number.

"I've got to run," he says, "but I'll be in touch. See you later Oscar."

Oscar stops eating long enough to look over at him and blink.

I follow Grayson to the door and close it behind him. I walk slowly back over to the island where Oscar is still eating, lean my elbows on the counter, and look at the pretty pink tulips.

I feel like my day has been a whirlwind. Starting this morning with my aunt's parakeet to eating strange, but good food, at a French restaurant, to going shopping with Grayson.

He was so generous. Paying for everything at the pet store. I think he might have paid for my groceries, but I already felt bad enough for him paying for everything else.

It's barely five o'clock so I've got plenty of time left to get some work done.

I walk to my computer desk tucked beneath the staircase and sit down. Open my computer.

And blow out a breath.

There is no way I'm going to be able to concentrate enough to get any work done.

Grayson has me far too wound up to think about much of anything beyond what his hands might feel like on me. His lips might feel on mine.

With a groan, I close the computer and head upstairs to my bedroom. Time to change into my running clothes and work off some of this energy.

CHAPTER
SEVENTEEN

Grayson

I DIDN'T REALLY HAVE any errands to do.

But I did have a proposal to read over back at my condo.

As I navigate traffic back to the Arabella, I decide that next time I take Emma out, she's going to have to get used to being chauffeured.

All this driving around in traffic is for the birds.

I drive up in front of my building and hand my key fob off to the valet.

"Welcome back Mr. Whitaker," Juan says.

"Thank you Juan."

I step inside a lobby that can only be described as the

inside of jewelry box with its huge glittering chandeliers and wide open spaces and get on the elevator to head up to my floor.

The elevator opens and I step into my living room.

Going straight into the kitchen, I grab a bottle of water and take it with me to my little sitting area.

Owning the entire thirty-first floor of a high rise building gives me space to have lots of different rooms.

Besides this little sitting room with a gas log fireplace and a loveseat that I use for thinking and reading, I have a larger living room for entertaining. Entertaining for me mostly consists of having one or another of my siblings over. Usually one at the time with whoever they're dating.

Maybe I didn't really need to buy a whole floor of the building just for myself. But it keeps me from having neighbors.

I have a dining area. A breakfast area.

A pool table room.

A little sunroom with two live orange trees that looks out over my swimming pool.

Then there are the bedrooms. One of which I made into a staff room.

After flipping on the fireplace, I go to stand at the wall of floor to ceiling windows. My sitting area looks west across the 610 Loop onto Uptown. I can see the entrance to the Galleria from right here.

Out over the heart of the city. Even more so than downtown.

The sun will be starting its downward trek soon, drop-ping slowly over the horizon.

Being up here in my condo high above the city has always been my sanctuary. A place I enjoyed being, even by myself. Maybe especially by myself.

Being a pilot I'm accustomed to spending long stretches of time alone. It's something I need. Something I enjoy.

But now, after spending the better part of the afternoon with Emma, my sanctuary feels empty. Lonely.

I have a proposal I need to read. I'm never short of things I can be doing, but this has been a long day. A really long day.

It all started with my father's summons. And his announcement that I have to get engaged in the next couple of weeks. Married in the next six months. If not, I lose my portion of my grandfather's inheritance. It's his legacy that I'm more concerned with than the inheritance, but it all comes as part of a package deal.

If I stop and sit still, I know my mind is going to race with this new information. This new unwanted information.

And then there's Emma.

The funny thing is I liked her before my father gave me his ultimatum.

It was almost like she'd just slid into place. It was like a door opened and she walked right in.

I didn't want to think about the two things together. About the inheritance and Emma. I wanted to think about them as two separate things. They are two separate things.

But at this point, it's damn near impossible for me to separate them. I became aware of them too close together in time. Within about twelve hours of each other.

I chug the rest of my water and turn away from the window.

I have to be honest with myself. There's no way I'm going to be able to separate them.

And the truth of the matter is I don't want to separate them.

EIGHTEEN

Emma

Less than an hour later, I'm back from my run, drinking a glass of cold water when my doorbell rings.

I'm not expecting anyone.

I glance at my phone. No texts or calls from Grayson or anyone else.

My hair is pulled back in a high ponytail. I'm wearing running shorts and a sports bra beneath a tank top. Still sweating from my run.

Oscar is sitting on the window ledge soaking up some sun. He pretends not to hear the doorbell. A lot of help he is. Maybe I should have gotten a dog instead of a cat.

I go to the door and peek out. A courier van is sitting next to my car. I only know it's a courier van because I recognize the logo.

As I'm still trying to sort out why a courier van would be at my condo, the driver gets back in his car and backs out.

Whatever it is, it isn't something I have to sign for.

I open the door and a box wrapped in plain brown shipping paper with my name and address printed on a label on the front of it is propped next to the door.

I carefully pick it up and bring it inside.

Setting it on the kitchen island, I just look at it for a few minutes, trying to figure out what it could be. It's not anything I ordered. Nothing I ordered would be delivered by courier.

No phone messages to give me a hint of what it might be.

Giving up on trying to figure it out, I rip off the brown paper to reveal a plain white box.

I lift the lid and move the white tissue paper aside.

It's the gypsy dress. The beautiful white gypsy dress with the pink layers in the skirt.

How did this happen?

I hadn't given the salesperson my name and certainly not my address.

There was only one explanation.

Grayson.

Grayson had somehow done this.

But why?

This dress costs two months of my salary.

Two months.

Pulling the dress out of the box, I hold it up.

I can't accept it.

I'll send him a message telling him that I can't keep it.

He must return it.

I find his number in my phone. Grayson Whitaker.

My fingers hover over the screen.

Maybe I'll just take a shower and try it on again.

Before I put it back in the box to be returned.

It can't hurt to try it on again.

I can see about returning it tomorrow.

In fact, I can take it back to the store tomorrow and return it myself.

As I take the dress upstairs with me, I remember that he had sort of invited me to go to his family's home tomorrow for lunch.

He'd wanted me to wear this dress when he took me to meet his family so maybe he'd been serious about the invitation.

Why else would he have an expensive dress like this sent to me?

Grayson is a sneaky one. That's why he'd gone back inside the store. He hadn't forgotten anything. He'd gone back inside to buy this dress. Had arranged to have it sent here.

I hadn't really believed that he wanted to take me home

to meet his family. Not because I wasn't the kind of girl a guy could take home. That's not it at all.

It's just that he and I just met. Last night.

I step out of the shower, dry my hair, and pull on the dress.

It's just as beautiful now as it was earlier in the day when I'd tried it on at the little shop.

Maybe even more so. It looks good on me. It looks good in my house.

Damn it.

I didn't want it to look good. I'd hoped it would look out of place or maybe it wouldn't look good in my mirrors. That maybe the little shop had trick mirrors that make every-thing look better in the store.

But nope. It looks just as good. And it feels lovely.

Not daring to wear the dress long enough to risk some-thing happening to it, I take it off and carefully put it back in the box.

I put the box up high on a shelf in my closet.

Oscar has a tendency to get into boxes and sleep.

It would not be a good thing for him to find this box and take a nap on the dress. Not good at all.

Wearing some comfy lounge pants and a t-shirt, I go back downstairs to make myself some hot tea.

With my hot tea in hand, I go to my little desk under the stairs and open up my computer.

It takes me a good hour to answer all the emails from students that have accumulated since this morning.

By the time I finish up, it's time to make myself a light salad for dinner.

Still no messages from Grayson.

I need to say something about getting the dress.

I just haven't figured out what to say yet.

CHAPTER
NINETEEN

Grayson

AFTER I GET that proposal read, I take a glass of whiskey back to my little sitting room and prop my feet up on the ottoman.

It's night time in the city now and I watch the headlights of the cars as they zip up and down 610.

The moon is full and bright over it all. A Fall moon. They call it the Hunter's Moon to represent one of the best times for hunters to bring home game fattened over the summer. It also helps that leaves have fallen from the trees making it harder for animals to hide.

Just another piece of the wealth of useless trivia packed in my head.

Noah Worthington, my boss, the owner and founder of Skye Travels is a strong proponent of reading during those inevitable down times of waiting. He believes that playing games on our phones or iPad will cause brain rot.

So for the most part we all comply.

He often gives us recommendations of things to read. Things he's read and enjoyed that he passes along to us. Sometimes his wife Savannah will recommend something for us to read. Noah usually recommends nonfiction books that he finds of interest and usually put me to sleep. His wife recommends novels, sometimes smutty fairy novels that get my blood racing. The two of them make a good pair.

It's Saturday night, but I have no inclination to go out tonight.

I need to spend some time thinking about my grandfather's will.

It's going to be hard to get past the anger at my father for not telling me already.

I just hope he's civil tomorrow.

Tomorrow.

I need to confirm with Emma that she got the dress and that she's planning on going with me tomorrow. I wouldn't go, my family is the last people I want to see right now, but I need to make a showing and I need to do it with Emma on my arm.

I open up a text message to Emma.

> Hi

She writes back immediately.

EMMA
> Hi

I smile. I don't know why. She just makes me smile.

> What are you doing?

Thought bubbles.

Then they stop.

I watch the cars' headlights on the interstate below while I wait.

EMMA
> I'm trying to figure out how to thank you for a dress you shouldn't have bought for me.

> What dress?

EMMA
> Funny.

> It's easy.

EMMA
> Okay. Tell me.

> Come to lunch with me tomorrow. Wear the dress.

No response. I get up and walk to the kitchen to get a bottle of water. When I get back to my seat, I have a response.

EMMA

It seems a little soon to meet the family.

It feels like I've known you a long time.

EMMA

That's strange.

I've been looking at your photo for months.

EMMA

Now you're being creepy.

LOL

EMMA

I can't keep the dress. It's too much.

Okay. I'll come get it. My sister will like it.

EMMA

Okay.

Even better. Wear it tomorrow. Then I'll give it to my sister.

EMMA

That doesn't seem fair to her.

She won't notice.

EMMA

How is that possible?

She has about a thousand dresses.

Thought bubbles.

EMMA

I don't know how to respond to
that.

So really. What are you doing?

EMMA

Sitting in bed. Reading a novel.

I'm at home, too.

EMMA

After last night, I just want to have a
quiet evening.

Want me to come over?

CHAPTER

TWENTY

Emma

I'm sitting in bed reading a fantasy romance that one of my students got me hooked on.

Oscar is on his pillow on his side of the bed. He sleeps with his head on a pillow like a little person.

Maybe I shouldn't have admitted to my exceptionally dull Saturday night activity to Grayson.

But there's not much point in pretending to be something I'm not.

Grayson had, after all, gone grocery shopping with me. Doesn't get much more mundane than that.

He really does want me to go to lunch with him tomorrow. At his family's house.

And he really wants me to wear the gypsy dress.

I really want to wear the gypsy dress.

I stare at the message on my phone.

GRAYSON

Want me to come over?

The words have me a little bit frozen. I don't know if he's serious or just playing around. What I do know is that him coming over here would not lend itself to me having a quiet evening.

What do you consider a quiet evening?

Thought bubbles. He's typing something.

I bookmark my page and set my book aside. Texting with Grayson is much more interesting than reading.

GRAYSON

Sitting in front of the fireplace. Reading a good book. Maybe watching a movie or streaming something.

Which one are you doing now?

GRAYSON

None of the above. Just texting a pretty girl.

His words make me smile.

Okay.

GRAYSON

Okay. I can come over?

No. Okay. I'll have lunch with you. Tomorrow. And your family.

I try not to cringe. Really? Lunch with Grayson's family. Something must be wrong with me for even considering it, much less agreeing to it.

GRAYSON

I feel like I twisted your arm.

You did. But you also bribed me.

GRAYSON

So now I know your price. Just buy you a pretty dress and you'll agree to meet my family.

They say everyone has a price.

GRAYSON

We'll talk more about that later.

What does he mean by that?

If he's trying to buy me, I think he needs to back up and rethink. In fact, I need to think about what he means by that.

I plug in my phone and set it on the nightstand. Maybe I just won't respond.

I turn off my lamp, lay my head back on the pillow and close my eyes. An image of his smoldering blue eyes is the first thing I see. I remember the feel of my hand in his.

My phone chimes with a text and my heart slams against my chest.

I pick up my phone and read the message in the darkness.

GRAYSON

I'll pick you up around 11:30 tomorrow.

Biting my lip, I smile to myself.

Okay. Goodnight.

GRAYSON

Goodnight.

Grayson Whitaker is a very confusing man. I can't figure out what he wants from me.

I almost feel like he's trying to buy his way into my bed. But it doesn't add up. If he was doing that, surely he wouldn't invite me to have lunch with his parents.

I want to see him again, but I'm nervous about meeting his parents.

Knowing I'm not going to be able to sleep, I turn the lamp back on, open up my book, and keep reading.

I need something to get my mind off Grayson.

Not that reading really works. My thoughts keep

winding back to his smoldering blue eyes and handsome lips. Handsome everything. There's nothing about him that I don't find handsome.

Including just talking to him. Even by text.

I've been known to overthink things. And this might just be another one of those things.

I'll just try not to think too much. To wait and see what tomorrow brings.

I close my eyes and my book slides out of my hands falling next to me.

Sliding a hand beneath the waistband of my pajamas, I slip a finger beneath my panties and with just a couple of circles, I'm slick with wanting.

Parting my knees wide, I slide a finger inside myself and imagine Grayson's hands being on me. His finger inside me.

Seconds later, my body explodes with shock waves and I whimper as I drift back to earth.

Grayson Whitaker is trouble.

TWENTY-ONE

Grayson

I STARE at the last text message from Emma.

EMMA

Okay. Goodnight.

Summarily dismissed.

She'd dismissed me just like that.

Sassy. I like it.

But I don't mind being dismissed. As long as I know I'm going to see her tomorrow, I'm good. Better than good.

From staring at her photo for months, her image is seared into my brain.

The real life version of Emma and the timeless photo of Emma have somehow seamlessly blended together into one version.

I picture her siren green eyes. Framed with dark, thick lashes.

Her lush kissable lips.

Her cute little nose and high cheekbones.

I need a shower. Probably a cold shower.

I head to my bedroom and turn on the water.

Somehow I'm not in the mood for a cold shower. Instead I turn on the hot water. Love my shower with the multiple shower heads.

With the water blasting from all different directions, the glass fogging up from the steam, I can't help but think about having Emma in here with me. I squirt some liquid soap on my loofah and lather up a foamy scent of sandalwood and old leather.

I scrub my arms, working my way down, imagining the way her cute little bottom looked in her blue jeans. In the white gypsy dress with hints of a pink underskirt beneath the flowing skirt.

My hands sweep over my arousal. Touching myself, I imagine Emma's hands on me. I press one hand against the shower wall and close my eyes, letting the sensations sweep through me.

Everything outside this world of hot water and steam and soft foamy soap vanishes.

I lean my head forward, thinking about the feel of Emma's hand in mine. Imagining her hand being on me.

As I take my release, her name tumbles out on my ragged breath.

CHAPTER
TWENTY-TWO

Emma

THE NEXT MORNING I take my time getting ready. I take a bath. Blow dry my hair. Straighten it to smooth it out. Then add some loose curls.

It's a process.

Every time I put mascara on my lashes, I think about Trey.

I shove him out of my thoughts. He doesn't get to live in my head rent free like that.

He and I are over and done with.

Finally, after doing my hair and makeup, I put on the dress. The soft silk feels good against my skin.

Oscar sits on the bed and admires the way the skirts sway as I examine the dress in the mirror.

"Do you like it?" I ask him.

"Meow."

I run a hand down his back. He stands up and purrs.

"Are you hungry?" I ask him.

He meows again.

"Come on then," I say. "Let's go check your food bowl. I'm going to be gone for a little while."

I walk downstairs, Oscar running along beside me, his tail high.

After I fill Oscar's food bowl, I wander over to my desk and open up my calendar to check next week's schedule.

I sit down in my office chair and make a few adjustments. Shift a couple of things I need to do to next week.

I didn't spend my weekend catching up on work like I usually do so I'll have to make up for that later.

When the doorbell rings, I jump, startled, and look at the clock.

It's only ten forty five.

Grayson specifically said he'd pick me up at eleven thirty.

He doesn't seem like the kind of guy who would show up forty-five minutes early.

I go to the window and peek out.

Trey's Mercedes is sitting in my driveway.

My stomach drops and I suddenly feel sick to my stomach.

I consider not opening the door. He'll just go away. But he knocks.

Whatever. I'll just see what he wants.

I open the door.

"What is it?" I ask.

He's wearing shorts and sun shades along with a decidedly unfriendly expression. Something about Trey in shorts always makes me think of him as a player.

"Can I come in?" he asks. It actually sounds more like a statement than a question.

"Why?"

I stand with one foot in the doorway, one hand still on the doorknob.

Maybe he wants to apologize.

"I think I left my Dallas Cowboy's sweatshirt here."

"Seriously? That's why you're here?" So much for an apology.

He had left it here. I had just washed it yesterday and put it in my closet.

It was one of those rules everyone understood. When a guy cheats and leaves things behind, the girl gets to keep those things.

"Yes," he says. "Do you have it?"

"Yes. I have it."

Fine. I don't want his stupid sweatshirt anyway.

"I'll go get it."

I start to close the door, but he pushes his way past me.

"I said I'd get it," I say.

"I'll wait," he says, crossing his arms.

I have to go upstairs to get his sweatshirt, leaving him alone down here.

Oscar is sitting on the kitchen counter. With a glance over my shoulder, I swing by and pick up my cat, taking him upstairs with me.

"Wait here," I tell Oscar as I close him up in the guest room.

I feel my blood boiling as I stride to my bedroom closet to pull out Trey's sweatshirt.

He's not supposed to be here. I'm waiting for Grayson to pick me up. I just need Trey out of here.

I grab the sweatshirt and head back downstairs.

Oscar meows from behind the guestroom door, wanting out. Not understanding. I just don't want Trey around him. Not the way he's acting right now. Like an ass.

"I'll be right back," I tell Oscar.

I get downstairs and find Trey standing in my kitchen. Still wearing his sun glasses.

"What are you doing?"

He leans back against the island. "You embarrassed me the other night."

"Wait." I hold his sweatshirt close like a shield. "I embarrassed you? You're the one who was humping the hostess on the patio."

He has the decency to look surprised.

"That's right," I say. "I saw you."

"That's not your business," he says. "Why are you so dressed up? Where are you going?"

"That's not your business." I throw his words back to him. "Something's wrong with you. You need to leave."

"Give me that." He steps forward, but I take a step back.

Maybe I'll just keep the sweatshirt. He's being an ass and he doesn't deserve to have it back.

"I think I'll keep it."

"Like hell you will."

I turn around and walk into my living room, the skirts of the pretty dress swirling around me.

Trey grabs my arm, stopping me.

"Ouch. You're hurting me."

"Give me the sweatshirt." His fingers dig into my arm.

"Fine. Just let go of me."

I turn and thrust the sweatshirt out to him at the same instant he grabs for it.

His fist slams into my eye.

He grabs the sweatshirt and I fall backwards landing on the unforgiving hardwood floor.

Stunned, I look up at him.

"Get up," he says, holding out a hand.

I shake my head.

"Whatever. Stay there then." He stomps toward the front door, muttering something under his breath. I don't hear most of it, but I hear the words *stupid bitch*.

Somewhere in the back of my mind, I realize he just left the door open.

Oscar. Oscar is safe. Oscar is in the guest room.

I sit up and press my fingers against my eye, but it hurts too much to open it, much less to touch it.

I will not cry. I will not cry. I will not cry.

Grayson will be here any minute and I don't want to look like a racoon again.

I will not cry.

I don't know how long I sit there, but I cringe when I hear someone walking up to my door. My open front door.

Maybe Trey isn't finished beating on me yet. Maybe he's here to kick me while I'm down.

I hug my knees to me, my head down.

"Emma? Emma? Are you okay?"

It's not Trey.

I recognize the voice.

The next thing I know, Grayson is kneeling next to me.

"What happened, Baby?" he asks, gently lifting my chin.

I can't open my right eye.

I feel the change in him. The anger coursing through him.

Unable to answer him past the lump in my throat, I just shake my head.

He puts one arm beneath my knees and another beneath my shoulders and picks me up.

He carries me to the sofa and sits down, keeping me in his lap.

"Where's Oscar?" he asks.

"Guest room."

"Let me see." He gently uses his fingers to nudge my chin up.

I look at him with one eye.

He takes a deep breath.

"Are you hurt anywhere else?" he asks, his voice so gentle it just somehow makes everything worse.

And that's when I feel the tears slipping out.

I'm going to cry.

I shake my head. I'm not crying because of Trey. I don't care about him. I don't even want to see him again.

But my eye hurts and Trey messed everything up.

I had a date with Grayson and I'm still wearing the pretty gypsy dress. The very expensive pretty dress.

"I'll get some ice," he says, his voice too calm.

And now tears are flowing.

"Shhh." He pulls me close and holds me while I cry.

I put my arms around him and fist my fingers in his crisp white button-down shirt.

He soothes me while I cry, my face against his chest, holding me close and making little circles on my back.

When my tears are spent, I realize I've ruined his white shirt with the mascara that is waterproof, but not tear proof.

"I'm sorry," I say, pressing my fingers against his soaked shirt, inadvertently touching his firm chest beneath.

"It's nothing," he says.

He gently shifts me so I'm sitting on the sofa as he

stands up. He studies me a moment, then puts my feet up on the sofa, too.

"Wait here, okay?" he says, his voice soft and firm at the same time. "I'm going to go upstairs. Get a wash cloth and then some ice from the freezer. I closed the front door. Can I let Oscar out?"

I nod again, but stop because it makes my head hurt.

"I'll be right back," he says. "Don't try to move."

As he leaves me and walks upstairs, I rub my arm where Trey had grabbed it.

He doesn't know where to go. He doesn't know where to get a wash cloth.

I start to get up, anyway, to help him, but the movement makes my head hurt.

Oscar comes bounding down the stairs and jumps right into my lap.

I hug him close and he just purrs.

I hear Grayson come back downstairs and open my freezer. I'm feeling thankful right now that I keep my house clean and organized.

He seems to have no problem finding his way around. It feels quite intimate having him poke around in my house. Actually it doesn't feel a lot different from going grocery shopping with him. He knows what I eat and he's been all over my house.

But it seems okay. I trust him.

I rather like the feeling.

He comes back and kneels in front of me.

"Let me see," he says, nudging my chin up. "That's quite a shiner."

"Right," I say, rubbing my upper arm. "Can you believe I've never been hit before?"

"I'd be worried if you had been hit before. Can you open it?"

I blink and open my eye. He leans close, taking a look.

"Are you a doctor, too?" I ask.

"No. but I have three brothers. Black eyes are a way of life."

"I'm glad I don't have any brothers."

He smiles. "Girls are supposed to be safe from all this. Can I sit with you?"

I nod before I remember not to.

I lean up and he sits down behind me, settling me against his chest, one arm holding me close against him.

"Let's put this ice on it," he says, pressing the cool cloth gently against my closed eye. "This should help the swelling."

I let out a slow breath.

Oscar jumps down and goes to find something more interesting to do.

My heart rate should be going back to normal now, but it's still beating too fast.

This time it's not from the trauma of the punch in the eyes.

This time it's from being in Grayson's arms.

CHAPTER
TWENTY-THREE

Grayson

I sit with Emma on her sofa, holding her until I feel her relax a little against me.

I need to go find some Tylenol for her, but I don't want to get up yet.

Then I need to take care of the person who did this.

"We're going to be late to lunch," Emma says.

"We're not going."

"You should go," she says.

"Not without you."

She looks up at me with one eye. "It's not fair to you. You should go."

"I'm not leaving you." Yet. "The dress looks good on you."

"I hope it's not ruined."

"If it is, it's nothing that can't be fixed." I take the cloth off her eyes for a few minutes. "Are you going to tell me what happened?"

"It was Trey."

"I know. But what happened?" I didn't know one hundred percent, but now I do.

"How do you know?" she looks up at me.

"I saw his car pulling out. He didn't even see me. Has he hit you before?"

"No," she says. "I sort of think maybe it was an accident." I put the ice back on her eye.

"Is that why you were still sitting on the floor with your front door open?"

"I suppose it is." She sighs.

"What happened?"

"He demanded his sweatshirt back."

"All this over a sweatshirt?"

"He was being nasty, so I decided to keep it, but..." she rubs her upper arm. "He grabbed me."

I can see the beginnings of bruises on her arm. Trey's hand. I bite the inside of my lip to keep from cursing.

"It happened so fast. I turned and..." She looks away, biting her lip.

"It's okay," he says. "Do you want to press charges?"

"What? No."

I remove the ice. Examine her eye. It looks like it's going to be okay. Just ugly bruises for a few weeks.

"I'd be inclined to let it go. Maybe," I say. "Except that he left you sitting in the floor with the front door open."

"I know."

"How did you know to put Oscar up?"

"Not sure. Trey was acting... nasty."

"Can I make a suggestion?" I ask.

"Of course."

"Does Trey have a key?"

"No."

"If he comes back here, don't let him come inside."

"Okay."

"Promise?"

She smiles a little, wincing as the smile reaches her eyes. "I promise."

I remove the now soaked cloth and set it on the floor.

"How do you feel now?"

"I feel a little better. I think."

"Can you eat something?"

"Maybe. I feel bad about your lunch."

"Don't. I see them often enough as it is."

"You're lucky."

"Why? Where are your parents?"

"Portugal," she says. "My parents and my little sister."

"Why Portugal?"

"I don't really know. They wanted a simpler life."

"You didn't want to go with them?"

"Leaving the country is something I never wanted to do."

"Me either." I kiss her on the forehead and feel her relax in my arms.

She tilts her head back so she can see me.

"Thank you," she says.

"For what?"

"For being here."

"I'm just sorry I didn't get here a little bit earlier."

"You still got here early."

"Actually James drove. I was going to sit in the car and do some work, but then we saw Trey driving off and your door was open."

"I'm glad you're here," she says, squeezing my hand and looking up at me again.

I lean forward and kiss her on the cheek.

When I straighten, she blinks and looks up at me.

"James is still outside waiting?" Her voice is full of concern.

"It's what he does. He drives and waits."

"I don't think I'd like that job."

"He doesn't complain."

"Hmm. Does he work for Skye Travels, too?"

I know where she's going with that question. She's trying to figure out why I have a chauffeur.

It's understandable that she would try to make sense of why a pilot has a chauffeur for everyday transportation.

"No," I say. "He works for me."

Her brows crease as she looks back up at me.

"I do okay," I say with a little shrug.

She closes her eyes.

I kiss her near the corner of her lips.

It would be so easy to kiss her right now. To really kiss her.

But it doesn't seem right. Not with her being so vulnerable. Not now. Not yet.

Right now I have to stay focused.

"Pizza delivery?"

"Okay."

I order pizza. "It's on the way. After we eat, will you be okay for a little while?"

"I think so."

"I need to go take care of something."

"Will you wait while I go to the restroom?"

"Absolutely." I help her sit up. "Tell me if you feel dizzy or anything."

"I will."

"I'm not leaving yet," I remind her.

She gives me a little smile. "Okay. I'll be right back."

I watch her walk down the hallway, past the kitchen. The dress looks fine on her.

While she's in the restroom, I open a can of food for

Oscar. He rubs his face on my hands as I empty it into a plate just as I'd seen Emma do.

I've got something I need to do, but I have to make sure Emma is okay first.

Trey is going to regret laying a hand on her.

TWENTY-FOUR

Emma

I LEAN against the sink in the downstairs half bath and examine my eye in the mirror. It looks nasty.

It looks even worse because of the mascara smudged beneath my eyes.

I wipe at the mascara, getting some of the black off my face. If I weren't feeling so wobbly, I'd go upstairs and use my special mascara remover.

The next time I go shopping, I'm going to search for *tear*-proof mascara. In fact, I'm going to check the Internet instead of trusting the salespeople at the stores this time.

So far two out of three times I find myself with Grayson,

I have mascara smudged around my eyes. It's not Grayson's fault. It's all because of Trey.

The ice on my eye seems to be working. It doesn't hurt right now unless I touch it. But it looks nasty. Red and puffy.

I hate I caused Grayson to miss lunch with his family, but he doesn't seem concerned about it.

Nonetheless, I'm glad he's here.

I replay his kiss on my forehead. The kiss on my cheek. The kiss on the corner of my lips.

He'd come so close to actually kissing me.

If I weren't in such a state of distress right now, with the black eye, that would be driving me insane. And even now, it's all I can think about. I'm thinking about that more than Trey punching me in the face.

I honestly don't know how much longer I can take of the torture of waiting for him to kiss me.

Leaving the restroom, I walk past the kitchen where Oscar is sitting on the island eating from one of his little plates.

Grayson is sitting on the sofa where I left him.

"You fed Oscar?"

He shrugs. "He looked hungry."

I smile and sit back down next to him.

He puts an arm around my shoulders.

"How do you feel?"

"I'm okay." Safe. Safe with him.

He pushes the hair back off my face. "I got you some fresh ice. And some water." He hands me a bottle of water."

"Thanks. Are you always this kind and caring? To damsels in distress?"

"Always."

As I drink from the bottle of water, I keep my gaze on his. On his smoldering blue eyes. There's an edginess that wasn't there before. Not even when Trey had cheated on me at the bar.

"Are you going to say something to Trey?"

"Not a word."

"I—" The doorbell rings and I jump.

"It's the pizza," he says. "I'll get it."

I sit forward, my hands clasped in front of me.

I pick up the cloth with the ice and hold it against my injured eye.

This was not how I would have predicted my day would go.

Grayson comes back with a pizza box.

"Do you want me to get us some plates?" he asks, handing me the box wafting with the scent of hot cheesy pizza.

"To the left of the sink."

I slide the box onto my coffee table, one of the many pieces of furniture my parents had left with me when they'd moved to Portugal two years ago.

"Do you ever visit your parents?" he asks, handing me a plate.

"I visited once, the Christmas after they first moved."

"Did you like it?"

"I liked it okay. It's just so far away. I miss them not being here."

"I understand."

"You're lucky your parents are right here."

"Sometimes," he says, putting a slice of pizza on my plate.

I smile, then take a bite of pizza.

"I didn't realize I was so hungry. You should take James some."

"I had a pizza delivered to the car."

"Oh. Good." He really does think of everything.

"Tonight, when I get back, do you want to hang out and watch a movie?"

"Sure... but... my television went out and I haven't replaced it." I motion in the general direction of the spot where it used to hang on the wall. It had actually been my parents' television.

"Okay. Do you want to hang out anyway?"

"Are you afraid I might have a concussion?"

He looks over at me sideways. "If I thought that, I'd take you to an urgent clinic."

"Okay," I say.

"Okay. I'll let my parents know we've rescheduled lunch for next week."

"Can I wear this dress?" I ask.

"I hope you do." He looks at me with an appreciative glance that brings heat to my cheeks.

I pick up the ice pack wrapped in a washcloth and hold it against my eye.

Ten minutes later, he holds out a hand to help me up.

"Walk me out," he says.

I follow him to the door.

Stopping at the door, he turns and gently putting his hands on my elbows, looks into my eyes.

"I won't let this happen to you again," he says, his voice gravelly.

"I'll be okay."

"I know you will." He kisses me on the cheek. "I'll see you soon."

TWENTY-FIVE

Grayson

"Take me to the airport," I tell James.

We don't talk. James has been with me long enough to know when I don't want conversation. To be honest, that's more often than not.

The whole point of having a driver in the first place is so that I can work while riding in the car or, as in this case, so I can brood.

Leaning back against the smooth leather backseat of my SUV with James in the driver's seat, I close my eyes and let myself feel the anger that I've kept at bay while I was at

Emma's. The cold air blasting into my face feels good. It might be fall, but it's Houston and it's still hot.

Sometimes it's hot all the way through December.

I don't even pretend to try to get any work done on the drive. My head isn't in the right place.

All I can think about is Emma's beautiful green eye red and swollen. Obviously painful, especially when she tried to open it.

I never liked Trey, but this takes it to a whole other level.

He showed his true colors hitting a woman. And maybe, just maybe, I could have bought the whole accident story. Things happened.

But he left her there on the floor. And not only that, he left her front door open.

The man knows she has a cat. If she hadn't had the forethought to take Oscar upstairs and close him up in the guest room, he probably would have gotten out.

What kind of man does that?

I can't even wrap my head around what kind of person does that.

Trey has a flight leaving in two hours. I know. I checked the schedule.

I'll be there waiting for him.

James hops on the interstate and makes good time with the light Sunday afternoon traffic.

As we pull into the parking lot of the Skye Travels terminal, a commercial jet takes off from the main runway, flying directly overhead, filling the air with the loud roar of the engine.

As James parks the car, I can already smell jet fuel permeating the air. Nothing like it. Being at the airport always gives me a little boost. Sometimes I think maybe some of us pilots have jet fuel running through our veins.

I don't see Trey's Mercedes, so I did well getting here before he did.

"I won't be long," I tell James, grabbing my briefcase as I get out of the SUV.

"Call me if you need me," he says as I close the door behind me.

I go inside the building, get on the elevator and head up to my office on the second floor. There's no one else in the building at the moment. The receptionist works remotely on Sundays.

I head straight back to our little office, a small space with a what passes as a window looking out toward the highway. There are four desks in here. Enough space for eight pilots to work when they need to, even though it's rare for more than a couple of people to be working in here at one time.

I pick up Emma's photo and tuck it, frame and all, in my briefcase. I also add anything else that I claim as mine.

A notepad and some pens. All in all, I don't keep anything personal here. I won't be using this desk again.

I send James a text message, then I sit down in the office and I wait.

TWENTY-SIX

Emma

IT's late afternoon when I wake up from a nap. It takes me a second to figure out why I was sleeping on the sofa. As a rule, I'm not a daytime napper.

After Grayson left, I'd gone upstairs, changed into sweatpants and a t-shirt and cleaned up my face, using the mascara remover, then the rest of my makeup.

I decide to go without makeup for the rest of the day even though Grayson alluded to the possibility that he'd be back later tonight for a movie.

After due consideration, I decide that my bruised eye is makeup enough for the time being.

Standing up and stretching, I realize I'm sore from being knocked down. My arm especially is sore where Trey grabbed me.

Grayson made me promise not to let Trey back in my house. He doesn't have to worry about that.

In fact, I take a few minutes to go around and check both doors and all the windows. Just in case.

I find Oscar curled up on my bed taking a nap himself.

Standing at my bathroom mirror, I brush my hair and study my eye. It's tender to the touch and swollen.

I think it would have been even more swollen if Grayson hadn't put ice on it.

As I walk back downstairs, I keep thinking about how gentle and caring he'd been.

I don't think I've ever known a man so gentle and caring, especially not one who looks like Grayson.

Grayson is heartbreakingly handsome. When he looks at me, his smoldering blue eyes send all sorts of delicious chills through me.

Since it's possible he really will come back tonight, I go back downstairs and spend some time straightening up.

When Oscar wakes up and comes downstairs, I give him fresh water and fill his dry food bowl.

"Don't look at me like that," I tell him. "I know you talked Grayson into another can of cat food."

He lifts one paw, then the other in the cat version of a shrug and goes back to eating his dry kibbles.

As the sun sets, I turn on the tea kettle, make myself a

cup of hot tea with honey, and sit down at my desk to check my email.

Students send constant emails and they expect immediate answers. I think they forget that there is a real person on the other side of the emails.

I contemplate setting up an automated reply telling them I'll be back in touch within twenty-four hours, but my gut tells me that even twenty-four hours is too long for them in our instant gratification society.

I have an automatic reply drafted when my doorbell rings, making me nearly jump out of my skin.

This thing with Trey has me on edge.

Peeking outside, I see Grayson's SUV sitting next to my car.

"Who is it?" I ask before opening the door.

"It's me," Grayson says.

Definitely not Trey.

I open the door to find not only Grayson, but James standing next to him.

"Good evening, Miss Emma," James says with a little tip of his cap.

"We have something for you," Grayson says.

TWENTY-SEVEN

Grayson

WHILE I WAS at the office, I had James find and arrange to pick up a new television. One of those new ones. Very thin like a wall painting.

After I dealt with Trey, we stopped and picked it up on our way back to the condo at the Arabella.

Always looking for a solution to problems, I'd figured out the best way to watch a movie at Emma's place involved replacing her television.

If it hadn't been for the black eye, I would have invited her to my place, but I didn't want to put her through meeting new people—the valet, the concierge, possibly my neighbors on the elevator. Not until her eye was better.

Speaking of her black eye, Trey won't be going near Emma again.

I never made a threat I couldn't carry out.

If Trey has any sense at all, something still debatable, he's figured that out by now.

Probably the most effective way to get a pilot in line is to threaten his pilot's license.

He might believe that I know someone who can have his removed or he might not believe me. I do think he knows better than to take the risk of finding out.

He's going to need a new shirt, too.

"What's that?" Emma asks, opening the door wide enough to let us inside.

"You said your television went out, so I brought one to you."

"You're going to like this one," James says, not commenting on her eye. He was forewarned and more than understanding.

In fact, when I finally told him what had happened on the way back from the airport, he'd offered to drive back up and show Trey what it felt like to have not just one, but two black eyes.

"Permission to set it up?" I ask, looking at Emma.

Emma looks beautiful.

She's wearing comfortable looking sweatpants and a t-shirt. Her hair is pulled back in a messy ponytail and she's not wearing a stitch of makeup.

Even with one eye swollen, she's so pretty, I can barely look away from her.

It takes no time for James and me to get the television out of the box, hung on her wall and set up.

"Are you sure this is a television?" Emma asks, running a hand alongside the side of the television. "It's so thin. It's like a painting."

"Wait until you see the screensavers," James says.

"It's really kind of you to loan me a television," Emma says. "I hadn't realized just how portable they'd gotten."

James looks at me and I can see what he's thinking.

She has no idea.

"How else can we watch a movie?" I ask, not wanting to go into it right now. Not in front of James.

I'll tell her later that I didn't bring it over as a loaner. That it's a gift. I know Emma can see that it's a new television. Maybe it just hasn't clicked for her or maybe she doesn't want to be presumptuous. I'm going with the latter. She's one of the smartest people I know.

"Grayson is generous like that," James says. I shoot him a look that tells him he's saying too much.

He just whistles to himself as he gathers up the box the television came in.

"I'll just take this with me," James says.

"You don't have to hang around," I tell James. "I'll text you when I'm ready to go home."

"Yes sir," James says. "Don't worry. I won't be far." He looks over at Emma and gives her a wink. "I'll see you later."

I walk him out while Emma plays with the remote.

"This television is amazing," she says when I get back.

"I know. Let me show you something."

I take the remote and show her how to turn the screen into a Monet painting or a window looking out at the rain or a flock of birds.

"Oscar will love these birds," she says.

"Then I'll leave it there," I say. "But..." I click the remote. "It's also a streaming device."

"I'm officially impressed," she says, sitting on the sofa.

"Have you had anything to eat?" I ask her.

"Not since lunch."

"How about I send out for some shrimp po'boys?"

"Okay," she says, her face lighting up. "My favorite."

"Yeah? What's your next favorite?"

"Tacos."

"I'm putting together a good list of things you like."
She smiles.

"Yes. You are."

"And... maybe things you don't like so much. Like French food."

"I could learn to like French food," she says.

"We'll see." I sit down next to her, get on my phone and order two shrimp po'boys for delivery.

"Let me see your eye," I say, setting my phone aside.

I put my finger lightly on her cheek and take a look at her eye. I try not to cringe at how it's blood shot and swollen.

"Does it hurt?" I ask her.

"It's a little sore."

"I wish I could make it better," I say, putting my arm around her.

She leans her head against my shoulder.

I kiss the spot right next to her eye, then right below it.

"It's better now," she says.

"Is that so?"

She nods.

My gaze dips to her bow shaped lips. So full and pink.

She tilts her face up in what I see as an invitation.

I slowly lower my lips toward hers, giving her plenty of time to turn away.

But she doesn't turn away.

I put a palm on her cheek and tangle my fingers in her hair.

As our breath mingles, I press my lips against hers.

So soft. So sweet.

So sexy.

She tastes so good.

I deepen the kiss, unable to get enough of her.

I nudge her lips apart with my tongue and explore the depths of her mouth, caressing her tongue with mine.

Going deeper, I touch the roof of her mouth with my tongue.

She makes a little sound something between a whimper and a groan.

Our mouths are made for each other. She follows every nuance of my kiss, her lips melding with mine. Her tongue moving with mine.

I can't get enough of her.

She tastes like mint and honey.

I never knew how turned on I could be by mint and honey.

Pulling my lips from hers, I trail kisses across her cheek to her ear.

She arches back as a little shiver runs through her as I run my tongue over the curves of her ear. Nibble her earlobe.

Then I make a trail of kisses back to her lips.

I don't want to stop kissing her. Ever.

We must have kissed for quite a while because the delivery guy comes to the door with our food.

We untangle ourselves from each other and I go to the door to collect our food.

We sit on the floor in front of her coffee table and as I unpack our food she finds the Weather Channel on the television and leaves it on as we eat.

"You like the Weather Channel?" I ask her, dipping a French fry into a cup of ketchup.

"I do. Is it weird?"

"I don't think so. I think you're a woman after my heart."

"Because of the Weather Channel?"

"I'm a pilot," I say. "We have to be part meteorologist."

"I can't say the same for college professors."

"What is it you like about it?"

"I think I like knowing what's going on in the rest of the country. It makes the country seem closer somehow."

"Flying does that, too."

"I've never flown in a private jet," she says.

"That is something we have to fix."

She smiles.

"Can I admit something?" I ask.

"You can tell me anything. I'm a psychologist."

"Right. I forgot. Well. I think I like shrimp po'boys and fries better than French food."

"Now you're a man after *my* heart."

I grin like a loon.

And she grins back.

Biting her bottom lip as she looks at me with her mesmerizing siren green eyes.

My breath hitches as I gaze at her. Wanting her. Wanting to protect her.

I'm a besotted sailor ready to climb over the rocks to get to her.

She beckons me with her gaze. Her lips. Her everything.

TWENTY-EIGHT

Emma

THE TELEVISION IS AMAZING. I'm truly impressed.

I find it quite confusing that he brought his television over for us to watch a movie. It makes even less sense when I note that it came as a new in the box television.

When it's just hanging on the wall in screensaver mode, it looks like a painting on the wall. It look absolutely nothing like a television.

I'll look it up later, but I can only begin to imagine just how expensive it must be.

As a college professor, I have all the basics I need. A nice place to live. A decent car. An Apple computer and an iPad.

But I live within my means. I have furniture my parents left behind when they moved to Portugal and I drive a used car.

In just the one weekend that I've known Grayson, he bought me a dress that would have cost me two month's salary, bought a month's supply of cat food for Oscar, and now thanks to him, I have a fancy television hanging on the wall. Not to mention the French restaurant and the delivery.

I got the sense from Trey that pilots make a lot of money and I know that people who come from working classes rarely become pilots. They can't afford the extra flight fees required to get there.

Grayson has the look of a wealthy man in his late twenties. Even in blue jeans and a—clean, mascara-free—white button-down shirt, everything about him screams professional man with a lot of wealth. The expensive haircut. The silver designer watch on his arm. The fact that he has a personal chauffeur.

I might be out of my league. Not might be. I am out of my league.

But he's so kind and I can't get enough of his kisses.

After we finish eating, he gathers everything up and takes it to the kitchen.

"Hey," he calls from the kitchen. "Oscar's hungry. Can I feed him a can of food?"

"Okay. Sure." Bad Oscar. I'm going to have to have a talk with him later.

And besides all those things, he takes care of me. And Oscar.

I lightly press my fingers against the area around my black eye. It must look really bad for him to be so careful with me. So helpful.

I play with the remote while he feeds Oscar. I should ask him about the television. Clarify that it's just a loaner. Confirm that he's coming back tomorrow to unplug it and take it off the wall.

But I don't want to make things awkward by bringing it up.

So I spend a few minutes looking for a movie he and I can watch.

At this point, though, I'm not sure I want to actually watch a movie.

It just seems wrong, though, for him to have brought this television over, installed it, and then us not even bothering to watch it.

It seems crazy.

"Do you need anything else?" he asks coming back and handing me a water bottle.

"I think I'm supposed to be asking you that," I say.

"And take the pleasure of taking care of you away from me?"

He sits down on the sofa beside me. "I can't help feeling a little bit responsible."

"How could you possibly feel responsible?" I ask, opening my water.

"I guess because I know Trey. And even though I know how he is, I didn't know he could sink this low."

"Neither did I."

"It won't happen again," he says, something in his voice I can't ignore.

"Did you talk to him?"

"Yes. I did. He knows I know and he knows that if he so much as speaks to you again, I will end him."

"End him? I'm actually feeling a little concerned right now." And maybe even a little turned on.

"His career. I will end his career."

"Oh," I say, looking away. "I can see where that would keep him away. But I don't think he even really likes me."

Not after what he'd done. After cheating on me with the hostess at the Speakeasy and then *accidentally* hitting me. The more I think about it, the more I agree with Grayson that even if the punch in the eye had been accidental, leaving me sitting on the floor, leaving my door open, was not okay and didn't fall into the accidental realm.

"He's an idiot," Grayson says, putting an arm around me. He smells like sandalwood and old leather with just a hint of jet fuel beneath it all.

I pull my feet up on the sofa and rest my head against his shoulder.

He gently cups my face with his hand, a finger lightly sweeping across my lip, making me close my eyes on a little quiver.

"Did you find a movie?" he asks.

"What movie?"

"Good answer."

He presses his lips against mine and pulls me closer against him, wrapping his arms around me.

I snuggle in, my body melding as perfectly to his as my mouth melds to his.

As his lips devour mine, I wrap my arms around him and run my fingers through his soft silky hair.

I don't seem to be able to get close enough to him.

He picks me up and nestles me in his lap, his lips never leaving mine.

Something coils in my core. Like a little igniting spark. I shift, pressing closer, as though I could melt into him completely.

"Are you okay?" he asks, his lips against mine.

"Yes." My voice comes out breathlessly.

I'm better than okay.

I don't even think I have to worry about feeling guilty about having just come out of I loosely call a breakup with Trey.

Trey being a prick in so many ways has given me license to put him behind me. Without a shred of guilt. And turn my attention completely to Grayson.

I don't even think Grayson is worried about the fact that I used to date Trey.

I wonder what he means about knowing Trey.

As he nudges my lips apart and his tongue slides

between my lips, all thoughts of Trey vanish out of my head.

All my thoughts zero in on Grayson as his tongue touches the roof of my mouth, ravishing my senses and sending heat to my core.

CHAPTER
TWENTY-NINE

Grayson

THE FAMILIAR CHATTER of the Weather Channel on the television plays in the background.

A thunderstorm in Dallas. Maybe I should feel bad for hoping Trey gets stranded. Maybe. But I don't.

The man deserves whatever problems he gets served.

Emma is lovely and sweet and approachable.

Not to mention her guileless oh-so-sexiness that makes me want to toss her over my shoulder and cart her upstairs and feast upon her. Not that I've ever done anything like that before.

There's something about Emma that has me wanting to not only protect her, but to *possess* her.

Her eyes flutter closed as I run a finger along her bottom lip.

"So sexy," I say. Her lips curve into a smile against mine.

She slides her fingers across my cheek to my ears, slowly following the outline of my ear, sending little shivers along my spine.

I realize, a little belatedly that I'm playing with fire.

As much as I might want Emma, the timing is not right.

I have the whole thing with my grandfather's will to work out.

I'm not exactly in a position to start a relationship with anyone right now. Not with that hanging over my head.

"Do you have a flight in the morning?" she asks as though she senses my distracted hesitation.

"Actually, I do," I tell here. "But it's not early. What about you? Do you have a class?"

"Tomorrow afternoon. But I have a committee meeting in the morning."

"I know how much fun those are," I say, toying with her hair.

"You have no idea," she says, leaning her head back against my shoulder and closing her eyes.

"I should let you get some sleep," I say, kissing her forehead. "You're going to have to figure out how to explain this black eye."

"I didn't think about that." She bites her lip. "Maybe no one will ask."

"You must not live in the same world I do."

"I'll be the first one in my department, probably my university, to show up with a black eye," she says.

"I doubt that," he says. "Do you need help coming up with a good story?"

"I think I'll just tell them that as a result of..." she taps the side of her black eye. "I'm no longer dating anyone."

I take her hand in mine, link my fingers with mine. "I was rather hoping that you wouldn't say that."

She looks up at me. "You wanted me to stay with Trey?"

"God. No. Not Trey. I was hoping you would see that there are other options. Someone else to date."

"Do you have anyone in particular in mind?"

I rub my chin. "I was thinking... but no..." I don't think you'd like that so much."

"What would I not like?"

"You wouldn't want to trade one pilot in for another one. Not when you've probably got a bad taste left in your mouth for pilots."

"I wouldn't say that exactly. I don't like to generalize people like that."

"Then you, my dear, are most unusual."

"I am unusual," she says.

Laughing, I hug her close to me, breathing in the clean lavender scent of her hair.

"Walk me to the door," I say, after a quick glance at my watch.

"You brought your television all the way over here and we didn't even watch it."

"We have something to do next time I come over." One of many things and watching a movie isn't top on that list.

I send James a quick text telling him I'm ready to go, then I hold out a hand for her to keep her steady as she uncurls and gets to her feet.

"How long are you planning to leave it here?" she asks.

"What? You don't like it?" I pull her along with me to the front door.

"Are you kidding? I love it."

"Then consider it a gift," I say.

She stops. "Oh no. I can't accept a gift like that."

"Why not?" I look at her with what I know is something of a challenge.

"Because... Just because."

I put my hands on her elbows. "I'm not your student," I say. "Or your client. Right?"

"Right."

"We have no duel relationship."

"How do you know about that?"

"My boss's wife is a psychologist. I listen."

She looks at me, her head tilted to the side as though she can't quite decide how she wants to answer.

"Maybe I'm applying for the job of boyfriend." I hadn't meant to say that, but sometimes the truth just slips out.

"I don't think that's how it's done," she says.

"I think you've been hanging out with the wrong crowd."

"No one has any doubt about that," she says.

I pull her to me, putting her arms around me.

I kiss her on the forehead. "So tell me," I say. "How does one go about applying for the job of your boyfriend?"

"I wasn't aware that there was an application process," she says.

I press my lips against hers. "How about this?" I ask.

"Maybe," she says.

"I'll take maybe as an answer," I say.

She leans forward and kisses me back.

I don't know how long we stand there at her door, kissing.

Long enough for me to get a message from James which I reluctantly look at.

JAMES

I'm outside.

Just over thirty minutes. That's how long we've been standing there at the door kissing.

Even though I'm thinking about doing other things, I'm in the moment, just enjoying kissing her.

Time could stop right now right here and I would be perfectly fine with it.

But alas, time stands still for no one.

"Good night, pretty girl," I say.

She put a hand beneath her black eye. "I fear something is amiss with your eyesight."

"A man who can't see the beauty beneath the bruises is a blind man."

Emma is a siren. And I'm under her spell.

CHAPTER
THIRTY

Emma

AFTER GIVING Oscar fresh water and filling his bowl with dry cat food, I turn off the television and head upstairs.

It's been one of the strangest and longest days I've had in a very long time.

As I stand in the bathroom brushing my teeth, I contemplate just what I'm going to tell my colleagues tomorrow when they ask what happened to me.

I have no reason to protect Trey.

I decide I'll figure it out when the time comes.

Not much use in worrying about it until then. Maybe I'll just wear sun glasses for a couple of weeks.

Makeup should definitely help though and hopefully it won't be a big deal.

As for Grayson, I honestly don't know what to make of him.

He alluded to the possibility of being my boyfriend in both words and deeds.

I've never heard of anyone applying for the job of boyfriend.

But then Grayson isn't like anyone I've ever met.

He's kind and thoughtful and sexy.

Speaking of sexy, my lips are pleasantly swollen from his kisses.

I don't quite know what he wants from me.

Most men would have been trying to get me upstairs.

Maybe he's just taking things slow because of the thing with Trey.

There were so many things with Trey. The cheating. The black eye. The recent breakup, loosely defined.

Oddly enough, Trey and I had never defined our relationship. For all I know, he had other girlfriends. I'd have no way of knowing whether he did or not.

Or maybe the fact that we hadn't defined our relationship explained a lot of things.

Maybe he didn't see dry humping the hostess as cheating.

He and I had never agreed that we were exclusive.

I had just sort of assumed it because that's the way I'm

built. It doesn't occur to me to date more than one guy at the time.

Lesson learned. Maybe I'll make sure to clarify things with Grayson before I make assumptions. Or if not Grayson, the next guy I date.

If not Grayson, I think I'll wait awhile before I date anyone else.

Sitting at my vanity, I brush out my hair, enjoying the quiet time to just think.

Such an odd day. I guess I have a new television now.

How is a girl supposed to turn down a gift... or two... from a guy she wants to date without offending him?

Maybe he just happened to have an extra television sitting around. It could happen, I guess.

Now I'm even more curious to meet his family than I was before. Before today I was just a little nervous about meeting them, but now I'm curious about what kind of people he comes from.

Maybe it's the psychologist in me wanting to understand him.

Maybe he'll invite me again and I'll have less drama in my life and can go.

I change into my pajamas and climb into bed.

I have two text messages.

One from Grayson which makes me smile.

And one from Trey that makes my blood run cold.

THIRTY-ONE

Grayson

"How's she doing?" James asks as he merges onto the freeway heading back to the Arabella in River Oaks.

"She's doing okay."

"That eye looks bad. Just say the word and I'll give Trey a taste of his own medicine and I'll do it with the utmost delight."

"I have no doubt that you would," I say, sitting back against the seat. "Don't think I didn't consider doing the same myself. But my ammunition might be a little bit stronger."

"Threatening to suspend his pilot's license."

"Exactly."

"Maybe. But not nearly so satisfying."

"Probably not. But still. More effective in the long run."

A police car, siren blaring, passes by going the other way.

"I hope you're right," James says. "I've known guys like Trey. Sometimes it takes a good ass kicking for them to really get the message."

"We'll hold that in reserve," I say.

"The offer stands."

"I know," I say. "I appreciate it."

"It's not for you," James says. "I never did like the guy."

"You have good instincts about people," I say.

"It's my super power," James says cheekily as he exits off the freeway.

I smile to myself. James is a good man. I'm lucky to have him as an employee and as a friend.

Once I expand my company by buying my own airplane, I'm going to promote James to vice-president of something. Maybe vice-president of fleet operations. Eventually. It depends on how fast the company grows.

I'm certain I'll think of something.

I'm make it a point.

Everything seems to be falling into place.

I send Emma a message.

Good night pretty girl.

James turns into the circle drive at the Arabella and the valet opens up my door.

"Thank you Owen."

"Have a great night, Mr. Whitaker. James."

James and I are just stepping onto the elevator when I get a return message from Emma.

EMMA

I just got a text message from Trey

"What the—?"

"What is it?" James asks, pushing the button for the thirty-first floor.

"Emma. She just got a text from Trey."

"I knew I should have given that guy a couple of black eyes," James says, flexing his fists.

I'm in the elevator. I'll call you as soon as I get to my floor.

"Let me know if we need to go back over there," James says.

"I will," I say distractedly.

The elevator stops and we step off into my living room.

"Don't go far," I say to James.

"I'm right here."

Maybe James will be my head of security. With instincts like his, he'll be more than invaluable. He'll be a secret weapon.

I go to my little sitting room and dial Emma's number.

"Hey," I say.

"Hey."

I can hear her pacing and I can hear the fear in her voice.

"Read me the message."

THIRTY-TWO

Emma

"You think hiding behind him keeps you safe? You don't know what I'm capable of. Neither does he." I read the words slowly.

I could have recited them word for word from memory already. I'd read them a dozen times before I decided to tell Grayson.

"Hold on a minute," Grayson says.

He puts me on mute. I keep pacing my bedroom.

I don't even feel safe in my own home right now. I'm in my bedroom with Oscar, the door closed.

It doesn't matter that I have good locks on the doors. It

doesn't even matter that I checked them half a dozen times before giving up and bringing Oscar upstairs with me and locking us both in my bedroom.

None of that matters right now.

"He's here," Grayson says, taking me off mute. "His flight got turned around due to the storm in Dallas so he came right back to Houston."

"He's here?" I hadn't even known Trey was on a flight, but somehow knowing that he was definitely in Houston and that Grayson thought it was important enough to check chills me to the bone.

"Yes. You're not staying there tonight. Pack a bag."

"But..."

I sit down hard on the edge of the bed and Oscar puts his head in my lap.

Trey might try to hurt me... Had hurt me. But if he so much as touches a hair on Oscar's head... "Okay," I say.

I hear Grayson walking.

"We have to go back," he says to someone, his voice muffled. James. He's talking to James. "Get the car."

James says something I can't understand.

"Where are you?" Grayson asks me.

"I'm in my bedroom."

"Does the door lock?"

"It's locked."

"Okay. Don't move. Stay on the line until we get there. James. Call the police department. Send a patrol car over to Emma's place."

"Do you really think all that is necessary?" I ask. "Surely Trey isn't stupid enough to break into my house."

"He threatened you. Nobody in their right mind makes those kinds of threats."

He's quiet as they ride down the elevator. Get back in his SUV.

"Grayson?" I say.

"I'm here." His door closes and I hear his car moving.

"I don't have anywhere else to go."

"You always have somewhere to go. You're staying with me."

"But..." I stroke Oscar on the head and swallow the lump in my throat. "I won't leave Oscar."

"He's coming, too. Oscar is more than welcome in my home. Don't even think about leaving him."

I take a deep breath. "Okay," I say. Now is not the time to worry about details. "I'm putting you on speaker so I can pack."

"Good. You do that. Call out if anything sounds off."

"I will. I have to get Oscar's food and his litter box and—"

"Emma."

"Yes?"

"Take a deep breath. James and I will be there shortly. We'll help you pack up all those things. Just pack up what YOU need for a few days until we get this figured out."

"Right. Okay."

I drag my suitcase out of my closet and start filling it. I need work clothes. And my computer.

"My computer is downstairs," I say out loud.

"We'll get it. We'll get everything."

"I need to make a list," I say. It sounds so silly to think about writing it all down, but I'd feel so much better if I could do just that.

"I'm writing it down for you," Grayson says.

"Really?" I stop, my hands full of clothes.

"Typing in my phone as we speak. It helps to have a driver." I hear the hint of a smile in his voice.

A half-hearted little smile tugs at my lips as I drop the handful of clothes into my suitcase.

"We'll be there in seventeen minutes," Grayson says.

"I've never packed so fast," I say to no one.

Even though my hands are shaking, I still think I'm overreacting. But if Grayson and James are coming to get me out of here, then maybe I'm not overreacting.

It's better to be safe than sorry.

I move into the restroom and pack my toiletries and cosmetics.

I'll have to go to work from Grayson's place. Hopefully I'll have my own bathroom and space for my things.

"The patrol car is there," I hear James says. "Do you want them to go inside."

"No. Just have them wait. We'll be there shortly. I want her to stay in her bedroom."

"I think I have everything from up here that I need

packed," I say, walking back to my closet. Maybe not. I grab the gypsy dress, fold it, and lay it in the suitcase, too. I have no idea how long I'll be gone

"Any other messages?" Grayson asks.

"Let me check."

I scroll to my messages.

"No. Nothing."

"Good. Just sit tight. I'll let you know when we're outside."

I zip up my suitcase and make one more run around my room to make sure I'm not leaving anything I need for an overnight stay. It takes as much to stay one night as it does to stay a month.

And the truth of the matter is I don't see how one night or even two or three is going to make a difference.

If Trey is threatening me tonight, what's going to change between now and tomorrow night? Or next week for that matter?

"We're pulling into your driveway. Don't be alarmed. There are policemen here," Grayson says. "Come downstairs and open the door when you're ready."

"I'm ready." I think.

I put Oscar in his little carrier, throw it over my shoulder, and open the bedroom door.

Blue police lights are slamming through my windows. It looks like a crime scene.

THIRTY-THREE

Grayson

"Let's go," I say as James stops next to Emma's car.

Two police cars are stopped on the side of the road, lights shooting everywhere. Neighbors are peeking out their windows. This is probably the most excitement this little community has ever had.

"I'll have the police stand at the door," James says, getting out with me.

I head straight for the front door while James stops to talk to the police officers.

My fist no more than connects once with the wooden

door before it opens and Emma throws herself into my arms.

"Hey," I say, hugging her tightly against me.

"I'm sorry for all the trouble. It's probably nothing."

I take her hand and pull her inside. "Let me see the text."

Juggling something on her shoulder, she reaches into her pocket for her phone.

"What's that?"

"Oscar."

"Give me that," I say, taking the cat off her shoulder and putting the bag over my own shoulder. "He must weigh twenty pounds."

"Fourteen. But he keeps moving around." She shifts her shoulders in relief.

"I'm glad you called me."

"Here's the text." She holds her phone up for me to see.

TREY

You think hiding behind him keeps you safe? You don't know what I'm capable of. Neither does he.

Fucker. Trey is a God damned prick and I should have torn him to shreds instead of threatening his pilot's license. The only thing I can take solace in is I'd ripped off a couple of buttons when I'd grabbed him by the shirt collar.

Probably just enough to set the fucker off.

Why is it James is always right about these kinds of things?

But right now my focus is on getting Emma out of here and into my high rise fortress where no one can get to her.

James comes inside. "What can I do?"

"Let's put everything on the island," I say. "Then we'll pack it up." I turn to Emma. Open up my phone to the list I'd been making for her while we drove. "What's first?"

She reads my list, then glances up at me. "You thought of more than I did."

"Cat litter," I tell James. "It's in her laundry room."

Emma looks at me as James takes off toward the laundry room where the cat box, indeed, is.

"How did you know that?" she asks.

"While you were... recovering... I went on a scavenger hunt of sorts."

"Right."

"Is it okay if I wrap this in a garbage bag?" James asks, coming back carrying Oscar's litter box.

"They're under the sink," I tell him. "Help yourself to whatever you need."

"Computer," Grayson says.

I peek into Oscar's carrier. He looks back at me, his big golden eyes wide. "I'll be right back," I tell him.

Grayson helps me pack up my computer and I toss in most of my office supplies. Again, I really hope he has some space for me to work. Either that or I can work at the office.

I tell him so.

"I'll probably work mostly at the office."

"You probably won't."

Straightening, my hands full of pens and pencils, I look at him. "What do you mean?"

"It means you're getting a leave of absence. If you want to go on campus to teach your classes, either I'll be with you or James will."

"I don't think I can get a leave of absence over a text."

Grayson looks right into my eyes.

"With that text and that black eye, you'll get a leave of absence. Don't worry. I know people in high places."

I drop my pens and pencils into my leather satchel and decide not to answer. It seems best to hold off on any further decisions for the moment. As odd as it is, I trust Grayson to be in my corner.

After we take my computer and office supplies to the kitchen island, I stand in my living room and look around. Looking for anything I might possibly need until it's safe to come back.

The super thin television hanging on the wall catches my attention.

"We should bring the television," I say.

"It's not a big deal," I say. "Just—"

"I'll get it," James says with a glance at Grayson. "Not a problem."

Grayson just shrugs.

Walking back into the kitchen, I notice a loaf of bread sitting on the counter. I just bought groceries. Yesterday.

I take a deep breath. I have to let that go. Grayson probably doesn't have room for my food at his place.

"Is this everything?" Grayson asks as James comes downstairs with what had turned out to be two suitcases and a toiletries bag.

"It looks like a lot," I say.

"It'll be okay," Grayson says, picking up Oscar's carrier and draping it over his shoulder.

Taking my hand, he leads me outside to his SUV.

First, he holds the door for me while I climb in, then settles Oscar in the backseat next to me.

"I'll be right back, he says.

While he talks to one of the police officers, James gets everything loaded into the back of the SUV.

It's not ten minutes later that we're driving off.

I don't really understand what just happened.

All I really know for sure is that Trey threatened me and Grayson deemed it serious enough that he doesn't want me to stay home alone.

He reaches over Oscar's carrier and takes my hand in his.

This was not how I intended my day to go.

From start to finish. This is not what I had planned.

And yet, I'm not complaining. I'm with Grayson and I can't think of a better way to end my day.

THIRTY-FOUR

Grayson

I HADN'T PLANNED on taking Emma home with me today.

Not that I was complaining about that.

I don't mind. She can stay with me as long as she wants or needs to and I hope she does.

Even though James puts the divider up to give us privacy, Emma and I ride in silence.

As we zip down the interstate, Emma looks over at me.

"Do you really think Trey is dangerous?" she asks.

I look over at her black eye in the dim light coming from other cars' headlights.

"I don't not think he's dangerous," I say.

"You think he could be."

"I think I'd rather not risk your life to find out."

"So what happens next?"

"I don't know," I say. "We'll get you settled in to my condo, then I'll do some research. Find out what our options are."

James exits off the freeway, heading toward my building and lowers the divider.

"I'll drop you off," he says. Then I'll park the car in the garage and use the cart to bring everything up."

"I'm sorry to be so much trouble," Emma says.

I squeeze her hand. "You couldn't be trouble if you tried."

She shoots me a doubtful look, but when we turn into the Arabella's circle drive, she turns back to me with disbelief.

"You live here?"

"Thirty-first floor."

"Thirty-first," she says, looking out the window again.

The valet, Juan, opens up her car door.

"Good evening, Miss," Juan says.

Emma automatically turns back to get Oscar.

"I've got Oscar," I say, bringing him with me out the other door.

Emma is waiting for me as I come around.

Juan holds the front door to the building open and Emma looks at me with uncertainty.

I take her hand and we walk inside together.

We walk across the lobby where I scan my fob to summon my private elevator.

We wait in silence for the elevator. Inside, she watches the numbers as we travel up to the thirty-first floor.

The elevator doors open and we step off directly into my living room.

Emma looks around at the walls of floor-to-ceiling windows with views across the city adorned in its night life all the way over to the horizon. There are no shades on the windows. No need for anything to obstruct the view.

She looks right, toward the door leading outside to the pool, then left toward the kitchen.

"This is where you live?" she asks.

"Yes. Can I show you around?"

"Okay. Where can I put Oscar?"

I slide the cat carrier off my shoulder and set it on the floor. "Anywhere," I say.

She kneels down, unzips the carrier, and pulls Oscar out.

"I'll just hold him," she says. "until he gets used to being here."

"Okay."

I lead her around to the main guest room. It's actually one of two primary bedroom suites on the floor on opposite sides of the floor.

"This will be your room," I say, sweeping a hand to motion her inside.

She looks around at the king sized bed with a white

comforter. A blanket folded at the feet. A dresser. A desk. Nothing on either except for a phone charger on the desk.

Normally I would have fresh flowers on the dresser, but I hadn't known she was coming.

She peeks into the ensuite bathroom with its walk-in closet. Free standing bathtub.

Designer shower just like mine. The two bedroom suites are mirror images of each other except that mine is lived in. This one isn't.

Then she turns back to me.

"This is the your guest room?"

"It's your room as long as you need it," I say.

"Where is your room?"

"On the opposite side of the floor."

Oscar starts to squirm.

"It's okay if he gets down?"

"It's okay with me. I don't have any pets to bother him."

She sets Oscar on the floor and he cautiously walks around the room.

"How many bedrooms do you have?" she asks.

"Two main bedrooms. This is one of them. And several guests rooms that serve various purposes."

"I see," she says.

James comes down the hallway noisily rolling a cart.

"This is everything," he says as he unloads my suitcases and other bags from the cart. "I'm just going to put the litter box across the hall in the maid's quarters."

Emma looks at me with one eyebrow raised. "Maid's quarters?" she asks after James walks out.

"It's just an empty room."

"So Oscar has his own bathroom." A hint of a smile quirks at the corners of her lips.

"Yeah. You could say that. I guess he does."

I smile. I can't help it.

I like having Emma here.

Maybe a little too much.

"I'll let you get settled in. Everything you need should be here, but if you need anything else, just text me."

She watches me walk toward the door.

I stop and turn back around, my hands in my pockets.

"No one can get up here. Not without a fob or permission from the concierge. Which Trey will never get."

"Okay," she says.

"Good night."

"Good night."

I want to hug her, but I don't. I want her to feel comfortable here. The last thing I want her to feel like is that I brought her here with expectations.

Because I didn't.

I brought her here to protect her.

CHAPTER
THIRTY-FIVE

Emma

After Grayson leaves me there, standing in the middle of the bedroom—his guest bedroom that's as big as the entire first floor of my condo. My luggage stacked off to the side, I stand there a minute trying to get my bearings.

Oscar is already on the bed, scoping out a place to sleep. Probably checking out the pillows.

I walk to the window and look out toward downtown.

The skyline is so far away, it looks like a pile of children's blocks stacked up down there. So many lights between here and there.

It really is like living in the sky.

We're so high, I can't even hear the traffic below.

What must it be like to live like this? It's like living in a castle. Safe. A place where no one can get to us.

I'm a little rusty on my fairy tales, but it reminds me of one of those fairy tales. A maiden locked away in a tower to keep her safe.

Whatever mischief Trey might be brewing won't be happening while I'm here.

Grayson has brought me to his castle.

A place where no one can give me black eyes or do any other kind of damage.

With a sigh, I drag my suitcases into the closet and open them up.

I'll start unpacking them tomorrow, but for tonight, I just need my pajamas.

I'd already been dressed for bed once tonight before I'd gotten the text from Trey.

Standing in the closet that's as big as my bedroom, I change out of my jeans and t-shirt into my pajamas. I'd forgotten my slippers, but I don't need them. The carpet in the closet is soft and plush and the wooden floor of the bedroom is warm.

I take Oscar across the hall to show him where his litter box is, then I get busy assembling his water fountain.

Not wanting to spread my things all over Grayson's condo, I set up his water bowl in a little alcove in front of the windows in the bedroom and fill his bowl with dry food.

I climb into bed... literally climbing up... before I realize I don't have any water for myself.

Getting up, walking barefoot on the cool clean wooden floor, I venture down the hallway toward the kitchen.

As I near, I hear voices I immediately recognize as Grayson and James.

Rounding the corner, I see them standing at the bar, sparkling whiskey glasses in hand, looking out over the city.

I stop, not intending to overhear, but somehow it's unavoidable. I'm acutely aware that I'm wearing my pajamas and I'm barefoot, both of which seem sacrilegious in such an upscale place as Grayson's condo.

I'd been worried that he wouldn't have room for my office supplies, but there's a desk in my guest room. I'd been completely off base on that one.

The kitchen off to my right has shiny white floor to ceiling cabinets. I'm sure there's a refrigerator behind one of them, but I don't even know where.

Everything is so clean and fresh smelling.

"I need to get an early start tomorrow," Grayson says.

"Have you figured out what you're going to do?" James asks.

"Not sure what my options are," Grayson says, taking a sip of his drink.

"I have something in mind."

"Don't worry, James. I know you've been wanting to take a swing at Trey. Try to just bide your time."

James laughs. "I'm so glad you're understanding."

I start to turn back. I can come back later in search of water.

But Grayson must have sensed me standing there.

"Hey," he says.

"Hi." I self-consciously run a hand along my pajamas.

After a quick glance, James looks away, but Grayson gives me a full head to toe assessment followed by a wicked little grin.

"Would you like a whiskey?" Grayson asks.

"No. I just wanted some water."

"I'm gonna head home," James says. "I'll be back in the morning."

"Later," Grayson says distractedly to James keeping his gaze on mine.

He steps behind the kitchen island and comes back, handing me a cold bottle of water. The space, the island, the counters, is flawless. No handles on the doors or draws. Appliances and dishes completely hidden behind those sleek cabinets.

The island, too, appears untouched and unused. Everything feels modern and expensive.

I tighten my fingers around the bottle. I've never stood in a place so perfect. And I've never felt more out of place.

Grayson watches me, his expression unreadable.

"This isn't for show," he says, with a little shrug, his voice low. "It's just... mine."

He reaches out, brushing his fingers over my black eye with a tenderness that makes my chest ache.

"And now, it's yours too. If you want it to be."

I swallow hard and nod, unscrewing the lid. "Thank you."

"There's always cold water in the wine refrigerator," he says, a small smile tugging at the corner of his mouth. "Make yourself at home."

"You're welcome," he adds softly, not talking about the water anymore.

"Skye Travels," I comment, looking at the bottle of water.

He shrugs. "The big boss likes to advertise."

"Subtle," I say.

"Do you have everything you need?"

"I think so." I put my right foot over my left toes. "I forgot my slippers."

"You look cute in your bare feet and pajamas," he says. "Like you belong here."

I glance around thinking just how highly unlikely that would be, despite what he says.

"You'll stay here until we figure out what to do about Trey."

I don't understand why he doesn't realize that if Trey is a threat to me now, he'll be a threat to me three weeks from now.

Maybe he's thinking a restraining order will work. A

restraining order only works on some guys. It's not a guarantee.

Surely he knows these things.

"Okay," I say. He tucks a strand of hair behind one of my ears, his fingers lingering in my hair.

"I like having you here," he says.

I swallow. "I never got my tour," I say.

"In that case, let's start with my bedroom."

THIRTY-SIX

Grayson

"Your bedroom?" Emma looks at me sideways.

"Yes," I say, taking her hand and leading her along toward my bedroom. "It's a mirror image of the large guest room. Your room. Except that I have a view of Uptown."

"What's that way?" she asks as we pass the small area overlooking the pool.

"North. It's not very interesting."

I lead her straight into my bedroom over to the windows. I don't have to worry about my room being in order. The cleaning service comes in every morning and cleans everything up. Makes sure all the clothes are picked up, washed and dried, and put back where they belong.

"You're right," she says. "I can see the Galleria from here." She stands against the window looking down.

"I like watching the traffic on 610," I say standing behind her, looking over her shoulder.

My gaze shifts from the traffic to our reflection in the glass.

We look good together. I'm about a head taller than she is, but compared to me, she's a tiny little thing.

It takes all my restraint not to wrap my arms around her and pull her back against me. I'd like to nibble on her ear. Kiss her neck. Trail kisses down her back.

Maybe see what, if anything, is underneath her pajamas. In fact, just thinking about her standing in my bedroom with no underwear. Just those cute little pajamas with ducks on them has all the blood pooling low in my belly.

I didn't even have to touch her. Just thinking about touching her has me hard and aching.

"Let me show you my favorite sitting area," I say, turning away before I yield to temptation.

"Oscar!" Emma says, turning around to find her cat in the middle of my bed, kneading his claws on my comforter. "You can't be in here."

I put a hand on her arm to stop her from rushing forward to grab her cat. "Oscar can sleep on my bed. He's welcome to go anywhere he wants to go."

She looks up at me. "Are you sure? I know you're not a cat person."

"I never said I wasn't a cat person. I just said I don't have any pets. There's a difference."

"Traitor," she says to Oscar as we walk past.

"I think he likes me."

She looks at me sideways but doesn't say anything.

"What's not to like?" I ask.

"I have to have a talk with him."

"Sometimes I get lonely," I say. "He'll be good company."

"Well now I'll be lonely."

"You know where to find us." Before she has time to react, I sweep an arm toward my little sitting area. "This is my favorite place in the house."

"I see why," she says. "I love the fireplace."

"I'm not supposed to have it," I say. "It took an act of congress to get gas run up here."

"Is there nothing you can't do?" she asks, mostly to herself.

"No," I say. "Do you want to see the rest of the house?"

"Tomorrow. I think I'm asleep on my feet."

"I can help you with that."

THIRTY-SEVEN

Emma

I SQUEAL as Grayson picks me up, one hand beneath my knees, the other beneath my shoulders.

Wrapping my arms around his neck, I hold on as he carries me back past the kitchen and down the long hallway leading to my room.

To my relief, Oscar runs past us, heading back to our room.

"See," Grayson says. "Oscar didn't desert you."

"Good." It's all I can think to say, my voice coming out breathlessly.

With no obvious effort whatsoever, he carries me to my

bed and deposits me on top of it.

"Is the bed to your liking?" he asks.

"I'm looking forward to finding out." I sit up, pulling my knees up to me.

Oscar jumps onto the bed and flops down on the other pillow.

Grayson sits down on the bed beside me.

"Now," he says. "I have a meeting first thing in the morning."

"About me?"

"Technically about Trey. But then I have to go by your university and have a meeting about you."

"You're not supposed to do that."

"Probably not."

"But you're going to do it anyway."

"Yes. If you need anything, James will be here. You can find him in the staff room."

"You have a staff room?"

"Of course."

I nod slowly. Of course he does.

I'm quickly coming to accept that Grayson's life is nothing like mine and along with that acceptance comes the realization that the dress he'd bought me and the television he'd given me were nothing to him. My year's worth of salary is just pocket change for him.

"If you need to go anywhere when I'm not here, let James drive you."

"I have a class tomorrow afternoon."

"Let James go with you. I'll be on a flight over to Austin, but I'll be back."

"Okay."

"I have to meet with the big boss, Noah Worthington, too. He needs to know about Trey."

I wince. I hate getting someone in trouble.

Grayson seems to read my mind.

"Don't even think about protecting him." He presses a finger lightly to the swollen area beneath my eye. "He left you on the floor. And then he sends you a threatening text."

"After you talked to him." I don't mean to sound accusatory because I'm not. "So now you're part of it."

"I was part of it from the time you walked out of the restroom at the Speakeasy."

"I guess you were." I wince again.

"Don't worry about me. I can't take care of myself. And I can take care of you, too. All you have to do is let me."

I nod slowly and bite my bottom lip.

"I believe you."

And the idea of letting Grayson take care of me has my blood racing through my veins.

I lean forward and press my lips against his.

"You did that," he says against my lips.

"I did."

Putting his hands on either side of my shoulders, touching me only with his lips, he leans over me and nudges me onto my back.

"Are you sure you wanted to do that?" His voice sounds more like a growl now.

"I try not to doubt myself."

His fingers move to the sides of my head, tangling in my hair as he devours my lips with his.

The only noise is a train passing by somewhere far below.

I don't hear any cars. No sounds of the city far below.

He tongue nudges my lips apart, sweeping through my mouth in what is quickly becoming a familiar manner.

With one hand still in my hair, cupping the side of my face, his other hand goes to my waist and finds its way beneath my pajama top.

His fingers skim my skin, warm and sure, sliding over my waist as if he's memorizing every inch of me.

"You're trembling," he whispers, his breath still mingling with mine.

"I'm not cold."

He smiles against my lips, a slow possessive smirk that makes heat swirl low in my stomach.

I arch into him as his hand trails slowly, painfully up my ribcage, just brushing the side of my breast as he discovers I'm not wearing anything beneath my top. He hesitates... a moment's pause... but I press a kiss to the corner of his mouth, giving him silent encouragement.

His lips are still on mine, but hungrier now, more certain. His body aligns with mine as he shifts over me, one thigh sliding between mine. My hands tug at his shirt, pulling it out of his pants. My fingers slip beneath his shirt, finding ridges of muscle and heat.

He groans quietly, low in his throat, the sound vibrating between us as he deepens the kiss.

I gasp as his thumb travels ever so slowly along the underside of my breast and his mouth trails kisses down to my neck. Slowly. Deliberately. Excruciating.

The world falls away.

The train rumbling past. The city below. The reasons we shouldn't.

There's just him. Just us.

And this moment neither of us wants to end.

A moment when time stands still.

His hand slides slowly back down to my waist, the warmth of his palm igniting sparks across my skin. He pauses again, giving me every chance to stop him. But I don't want him to stop.

"Grayson," I whisper, urging him for more.

That's all it takes.

Groaning softly, he moves over me, his weight pressing me into the mattress, solid and protective and right. His mouth is on mine again, his breath mingling hot with mine. I tug at his hair, needing more, pushing and pulling at the same time.

He finds the hem of my pajama top again, starting with the bottom button, slowly, deliberately unbuttoning each one. In the hazy moonlight coming in from those windows with no shades, his gaze travels down my body and for a moment everything stills. In this moment, we're the only two people in the world.

"You're beautiful," he murmurs against my lips.

Then his mouth is on mine again. Hot. Hungry. Tender. His hands and lips map every inch of my skin. Claiming me. As his hips settle between mine and I feel the hardness of him pressing against me, I moan. But not from pain. From how much I want him. From how much I need him.

I wrap my legs around his waist, urging him closer. I have no doubts. No hesitation.

Just a feeling that everything is right.

Time becomes fluid with no beginning and no end.

Minutes... hours... later when he finally enters me, everything else falls away. There is only his touch, his breath, and the passionate promise of something I never knew I wanted until now.

CHAPTER
THIRTY-EIGHT

Grayson

I'M up early the next morning, showered, dressed, and ready to get things done.

I'd slipped out of Emma's room just as the sun lightened the horizon, careful not to wake her.

If I'd had a rose in the house, I would have left one on her pillow. I could have asked James to bring one on his way in, but that would be too obvious.

So I had to console myself with planning something for later. Something I could do myself.

I want the intimacy we'd shared to be just between the

two of us. Not something to be bantered about with other guys. Not even James.

As far as I'm concerned, Emma is mine now. Mine to cherish and protect. Those are things I'm good at. And she deserves the best of what I can give her.

As much as I might have wanted to wake up with her, I have too much to do this morning. Too much to do, for her, before I have to make a quick flight over to Austin, drop off a passenger, and fly back.

I step out of the shower, dry off, and put on my pilot's uniform. black pants and a white button-down shirt. A uniform I've pretty much adopted as my everyday dress code.

Before leaving my closet, I grab a black blazer, and cap, both with the Skye Travels logo on them. I only wear the cap when I'm flying. It's a small detail that Noah insists on for all his pilots. A dash of whimsey perhaps.

Since I've given James the job of watching over Emma, driving her wherever she wants to go, and essentially being her bodyguard, I'll be driving myself around today.

I don't mind. I'll take the sports car I don't drive very often.

My first stop is the university.

I don't think they'll need proof of Trey's danger to Emma, but if they do, then I can get it for them. I'm really hoping that I don't have to put her through that though.

I have enough clout in the city that I shouldn't have to

do more than tell the President of the university what I need to have done.

That Emma needs some time off from hanging out at the campus and that she'll be working remotely until further notice.

If she wants to show up for her classes, she can do so, but she'll do it with either James or me with her. Today it'll be James.

I hate leaving her even just long enough to fly to Austin and back, but flying is my primary job. The one I don't want to give up.

Speaking of my primary job, I have to let Noah know what's going on. I'm fairly certain that Noah will be firing Trey over this matter. I'd be disappointed if he doesn't.

Either way, I still hold the trump card of pulling Trey's pilot license. Noah won't do that. He would do that if he caught Trey drinking alcohol and something else that put passengers in danger.

This thing with Emma is personal to me.

Dressed and ready to go, I head to the kitchen.

And then there's the matter of my father.

I make myself a strong cup of coffee and pour it into a travel mug.

I check my watch. I want to be at the university when the president gets there. Waiting is not something I have time for today.

What I do have time for is getting everything done to

ensure Emma's safety and get back to her as soon as possible.

She's mine now.

And I protect what's mine.

THIRTY-NINE

Emma

THE NEXT MORNING, sunlight spills across the luxuriously soft sheets on the heavenly soft mattress.

Stretching beneath the covers, I gaze out the window—no shades—across the city toward downtown. The sun peeks over the horizon, casting an ombré wash of orange across the morning sky.

Such a luxury to wake up to such a beautiful view.

I'm pleasantly sore in my core, a reminder of last night's passion spent in Grayson's arms. I'd gotten far more than protection from him.

I'd gotten something I hadn't even realized I'd needed. He was gentle and giving.

"Meow." Oscar pats my pillow as though to say enough with the reminiscing. It's time to get up and feed me.

Wearing my pajamas, I walk barefoot down the hall, a can of cat food in my hand and Oscar bouncing along beside me, tail high.

He seems to know just where to go. Hops up on the pristine kitchen island to wait while I search for a plate to dump his food in.

After a couple of false attempts, I finally open the right door to find a small plate and matching bowl, both solid white and heavy.

"I don't think you're supposed to eat up there," I tell Oscar, pulling him into my arms and taking all my supplies back to my room.

Making myself at home and spreading cat things all over the house seem like two different things to me.

As I feed Oscar, I debate whether to take a shower or a bath.

I decide on the shower.

It wasn't just a shower, it was an experience. There wasn't just the rain water falling overhead, there were half a dozen sprayers shooting water out at the same time. I spent some time playing around with the sprayers in what appeared to be an endless supply of hot water.

Out and dressed, one big soft towel wrapped around me and my hair wrapped in another, I send my department chair a message informing him that I won't be at the committee meeting this morning. A family issue.

I spend some time on my hair and makeup and by the time I've finished my makeup, my black eye is barely noticeable unless I lean over the counter and look closely.

No mascara today. I'm much too careful with my injured eye to put myself through that.

Fortunately I reserve mascara for going out so my students are accustomed to seeing me without it.

I get a message back from my department chair telling me to take all the time I need. Let him know how he can help. My job will be there when I'm ready to come back.

An unexpectedly odd response. I let him know that I'll be reaching my classes at minimum.

I put on a pair of black slacks and an emerald green blouse, my black ankle boots, and go in search of coffee.

I find a coffee mug and what I think is a built-in coffee maker, but figuring out how to use it is another thing entirely.

Thinking maybe James is around, I go in search of the staff room.

It's not hard to find. The whole condo is set up in one big rectangle. Depending on where one is standing at any given moment, one can see the city in any direction.

The staff room looks south, probably the least desirable view since the view is another, shorter, high rise.

"Good morning," James says, looking up from where he's typing on a notebook computer.

Even the chauffeur has more than one job, it seems.

"Hi. I was…" I hold up the coffee mug. "hoping for a cup of coffee, but…"

"Sure." He closes his computer and gets up. "The coffee machine is great, but it takes some getting used to."

"Good to know it's not just me," I say.

"Come on I'll make it for you."

"Thank you so much."

"Did you sleep well?" he asks as we walk down the hallway back toward the kitchen.

I hope he doesn't see the heat rise to my cheeks. "Considering it's a strange place, not too bad."

"Good. You'll sleep better tonight."

He flips switches on the mysterious coffee machine.

"How do you take it?" he asks.

"Anything resembling a cappuccino if possible."

"This baby can make any kind of coffee you want. Hot tea. Hot cocoa. You name it."

While the coffee brews, he watches me from the corner of his eye.

"Am I driving you to the university today?"

"I have a class to teach, but I'm skipping my committee meeting."

"Good idea. Just tell me what time we need to be there."

He hands me a cup of coffee with lots of caramel froth.

"This is better than I expected," I say.

"You should ask Grayson to give you a lesson working this thing. He knows it inside and out."

"I will. Thank you."

"Just come find me if you need anything else," he says.

I sit down at the little breakfast table and sip my coffee while I check email on my phone.

James seems to think I'm going to be staying here for a while. I wonder.

I just wonder.

CHAPTER
FORTY

Grayson

With my morning errands taken care of, I have time to stop by the flower shop before heading up to the airport.

The young lady behind the counter doesn't so much as bat an eye when I arrange to send a dozen roses to my own address.

It seems right. Sending Emma flowers after last night.

I've been thinking about her all day and even though she's okay and safe in my condo, I find it hard to resist checking in with James.

Knowing that James is with her is even worth the sacrifice of driving myself around.

The university president had been understanding as I'd known he would be.

It helps that he's been invited to a few of my family's social functions. It's a reminder to myself to invite people like him at random times to attend random events. It gives me more connections and we never know when those connections will come in handy.

Today is a perfect example of that.

After sending the flowers on their way, I start the drive up to the airport.

James will be the one the concierge will call when the flowers are delivered. He'll wonder about it, but he won't know. He'll suspect, but he won't say anything.

He won't judge. He likes Emma.

As I weave in and out of traffic, I wonder what I'm going to do about Emma.

With Trey's threat hanging over her, I can't let her go back to her place.

I'll ask Noah what to do. He'll know. He's the smartest man I know.

Greeted by the sound of a commercial jet coming in for a landing, I pull into the parking lot.

The airport is hands down my favorite place.

It takes a lot for me to want to be somewhere else. Emma's doing that. Emma is making me want to be some-where else.

Anywhere she is will do.

Right now, knowing she's in my condo, showering,

getting dressed, doing ordinary everyday things, makes me want to be there with her.

Going inside the Skye Travels terminal, I realize I don't want her to leave.

I shake my head as I push he elevator button that will take me up to the second floor.

She can't just live with me indefinitely. She has her own place. Her own life. I can't just uproot her and expect her to put down roots with me.

I've known her all of what? Three days.

And I did exactly what I promised myself I wasn't going to do. I took her to bed. And with everything hanging over me in an uncertain cloud.

I get off the elevator and walk straight toward Noah's office.

"I'm sorry," his personal receptionist says. "He's not in today. He won't be back until tomorrow. Can I take a message?"

"No," I say. "It'll wait." It can't, really, but it will have to.

Since I showed up early to talk to Noah, I have some extra time to work. Instead of going to my usual office, a place I vowed I'd never work in again, I set up my computer in the currently unoccupied conference room.

The room has a big floor to ceiling window overlooking the tarmac and another wall of windows along a view of the hallway.

I pay neither of them any mind as I open up a file and read over an acquisition contract.

Every acquisition... every sale... puts me that much closer to buying my own airplane. With my own airplane, I have a whole lot more options. I can continue to fly for Skye Travels, but I can also fly myself for personal business.

I can take pleasure trips, something I don't get to do. There are a number of places I'd like to take Emma.

The thought gives me pause. I swivel around in my chair and watch a small jet take off on the private runway.

I can't be making plans with Emma right now. Not those kinds of plans.

I have the thing with my father and my grandfather's will to get worked out before I can make plans like that.

Bringing Emma into that mess is not something I want to do.

I've got to find a legal loophole to get out of it. I check my watch. I was supposed to meet with my attorney about that today, but other more pressing matters came up.

Tomorrow. Tomorrow I'll meet with my attorney. See what kind of options I have.

And then right on cue I get a message from my father.

I swivel back around to the table.

FATHER

Missed you yesterday.

Not how are you doing? Everything okay. Just understated judgment.

Something pressing came up.

FATHER
Come to dinner tonight.

Again. No niceties with him. Not a request. Just a demand.

If I get back from my flight to Austin in time.

FATHER
Bring your girlfriend. Your mother and I want to meet her.

I stare at the message while sorting through all the implications of that statement.

First of all, what makes him think I have a girlfriend? If he's talking about Emma, how does he know about her?

There's no one else he could be talking about.

It's also possibly he's being a smart ass.

It's probably his way of telling me to get my act together and find a girlfriend or he'll find one for me.

Well. I've got news for my father.

I'm not interested in any of the women my father thinks I should be interested in.

Not a chance in hell.

I've already found the woman I'm interested in.

I'll take her to dinner. To meet my parents, but I'm not about to drag her into this whole inheritance business.

My phone alarm goes off before I figure out how to respond.

It's time for me to get down to the tarmac and start my preflight checklist.

Everything else has to go on hold until I get back from Austin.

As I'm packing everything up, I get a message from Monique, my girl from Dallas.

MONIQUE

Your father invited me to dinner tonight.

CHAPTER
FORTY-ONE

Emma

Teaching my class today goes into the bizarre category.

James not only drives me to class, he parks the car and walks me to my classroom. Okay. I can get behind that. No one bats an eye at me being escorted to class by a handsome man. Not *my* handsome man, but a handsome man, nonetheless.

It had been a little strange riding in the back seat of the SUV, but I'd used the extra time to go over my PowerPoint for today's lecture. Not a bad set up.

Grayson is on a flight to Austin. If he hadn't had a flight, would he have walked me to my class? The possibility distracts me as I set up my computer and log in.

When I look up and see James sitting in the back row of my classroom near the door, my heart slams against my chest.

I can't help thinking that maybe I missed something.

I get it that Trey was an asshole who gave me a black eye and left me there on the floor. In his defense, I had told him to leave me alone.

And, yes, he'd sent me a threatening text message, but I saw that as him lashing out in anger.

I'm definitely missing something somewhere.

I'm missing the thing that has Grayson and James, too, perhaps, taking Trey's threats to the limit.

It's possible they know something about Trey that I don't.

The thought gives me pause.

I'd dated Trey for long enough that I should know if he was mentally unstable. I'm a psychologist, for God's sake. Wouldn't I have seen it?

But in all truthfulness, we didn't see each other all that much when we were dating.

He was always out of town. Or resting from traveling.

After I put my phone on silent and slide it into the front pocket of my leather bag, I open up my laptop computer and just like I always do when I'm in front of the classroom, I shove all my personal stuff to a back room of my mind and close the door. For the next hour, my focus is going to be completely on my lecture and my students.

I am, aptly, talking about anxiety today. Something that engages my students. Something everyone experiences at one point or another at one level or another.

No one seems to notice that since last Wednesday's class, my life has changed to the point that I have what is essentially a bodyguard sitting in the back of my classroom.

But not all the things that had changed were bad.

I'd spent last night in Grayson's arms.

I found it hard not to think about, to replay it, over and over in my head.

I have to be careful though. Grayson, like Trey, is a pilot and Trey hadn't left a very good taste in my mouth when it came to pilots.

They're different, though.

In fact, they're so different that the only similarity between them might just be their choice of career.

But with stalwart determination, I put all that behind me as I pull up my first slide.

Generalized Anxiety Disorder.

"How many of you have ever been worried about something but you don't know what it is you're worried about and really there is nothing obvious to be worried about?"

I raise my hand and every hand in the room goes up.

Including James's.

This is good.

I'm in my element.

Standing in front of a classroom is where I'm most at home.

CHAPTER
FORTY-TWO

Grayson

My FLIGHT to Austin and back is uneventful as any good flight should be. It's a beautiful fall day. Perfect for flying. Not a cloud in the sky. Just forever blue sky in every direction.

I'd been planning on having a few hours of quiet contemplation for myself.

Dr. Savannah Worthington calls flying a positive addiction.

I have to agree with her. I need time in the air like a runner needs time on the track.

Flying time allows me to think my own thoughts without interruption. I don't count control tower chatter or even occasional questions from passengers. I certainly don't count monitoring gauges and computer screens. Those things are just part of the job. Those things keep me alert.

I'd been planning on using the fight time today to think about Emma. I'd been looking forward to it quite a bit.

But instead, the most coherent thought I keep coming back around to is *What the Hell?*

My father had somehow found out about Monique and he had then drawn the conclusion that Monique is my girlfriend.

He could not be further than the truth. Whether she is my friends with benefits girl or a booty call girl, she is not my girlfriend. Never was. Never will be.

I can't contact her. Not while I'm in the air and the flight is a quick turnaround, leaving me no time to contact her while I'm in Austin.

So I spend the entire flight there and back trying to figure out what the hell happened and even more importantly what I'm going to do about it.

If Monique is coming to dinner tonight with my family, then I certainly can't take Emma.

And yet Emma is the only person I want to take. I don't want to be apart from Emma for the evening. I don't want to be apart from her at all.

If Monique is going, I decide, I'm not going. Period. End of conversation. I'm not willing to spend an evening pretending to be with someone I'm not. Nor am I willing to spend an evening explaining to her and everyone else that she and I are, in fact, not dating.

Fortunately I don't have a passenger on the return trip, so I don't have to worry about trying to keep a calm demeanor.

I'm free to brood all I want. And that's exactly what I do.

I brood.

And I fret.

And try as I might, I can't figure out how my father and Monique crossed paths to begin with much less for my father to somehow mistake what I have... had... with Monique as her being a girlfriend.

I admit I haven't given any thought to Monique this weekend, but if I had given her any thought it was that I had not been planning on seeing her again.

Maybe I'd let her know at some point, but our relationship isn't the kind of relationship that requires us staying in touch between my visits.

For all I know, she has other boyfriends. I don't care. Never did.

But now I'm forced to care. Forced to think about Monique more than I've ever thought about her outside of when she and I were together for an evening's entertainment.

As soon as I'm back on the ground, I've got to figure out how to fix this disaster that has fallen in my lap.

My father has got to learn to stay out of my business.

Not even this inheritance thing gives him license to get into my love life.

By the time I land back in Houston, I have seven text messages on my phone and three voicemails.

CHAPTER
FORTY-THREE

Emma

CLASS GOES WELL and James waits patiently in his seat by the back door while I talk with the few students who come up after class.

One of them wants to ask about the upcoming test.

Two of them want to talk about their own experiences with anxiety.

And one male student feels the need to tell me that just coming up to talk to me gives him a panic attack. I refer him to the counseling center even though I don't expect him to go. I've referred this particular student before and he never follows through with counseling.

James takes my computer bag and throws it effortlessly over his shoulder.

"Good class," he says.

"Thanks."

"I can honestly say I learned something today."

I smile over at James. "Then I did my job."

As we walk across campus toward the car, he scowls at his phone.

"Everything okay?" I ask.

He glances over at me, then glances around us. Slides his phone back into his front pocket.

"It will be. Grayson landed back in Houston."

"Oh." A sudden rush of emotion flows through me at the thought of seeing Grayson again. An intoxicating mix of anticipation, nervousness, and a tangled ball of what I can only call anxiety.

Upon reaching the SUV, James opens the back door and waits while I settle in to the backseat.

"Do you need to go anywhere else before we head home?" he asks from the front seat.

"No," I say. "I'm good."

Home. He's taking me home.

It would be so easy to get used to calling Grayson's condo home.

"Any word about Trey?" I ask as James leaves the parking lot.

"No. Nothing."

"I guess that's good," I murmur to myself, relaxing

against the soft leather seat.

I pull out my phone and check my messages. None. No cryptic messages from Trey which is a relief. But no messages from Grayson either.

He sent James a message telling him he's back on the ground, but no message to me.

Maybe he knows that James will tell me. Maybe he doesn't want to disturb my class.

That's it, I decide, holding my phone in my lap.

Grayson knows I have a class this afternoon, but he doesn't know what time exactly. He's just being respectful by not wanting to disturb me.

While we sit in traffic on the freeway back to Grayson's condo, I send an email to my family telling them that Trey and I broke up. I don't go into detail why. And I don't tell them that Trey threatened me and now I'm hiding out in Grayson's thirty-first floor condo. They don't even know who Grayson is.

I don't want them to worry about me. There's nothing they can do anyway, especially being over in Portugal like they are.

They have my little sister to take care of. She'll be eighteen in... I check the date... a couple of weeks.

I make a note to call her on her birthday. It would be great if I could get over there to visit her, but her birthday is right in the middle of my semester so that's not going to happen.

I'll call her and send her a gift. If I'm going to send her an actual gift, though, I've got to move on that right away.

I send a follow up email to my mother.

Any thoughts on what I can give Michaela for her birthday?

"We're here," James says as he pulls into the circle drive of the Arabella.

I'm quickly getting used to having valets throw open the car doors and grabbing my computer bag. Extending a hand to help me out.

It wouldn't be hard to get used to this lifestyle.

Following James inside to the elevator, I remind myself that even though he calls it home, I have to remember that I'm just a guest here. I mustn't let myself get too used to living here. To living this lifestyle.

The elevator stops on our floor and we step off into Grayson's living room. The floor has three elevators. I counted them. But only one of them, this one, is private.

I wouldn't be able to get back up even if I rode down to the ground. I don't have a fob. No one can get upstairs without a fob.

So even though I'm safe, I'm also something of a prisoner.

Oscar, who doesn't seem to mind being a prisoner in the least, comes prancing down the hallway to meet me just outside the elevator.

There's a bouquet of red roses that wasn't there before sitting on the island.

James checks the card, then hands it to me without opening it.

"These are for you," he says, his expression blank.

"Me?"

He hands me the card with my name scrawled across the front.

My first thought is that Trey had done something.

My fingers tremble as I open up the card.

Welcome home.

Grayson

Well. James must have recognized Grayson's handwriting. He doesn't show any concern whatsoever at the bouquet of red roses sitting on the kitchen island that wasn't there when we'd left shortly after lunch.

Everything is cleaned up. Coffee mug washed and put away. Floors and counters shining.

Having someone come in to clean the house would bother me, mostly because I'd worry about Oscar. But my cat seems unscathed by the cleaning service.

I pick him up and set him on the kitchen island while I examine the deep crimson, lush and velvety, petals that exude a warm honeyed scent.

Twelve red rose buds nestled among champagne-hued baby's breath and a whisper of eucalyptus in a sleek, modern crystal vase with subtle etching. A black silk ribbon tied in a large bow finish it off.

What am I supposed to do with them?

James has already disappeared down the hallway toward the staff room.

Left to my own devices, I decide that I should take them to my room.

I carefully slide the heavy vase of flowers off the counter and, holding them close to me, head down the hallway. Oscar hops off the island and runs alongside me.

In my bedroom, I find my bed made, my used towels washed and put away. And Oscar's plate washed and ready.

I put the flowers on the dresser, then go about the business of feeding Oscar.

He nudges my hand while I open up can of food and dump it out into the clean plate.

I sit on the floor next to him while he eats and rub a hand along his back.

"What are we supposed to do now?" I ask him. He just purrs in answer.

I can't go home and I can't stay here.

Sitting up, I cross my legs.

That's not entirely true. I can go home.

I have to go home. Eventually.

I'll get some kind of weapon. Some pepper spray or a taser gun.

I have a mortgage for God's sake. I can't just abandon my home.

But since I'm here, I'm not going to just rashly leave without more information.

I'll wait to see what Grayson finds out regarding the situation. Acting rash and impulsive is not my style.

I stare out the window across the city toward the cluster of buildings that make up the Houston skyline.

I'm not usually impulsive. I just hope that Grayson doesn't think I was being impulsive last night.

FORTY-FOUR

Grayson

I MAKE a smooth landing at the Houston airport and taxi down the runway.

It's my favorite time of day. The time just before sunset when the sun begins its downward trek, splashing an array of pinks across the horizon.

The scent of jet fuel fills the air along with the roar of jet engines.

Commercial jets come and go from the main runways.

Skye Travels is tucked off to the side of the airport with its own little three-story terminal. Although the light isn't right for me to see it, Noah Worthington's office makes up the second and third floors of the building's corner giving him an unparalleled view over his domain.

I'll have to drive back up here tomorrow to talk to the boss about Trey. The situation is one of those that demands a face to face conversation. No way around that one as far as I'm concerned.

I park the airplane, but before I start through my post flight checklist, I check my messages.

I read the texts from Monique first.

> **MONIQUE**
>
> Hey
>
> **MONIQUE**
>
> I haven't heard from you lately.
>
> **MONIQUE**
>
> I called the Skye Travels office. Spoke to your friend Trey. He gave me your family's home number.

That son-of-a-bitch.

So that's how Trey decided to get back at me.

That. Devious. Asshole.

Trey's vindictiveness is off the chain.

Everyone who works here knows that it's against policy to give out private numbers. Hell. That's common knowledge at any place of business.

Trey is just a son-of-a-bitch.

My father, instead of sending text messages, left me a voicemail.

Grayson. I talked to your girlfriend. Monique. Sounds like a very nice young lady. I'm sending a helicopter up to Dallas to bring her down to dinner tonight. The sooner she meets the family, the sooner we can move things along.

I know exactly what he means by *things*. He means the inheritance.

I've always heard the expression "seeing red," but I never quite grasped the emotion. Until right now.

Right now I see red.

Trey did this.

Because of Trey my father thinks I'm dating Monique. He's sending a helicopter to pick her up.

I let loose a string of curse words that would make a sailor blush.

And to think that I was planning on taking Emma to meet my family tonight.

Either that or I was going to spend a quiet evening at home with Emma.

Either way my plans involved Emma.

But now, instead of spending the evening with Emma, one way or another, I'm stuck spending the evening pretending that Monique is my girlfriend.

This won't do.

I'm going to fix this once and for all.

Taking a deep breath, I dial my father directly. My voice is calm, too calm, but even I hear the controlled fury simmering just beneath the surface.

"Father," I say evenly. "You're not sending a helicopter for anyone tonight."

My father's voice comes back through the line, sounding bored and weary. "Your mother and I need to meet any woman you date at this point in order to vet her. You're past the point of wasting time playing games."

"You don't need to meet Monique. There is no Monique. I'm not dating her." I'm with Emma and she's the only one who matters to me, but my father hasn't earned the right to hear that yet.

"It's too late," he says, his voice loud and clear. "Monique is already here."

FORTY-FIVE

Emma

I'm sitting in Grayson's favorite sitting area looking out over 610 and the Galleria as the sun sets, playing around with a PowerPoint for Wednesday's upcoming lecture.

A cup of coffee sits on a glass-topped table next to me. Oscar curled up on the ottoman.

I figured how to turn on the gas fireplace.

It's ridiculously cozy.

I miss my little house. Sort of.

Being here is... different.

I know it's a novelty and it will probably wear off, but right now I like it. A lot.

I finally got a text from Grayson about an hour ago.

GRAYSON

Had to take care of something, but
on my way home. See you soon.

He calls this home, too, but it is home for him.

I'd taken one of the roses from the bouquet in my room and brought it with me. It's lying across my textbook so I can enjoy just looking at it while I work.

I'm deep in edits when I feel someone standing behind me. I hadn't heard footsteps.

I look over my shoulder.

Grayson is standing there, leaning against the door-frame, watching me.

"Hi," I say, closing my computer and putting my feet on the floor.

"Hi," he says, pushing off the doorframe and coming to sit next to me.

He picks up the rose and examines the petals.

"They only brought you one?" he asks.

"What? No. The others are in my room."

"Good."

"They're beautiful," I say. "And very unexpected."

"Are you okay?" he asks, looking at my eye now.

"I hardly even notice it anymore."

"Well, that's something," he says.

His mood is different now. Something is bothering him.

"What about you? Are you okay?" I ask.

"I had to take care of some family business. Annoying more than anything else."

"Do you want to talk about it?" I ask.

He looks at me with an odd expression.

"Psychologist mode?"

"Second nature."

"Hmm. As much as I might want to... no."

"Okay," I say. "How was your flight?"

"Uneventful."

Oscar stands up, stretches, and walks over to him to get his head scratched.

I just shake my head. Not that I blame him.

I can't decide if this is just his mood being weird or if this is the awkwardness of the morning after. Maybe it's weird with me being here in his house. On the morning after.

We both speak at the same time.

"Maybe I should go back to my house."

"Do you want to get tacos?"

He smiles and I smile back.

"I don't think you should go back to your house," he says.

"Tacos sound good," I say.

He cups my face gently, his expression softening.

Then his lips seal against mine.

I sigh, my breath mingling with his.

His fingers tangle in my hair as his thumb scrapes across my bottom lip urging my lips apart.

His tongue caresses mine. Exploring. Memorizing. Claiming.

CHAPTER
FORTY-SIX

Grayson

AFTER HAVING TACOS DELIVERED, Emma and I settle in at my marble dining table to eat.

As I'm pulling everything out of the bags, James stops by on his way out.

"If you don't need me any more today, Boss," James says. "I'm going to head out."

"Have some tacos first," I say, shoving a chair out with my foot. "I ordered enough for all of us."

"Can't," he says. "I've got a date."

Both Emma and I stop what we're doing and look at him.

"With who?" I ask.

"An old girlfriend from high school. I haven't seen her in ten years."

I look over at Emma then back to James.

"I can't decide if you're brave or crazy."

"Maybe both," he says, but I can see the nerves in his eyes.

"Hey," I say. "Take the Ferrari."

"I can't do that," James says.

I try not to notice Emma's raised eyebrows.

"I insist."

James looks over at Emma. "I don't want to frighten her."

Emma looks at me with an expression I can't read. "You have a Ferrari?" Without waiting for an answer, she turns to James. "Take the Ferrari. Impress the girl."

"See," I say. "We want an invitation to the wedding."

"Setting expectations like that," he says, grumbling. "You'll be paying for the wedding."

"Don't think I won't," I say as James grabs the keys to the Ferrari on his way out.

"You're a good man," Emma says as she unwraps a taco.

"Second nature," I say with a little wink.

But the truth is, I hope she still thinks so after she meets my family.

"So... sort of related to what I had to take care of," I say, unwrapping a taco for myself. "My parents want to meet you."

"Why?" she asks.

"You know how parents are," I say. "They're desperate for grandchildren and I'm the oldest."

She turns all different shades of green and her eyes widen.

"Just kidding," I say. "I had them all primed to meet you yesterday and now I have to make it up to them."

"Okay," she says, clearing her throat. "I'm not going in to the office tomorrow. My department chair was unusually understanding."

"Yeah? What did you tell him?"

"I just told him I had a family issue. I think he would have found someone to cover my classes if I'd asked. Very odd."

"Huh. I'm glad to hear it."

And it's good to know that the university president did what he promised he would do.

Emma doesn't need to know that I took care of it for her.

She's got enough to deal with.

And there are so many things I haven't told her about yet.

So many things I have to deal with before I'm free to be myself with her.

CHAPTER

FORTY-SEVEN

Emma

AFTER DINNER we go into Grayson's movie room.

The movie room is small. A little room with no windows.

"I call it my movie room for one," he says.

It appears to be aptly named. The only place to sit is a chaise lounge.

"Do you watch a lot of movies in here?" I ask. I don't understand the concept of the movie room. He has a perfectly good flat screen television that looks like a painting on the wall in his living room.

"I've watched two movies in here," he says.

"Why just two?"

"It just seems silly when I have televisions in my living room and my bedroom. The funny thing is I rarely watch any of them."

"That's too bad," I say. "But I'm the same way."

"Hard to watch television when you don't have one, huh?"

"Chicken and the egg." I sit on the edge of the chaise. "Can we both fit on here?"

"I'm looking forward to finding out."

Sitting down next to me, he pulls me close and turns on the television. Then he hands me the remote.

"You drive," he says.

I go back to the movie I'd picked out the other night. The one we hadn't watched.

"I hope you like drama," I say.

"I love drama as long as I don't have to deal with it in real life," he says. "Alexa. Turn off the light."

The room goes dark. With only the light from the television to light the room.

Grayson kisses me on the cheek.

I lean into him and wonder just how much of the movie we're going to actually watch.

Truth is. Although I really want to see the movie, I hope we don't watch much of it tonight.

There are so many other things I'd far rather do.

I snuggle closer to him, my head resting against his chest, listening to the steady beat of his heart. He drapes his arm around my shoulders, his thumb tracing slow circles on the sensitive skin near my earlobe.

The movie flickers across the screen, but I barely notice it. Cinematic music fills the room, but I barely hear it. My blood pounds through my veins, taking all my focus. Every thought is on the way he feels pressed against me, bringing every one of my nerves to life. Every beat of his heart is a promise.

"Are you paying attention to the movie?" he teases, his voice low and masculine, sending a little shiver through me.

I tilt my head up, meeting his gaze in the flickering light. "Should I be?"

His lips curve into a smile and he captures my lips with his. The kiss is gentle, so gentle, at first. We're still testing... learning... sharing.

It takes no more than mere moments, though, before need kindles and ignites, pulling us under.

I shift closer, impossibly so, pressing against him. I can't get close enough to him. His hands slide down to my hips as he deepens the kiss.

My fingers tangle in his hair and I sigh as our breath becomes one.

The movie is no more than background. He touches me as though I'm the only thing that matters. I feel his control slipping. Can feel it in the way his breath hitches.

Although my body burns for him, I want to savor the moment. To make it last. When he lifts me into his lap, I pull back a little, slowing things down. Savoring the feel of his lips against mine. His body beneath me.

His hands roam lazily over my back, finding their way just beneath the hem of my shirt. He groans as he finds bare skin and I shiver.

"I thought about this all day," he murmurs against my lips. "About you."

"Me too." My voice hitches, making it hard for me to catch my breath as his fingers roam ever so lazily up and down my back.

With the movie playing in the background, the light flickering with unseen images, time moves at its own pace. Not rushing. Not too slow. Just a lazy river that we float along on.

I shift again so that I'm straddling him, pressing my core against his hardness.

With a little moan, I tear my lips from his and arch my back, rubbing myself against him in little circles, our pants the only thing between us. My panties are wet. My body aches with need.

He moves tortuously slow in contrast to my sudden urgent need. Slowly unbuttoning my shirt, his fingers brush the skin beneath as he tortures me with those slow steady movements.

There is no hesitation this time. I feel wanted by him and that feeds my need.

He flicks my bra open, sliding the straps off my shoulders. His fingers circle my nipples, making them hard without even touching them.

When he takes one nipple in his mouth and licks the tip with his tongue, I lift my arms and lean into him. He replaces his lips with his fingertips as he moves to devour my other nipple.

I open my legs wider, grinding against his hardness.

I nearly come undone when he slides a finger beneath my waistband, sliding beneath my panties, down my butt, and finds the source of my wetness.

When he slides a finger deep inside me, I grab his shoulders and put my mouth back on his.

He thrusts his finger in and out, just the way I need, and the tension inside me coils tighter and tighter until I can no longer bear it. My moans mix with the sounds of his ragged breathing.

"I've got you," he murmurs, his lips against mine, two fingers inside me now, and it's those words—those simple, perfect words—that send me over the edge.

My body shatters against him, around his fingers, my climax crashing through me in waves. I whimper against him as I ride out the pulses of pleasure.

He holds me through the storm, his fingers slowing until I'm gasping and spent, my head falling forward onto his shoulder.

When he lays me back against the soft chaise, his hands gentle and his mouth hot against my skin, I feel cherished.

I don't care about the movie playing in the background or the millions of people in the city below us.

The world fades away, the only story I care about is our story. Breath by breath. Touch by touch. Heartbeat by heartbeat.

And every sigh in between.

FORTY-EIGHT

Grayson

THE NEXT EVENING Emma and I sit in the back seat of my SUV with James driving in the front.

She and I sit side by side in the middle of the backseat, our shoulders and thighs touching, our hands clasped tightly together.

Emma is wearing her gypsy dress and I'm wearing my usual black pants and white button-down shirt.

I don't think anyone is going to be around tonight other than my parents, but I want us to make a good impression.

We look good, if I do have to say so myself. I just wish I

felt as confident about this evening with my parents on the inside as I look on the outside.

"Did your girl like the Ferrari?" Emma asks James as we sit waiting in traffic to get out on San Felipe Street.

"She did," James says with a little secret grin I haven't seen on him in forever and a day.

"When are you going to see her again?" I ask. That is now my new litmus test for the strength of a relationship.

Now that I had Emma in my life, I never wanted her out of it. Not for a second.

Having her move in with me two days after we met was by accident, but I didn't regret it in the least and even though it might have been mostly by accident, I know that I wouldn't have let just anyone move into my condo.

I'm not that philanthropic. I am, in fact, extremely private. Almost private to a fault, but I balance that out with protectiveness.

"Tonight," he says, after I get off work.

I feel a twinge of guilt that James is driving us around instead of going out with his girl.

"Should have said something. I would have given you the night off."

"She understands."

"There's going to be a wedding," I say to Emma.

"I hope so. I can't wait to meet her."

"You'll like her," James beams as the traffic starts moving. "She's the same person I knew in high school and yet it's all new."

"I'm happy for you," I say.

"Thank you, Sir. I'm going to give you privacy now." He taps a button and the divider slides into place.

"There's something you need to know about my father," I say.

"What's that?"

"He can be an ass."

Emma looks at me sideways. "You're saying you take after your mother."

"Temperament wise, I guess I do. They say I look like my father, but that's about it."

"Duly noted."

"Try not to be offended by anything he says to you."

"I'll try not to be."

"My mother, though, is a very kind lady."

"I look forward to meeting her," she says as she looks away with a little smile.

"Are you okay?" I squeeze her hand.

She nods. "Of course. It's just. It's funny. I'm usually okay with my parents living in Portugal. It makes them happy. But sometimes... like now... I just miss them." She lifts her chin. "I'm okay though."

"We'll make a trip," I say, the words sliding off my tongue as natural as breathing. "We'll visit them. the first time you get a holiday."

Only when I see the genuine delight on her face do I think about all the hurdles we have to get past before I can make a promise like that into a reality.

First there's the matter of my inheritance. The little detail that requires me to take a wife. Someone my parents approve of. Not to mention just how angry my father is with me after last night's fiasco. One that, in my defense, I did not cause.

And then there's Trey. I still haven't had a chance to talk to Noah. Fortunately, Trey hasn't made any more threats and I'd sent James over to Emma's house earlier today to check on things. There was no sign that he'd made any attempt to break in. It was almost like he knew Emma wasn't there.

If I was a betting man, I'd put money on him knowing exactly where Emma is. All the more reason for me to do everything in my power to protect her.

FORTY-NINE

Emma

I THINK I expected Grayson's family to live someplace like my parents had lived before they left the country. They'd lived in a rather large two-story suburban-style house with lots of windows and natural light. A yard smaller than the house, but alive with colorful flowers that changed with the season.

One of my mother's favorite things to do was to get out and get her hands in the soil as she changed out the flowers each season.

My father, not nearly so inclined to be outside in the

heat, paid a teenage neighbor to mow the grass once a week.

That was the life I'd grown up in and Grayson seemed enough like me that I made assumptions.

My assumptions had been ever so very wrong.

Grayson's family lives in a mansion in River Oaks. Since River Oaks is one of the most expensive areas of Houston, I can't even begin to imagine the cost associated with living there.

In order to just drive in, we had to stop at a guard gate —with an armed guard. I'd thought we were going into a gated community, again, like the one I'd grown up in, until we pulled up in the circle drive of the only house inside the gate.

The house is completely hidden from the road and no one would know it's here unless they knew and even then they'd have to get past the guard first.

James lowers the partition and meets my gaze in the rear view mirror.

"We're here," he says, obviously for my benefit.

"I'll come around," Grayson says. "Get your door."

I could have just slid out with him, but instead I wait for him to come around to open my door.

One thing I'm good at is adapting to my surroundings. If Grayson needs to been seen opening my door, then I'll let him.

While I wait for him to come around, I look out at the house.

Three stories. Dark gray stone. Lots of tall windows.

No flowers on the lawn. Just an expanse of perfectly manicured grass with tall oak trees lining the edges creating a natural fence of sorts.

As Grayson opens the door, I hear water running. A little stream or maybe a water fountain.

Grayson says something to James, then James drives off.

I guess he's leaving us here for a while. Somehow I was more comfortable with him around. But then Grayson tucks my hand in the crook of his arm and I know I'm safe with him.

Even if he did feel like he had to warn me about his father.

He rings the doorbell like a guest and a butler dressed in a black tuxedo answers the door.

"Welcome, Mr. Grayson," the butler says.

"Thank you, Oliver," Grayson says. "How are you?"

"Doing good. Arthritis is acting up a bit, but I'll be okay. Come on in here, pretty lady." He opens the door wide. "They're waiting for you out on the patio."

We walk through a house that closely resembles Grayson's thirty-first floor condo in décor. Spacious. Minimalist.

Everything in its place.

Every surface spotless.

There may not have been flowers in the front yard, but there are flowers inside the house. Fresh flowers in vases.

Daffodils on a little table just inside the front door fill the house with their fresh clean scent.

Grayson leads me across gleaming hardwood floors, past a wide staircase leading up to the second floor.

A tall grandfather clock, that looks like a well-maintained antique stands next to the stairway, steadily marking the minutes.

We walk down a hallway that opens up into a kitchen. Gleaming countertops that look unused just like Grayson's. Two kitchen islands. Perhaps not looking used, but definitely ready to be put to use.

"Don't let them intimidate you," Grayson says as he opens the back door and steps outside first as though to shield me from his parents.

His father is standing at an oversized barbeque grill wearing a red apron. His mother is lounging on a chair sipping a little pink drink.

At first glance, they look harmless enough. Normal.

At the sound of the door opening, his mother gets to her feet.

"They're here, Thomas," she says.

Thomas wipes his hands on his apron and turns to smile at me, ignoring his son.

His mother however, gives Grayson a welcoming hug.

"You must be Emma," she says, pulling me into a hug, too.

"It's nice to meet you Mrs. Whitaker."

"Please," she says. "Call me Alice."

"Alice. Okay." I glance at his father.

"Make yourself at home," Mr. Whitaker says as way of greeting.

He doesn't look the least bit intimidating to me. Perhaps Grayson just doesn't get along with his father. Or perhaps his father was being on his good behavior for the moment.

Whichever it was, they seemed to be most welcoming.

"Would you like some fresh strawberry lemonade?" Alice asks, sitting back down and holding up a glass.

"Yes. Lemonade would be nice."

"Sit," she says, motioning to the chair next to hers. "We've got plenty of time to get acquainted."

As I take a seat on the cushioned outdoor chair, I can't help thinking maybe Grayson should have warned me about his mother instead of his father.

CHAPTER
FIFTY

Grayson

I'M a little surprised to see my father at the outdoor grill. He's grilling steak, shrimp, and vegetables. The steak sizzles as he flips them over. Uses a brush to slather on some barbecue sauce.

"Is someone else coming?" I ask him, taking a bottle of beer from the little outdoor refrigerator.

"I doubt it," he says. Father looks nothing like the businessman that he is. He looks like a relaxed milled-aged suburban family man. "Your sister is at a friend's house. Your brothers were here Sunday."

That last part sounds like a dig to me, but I don't

respond to it. I'm well aware that my brothers were here and I wasn't. I'm also well aware that I had an excellent reason for not being here.

My sister is the only one of us still living at home and she's rarely here. She just started college and has a new crop of friends.

"You didn't have to go to all this trouble," I say. "We could have gotten takeout." I take a sip of the beer I won't be drinking much of. It's possible I have to fly tomorrow and Noah Worthington has a strict bottle to throttle rule. One that I don't even go near.

While my father slathers some kind of seasoning on the shrimp, I watch Emma sipping lemonade with my mother.

It's almost like they decided to present themselves as an ordinary relaxed couple on Emma's account. Instead of the tycoon society couple they are.

Emma looks a little nervous, but my mother is smiling.

Emma looks like she belongs here. That surprises me a little bit for no particular reason.

I'd bought her the dress she's wearing. Not because I don't trust her to dress in a way my parents would approve of, but simply because she looked so cute in the dress.

Glancing over at me, she catches me watching me. Her cheeks pinken and her eyes sparkle.

I wink at her, causing her to flush even more, inadvertently reminding me of last night in the little movie room.

She's so pretty I can hardly look away from her. She'd

done wonders with her makeup, disguising her black eye so that it's barely noticeable.

"I apologize for bringing Monique here last night," Father says.

It takes a bit of effort to keep my jaw from dropping. My father never apologizes for anything.

"Why?" I ask, It's the only response my brain can process.

Father glances over at Emma.

"I overstepped." It's as much of an admission of wrongdoing that I'm going to get from my father.

When I'd gotten here last night, Monique had not responded well when I'd insisted that I immediately drive her to a nearby hotel.

I saw the same thing my parents saw and it wasn't pretty. Monique sensed wealth and she had cried fake tears all while declaring her undying love for me. When that didn't work, she'd gotten mad.

The only good thing that came out it the whole situation was that Monique is now out of my life. She got the message loud and clear that what she and I had, whatever it was, was over.

"Come back tomorrow," Father said with a glance at Emma. "We'll talk."

"Sure." Sometimes I think I can read my father's mind.

He's looking at Emma as the woman I'm going to marry in order to get my inheritance.

But that's not my plan.

My plan is to get out of the inheritance.

Not to drag Emma into being a pawn in my family's drama.

"Have you proposed yet?" Father asks with a nod toward Emma.

I really, really wish I couldn't read my father's mind.

FIFTY-ONE

Emma

THE WHITAKERS HAVE two swimming pools in their back yard. Not one. two.

The sound of water I'd heard when we stepped out of the car was indeed a water fountain in one of the little pools. Crystalline blue water reflects the soft glow of the evening's fading light as it tumbles over rocks so artfully arranged, they look natural. Like a little mountain waterfall.

The soft splash of water cascades into the little cocktail pool creating gentle waves rippling across the shimmering surface.

Further back in the backyard that seems to go on forever is an infinity pool. Large enough to accommodate a big family like the Whitakers, their extended family, and friends.

Oak trees rustle in the light breeze, tossing red and gold leaves across the otherwise pristine lawn.

The icy fresh squeezed lemonade with fresh strawberries in my glass is delightful. Mr. Whitaker is grilling steak and shrimp and vegetables.

"You have a beautiful home," I say. "but you didn't have to go to so much trouble."

Mrs. Whitaker, Alice, puts a hand on my wrist. "We want you to feel welcome."

"You're very kind."

Mrs. Whitaker smiles. "How long have been dating Grayson?"

My lemonade goes down the wrong way and I fall into a fit of coughing.

Grayson is almost instantly at my side, rubbing my back.

"What did you do?" he asks his mother.

"I'm okay," I say, but I admit I don't sound okay.

"We were just talking about how long you've been dating."

I see the scathing look Grayson gives her and the innocent one she gives him in return.

It's almost humorous except that I can barely catch my breath.

"You're okay," Grayson says, gently rubbing my back.

I nod and wipe at my watering eyes.

Alice is leaning forward now, looking closely at me. Apparently coughing made my eyes water and when my eyes water, my waterproof—not tearproof—mascara runs. Between that and disturbing the well-orchestrated makeup that had all but hidden my black eye, well...

Alice looks from me to her son.

"You need to explain that," she says, obviously talking about my eye.

I take a ragged breath and prepare to defend Grayson. God help him if he ever did give a girl a black eye.

"It was Trey," Grayson says without hesitation.

My eyes focusing again, I see Mr. Whitaker standing next to his wife, also looking at me. He has a dishcloth slung over his shoulder, his hands on his hips.

"Trey, your friend the pilot Trey?" he asks.

"Not my friend," Grayson says. "We talked about this last night."

Mr. Whitaker makes a noncommittal grunt. "We did not talk about *this.*"

"Different issue," Grayson says flatly, his hand still on my back even though my breathing is even now.

Mr. and Mrs. Whitaker exchange a glance that tells me they aren't buying the separate issue thing.

Unfortunately, I'm not in on whatever happened last night, so I'm in the dark here.

"I hope you contacted the authorities," Mr. Whitaker says.

"It's complicated," Grayson says. "I haven't spoken to Noah yet."

"How is Noah involved in this?" Mr. Whitaker's flat tone says he's in charge now.

"Trey's employer," I say.

"I'll call the judge in the morning," Mr. Whitaker says, dismissing that excuse. "Get a restraining order in place." He takes a breath. "You talk to Noah."

Mr. Whitaker looks at me now. "Have you filed charges yet?"

I shake my head, glancing at Grayson, then back to Mr. Whitaker's stern face. "It was an accident."

Mr. Whitaker looks to his son. "Take care of it."

"Yes Sir."

I clamp my mouth shut, not about to get anymore into this than I already am considering a big part of it seems to be about me.

As Mrs. Whitaker, Alice, puts a hand on my wrist again, I realize I had not answered her question about how long Grayson and I have been dating.

No one seems to care about that anymore.

Instead, they rallied around me and that leaves me feeling cared for. Almost like I'm enveloped into the folds of Grayson's family.

"You'll stay here with us," she says.

"I can't—" I look at Grayson with a sense of panic. Oscar. I can't leave Oscar alone.

"She's staying with me," Grayson says, sitting down.

And that seems to say everything.

FIFTY-TWO

Grayson

FATHER BRINGS over a platter of steak and shrimp and grilled vegetables making everything seem back to normal again.

With tacit agreement, we shift the topic away from Emma's black eye and onto mundane things.

"Grayson's little sister just started college this semester," Mother tells Emma. "Maybe she'll be in one of your classes."

"What's her major?" Emma asks.

Mother waves a hand. "Who knows? It changes by the day."

"If she takes psychology, she just might end up in one of my classes."

"That would so much fun. I'm sure you're an engaging professor."

"I try."

"James sat in her class yesterday and I think he's ready to sign up for her classes," I say, making Emma blush.

"James?" Mother looks confused.

"My bodyguard by day," Emma says with a hint of a smile.

"You told them," Grayson says. "I didn't."

"It sounds like they know everything anyway," Emma says to me, then looks at my mother. "Your son is very protective."

"Then I raised him right, didn't I?"

"Yes," Emma says. "You did."

I stab a shrimp with my fork and stuff it in my mouth.

I feel like I'm losing a game and I don't even know the rules.

Emma's playing along, but I guarantee she doesn't even know there's a game being played.

I know my parents. I know what they're up to. And I can't say I blame them.

They just met Emma, but they like her.

Last night could not have set things up more perfectly. Monique made a fool of herself priming my parents to like Emma possibly even more than they would have otherwise.

Now they can't help but compare the two.

Monique was obviously conniving and manipulative, getting Trey to help her convince my parents that she and I were dating.

Emma, on the other hand, is the complete opposite. Emma is sweet and innocent and now my parents, through no one's fault, can the see the black eye that Trey gave her. They don't believe for a minute that it was an accident.

I was there and I know that what might have been an accident turned into not an accident.

It all seems like fate. The whole thing from the moment Emma stepped out of the restroom at the Speakeasy. Maybe even before. Maybe it started the day Trey set a photo of Emma on our shared desk.

Unfortunately, it just can't be that easy. My father made things difficult. He should have told me about the will. He should have given me the consideration of making things happen on my own timeline.

I'd be married by now and I never would have met Emma.

I can hear my grandmother's voice just as clear as if she was sitting here at the outside table with us.

"Everything happens for a reason," she'd say. "It doesn't always make sense at the time, but God has a plan for everyone. No one else can begin to pick apart the pieces that weave the fabric of our lives."

She and my grandfather had been so different in their philosophies.

Grandma believed in fate and Grandpa believed in making things happen.

I'd always thought they were on disparate ends of the spectrum.

But now I know.

They were both right.

Emma leans over and whispers to me. "I have to go to the restroom."

"Just go inside. There's one off the kitchen."

"That one's being renovated," Mother says. "Just go past the kitchen, turn left, and go down the hallway."

"Do you want me to go with you?" I ask her.

"I think I can find it," Emma says with an innocent little smile that somehow sets my blood racing through my veins.

CHAPTER

FIFTY-THREE

Emma

THIS EVENING IS nothing like what I'd expected. I'm not sure what I'd expected, but I hadn't expected to be enveloped into the Whitaker family's fold.

Especially not after Grayson had warned me about his father. His father is stern, but he's actually a kind man. His mother scares me a little, but that's a different thing altogether.

Following his mother's directions, I turn left after going through the kitchen and make my way down the hallway.

I find the restroom easily enough, tucked discretely off to the side.

Like the rest of the house I've seen so far, it's clean and could be in one of those house magazines where everything is perfect. The vanilla scented candle burning on the counter tells me the Whitakers do not have a cat. I can't leave candles burning with Oscar around.

I smooth out my makeup as best I can, but the cat's out of the bag, so to speak.

Everyone blames Trey. I'm the only one who was there and even I'm not sure what really happened. Can't dispute that it was Trey though. Definitely Trey's fist that connected with my eye.

Whatever it was, it has led to a unexpected chain of events that has put me here.

Not only do I like Grayson—a lot—I like his family.

They seem like they genuinely want to help me get out of this situation with Trey.

Leaving the restroom, I walk down the hallway the wrong way. It takes me a couple of seconds to figure it out. As I walk by what looks like a home office, a painting in one of the rooms catches my attention.

It's a beach in Portugal that I recognize immediately. It's the same little village where my parents and sister live.

So odd.

I've stood on that very beach.

In awe, not so much of the painting, but that the Whitakers have it right here in their home, I walk straight over to it and stand in front of it, taking in all the little nuances that I recognize.

What are the odds that the Whitakers have a painting of the very place where my family lives? It makes me a little dizzy to even think about it.

Realizing I've been gone too long and they must wonder what I'm doing, I whirl around nearly bumping into the large wooden desk, my gaze landing on a printed email.

I don't mean to read it. I don't consider myself a person who snoops in other people's business. But it's right there and it has Grayson's name on it.

Grayson S. Whitaker. I don't know what his middle name is, but I have no doubt that this email is about him.

In my defense I try to look away. Try. Fail.

Just to summarize the terms of the will in its simplest terms...

Grayson S. Whitaker must be married by the time he reaches the age of thirty...

I blink, looking away.

Surely this is not real. A work of fiction perhaps.

I try again to look away. Fail.

As a courtesy, we have agreed to the six month extension as per your request provided Grayson is engaged by the time of his 30th birthday.

The back door opens, jarring me away from the desk and the email I should most certainly not have seen, much less read, I hurry from the room and head back to the kitchen.

"Hey," Grayson says. "You okay?"

"I was just trying to clean up some of the makeup." I gesture to my black eye. Not a lie.

"James is on his way back if you're about ready to head out."

"Sure. Okay." Any disappointment I might feel at leaving already is overshadowed by the email I'd just read.

Mr. and Mrs. Whitaker are coming inside carrying platters of food.

"We'll have leftovers for days," Alice says.

"It won't last and you know it," Mr. Whitaker says. "One or another of the kids will stop by. They have a sensor about food in the refrigerator."

"You're probably right."

"We need to head out," Grayson says. "I've got a flight in the morning."

"You didn't tell us," Alice says.

"I didn't know." He holds up his phone. "You know how people are always deciding to go somewhere at the last minute."

"Your father wouldn't know anything about that." Alice sets her platter down and walks over to me. "You come back," she says, giving me a hug. "Even without Grayson, you come back."

"Okay," I say, forcing a smile. I so wish I hadn't seen that email.

It must be a mistake. It had to be a mistake.

"Watch your back," Mr. Whitaker says to me, then turns to his son. "Grayson. Take good care of this one."

Now I'm analyzing everything they say to each other.

What does he mean by "this one?"

Am I the chosen one?

I feel dizzy as we walk outside and Grayson opens the back door of the SUV.

We've no more than settled in and buckled up, when I turn to Grayson.

"Hey," I say. "When is your birthday?"

"My birthday? Why? Did my mother say something to you?"

"No. I just... I just realized I don't know when it is."

"A couple of weeks," he says.

"Two weeks and four days," James says from the front seat as we head down the driveway toward the armed guard.

I can't unsee what I saw.

I think I'm going to be sick.

FIFTY-FOUR

Grayson

EMMA DOESN'T SAY much on the drive home.

She's tired. She looks tired.

My parents are enough to tire anyone out, even though, I have to admit that they were on good behavior tonight.

Surprisingly good behavior.

I'm very proud of them.

They'd accepted Emma right into the family.

It was what I'd wanted them to do and yet I don't know what to think about it.

It pleases me and frightens me at the same time.

They don't understand how hard I'm trying to protect

Emma from the whole inheritance marriage thing that they're pushing me toward.

I want to get it nulled or at least postponed so Emma and I can move along a timeline of our choosing.

I would never want her to think she's merely a woman of convenience.

Because she's not.

She's so much more than that.

I reach over and take her hand, but she doesn't look at me.

I suppose she has a lot to think about. A lot to process.

Maybe I'd taken her to meet my parents too soon.

I hope they didn't frighten her away.

"I hope my parents weren't too much," I say. "They can be a little intense at times."

"No," she says. "They were wonderful."

"They were on their good behavior," I say. "They like you."

"I like them," she says automatically, glancing at me with a little smile before she turns back to the window.

I start to say something else, but decide against it.

I decide to let her be. To let her think and process.

"We're here," James announces as he always does as he pulls up to the door at the Arabella.

The valet opens my door and I pull Emma along with me, not wanting to let someone else get her door.

My protective instincts are running high right now.

James gets out and looks around. His instincts are also

on high alert. That bothers me more than anything because James has good instincts.

The two of us walk on either side of Emma as we go inside the building and head toward the elevator.

The concierge leaves his desk and hurries toward us.

"Mr. Whitaker," he says.

I always feel like I should look over my shoulder to see if my father is behind me when someone calls me "Mr. Whitaker."

"Yes, Jose?"

"A delivery came for Ms. White. I took the liberty of taking it up to your floor. I left it just inside the door."

James and I look at each other, but I show no other outward reaction.

"Thank you," I say.

Emma looks a little confused, but it's the same expression she's worn since we got in the car to come home.

James and I look at each other over her head.

CHAPTER
FIFTY-FIVE

Emma

As the elevator closes and the two men stand on either side of me, I see them look at each other over my head in the smooth steel reflection of the doors.

"Is it your birthday?" James asks with what I sense is restrained control beneath forced casualness.

"No." I shake my head. "My birthday is in April."

I can't think of any reason why anyone would send me a package, especially not here. No one knows I'm here at Grayson's condo. Not even my family.

The elevator comes to a stop on the thirty-first floor and the doors slide open.

Oscar comes bounding toward me, tail high.

Delighted and not a little relieved to see him, even though I know he's perfectly safe up here on the thirty-first floor, I pick him up and hold him close against my chest, my face in his soft fur. He purrs, happy to see me, too.

The train rumbles by on the ground, the only sound of the city life below, but twinkling city lights stretch to the horizon.

James picks up the solid black gift bag just to the right of the elevator and takes it to the table. It rather creeps me out when he takes a photograph of it before even looking inside.

He holds up the little tag hanging on the side. "It's addressed to you," he says. "Permission to open it up?"

"Please do," I say, holding onto Oscar like a lifeline. I don't recognize the handwriting.

James pulls out two sheets of black tissue paper, then a little brown box. The box shape a bracelet might come in, only bigger.

He takes more pictures, then folds up the bag.

"Anything look familiar?" Grayson asks me.

"No." I can't imagine why it would. Again, no one knows I'm here.

Except possibly Trey.

The realization makes my blood run cold.

Had I ever even seen Trey's handwriting? I can't remember.

He opens up the box, takes a photo, then pulls out a pet

collar. It's obviously not for Oscar. Too big for a cat. It looks more like a dog collar. A big dog.

I swallow and even though Oscar squirms a bit to get down, I hold him tighter.

"There's a note," he says, glancing over at me.

I bury my face in Oscar's fur. Grayson is standing next to me watching everything James does.

James reads the note to himself then looks up at Grayson, then me.

"What does it say?" I ask.

James looks questioningly at Grayson, reluctance evident on his face.

"Read it," Grayson says.

James clears his throat and reads the note. "How does it feel to be a rich man's pet? Maybe this collar will help you play the part."

"He's gone too far," Grayson says flatly.

Oscar squirms and I set him on the floor.

"How do you know it's Trey?" I ask.

They both look at me.

"Never mind."

"We need to figure out what we're going to do," James says, as he takes a photo of the note.

"We're going to take him down," Grayson says in a tone I've never heard him use.

FIFTY-SIX

Grayson

THE THREE OF us sit together at the marble dining table. I sit next to Emma and James sits across from us with a pad of paper and a pen.

Too organized for my blood. Too organized for the way my blood is boiling beneath my veins.

Emma sits quietly. Too still. So still it concerns me.

The dog collar, black with silver spikes, lies in the middle of the table in front of us.

Oddly enough... disconcertingly enough... it's big enough to fit around a person's neck.

I clench my fists together beneath the table.

I'm not a violent person, but right now, more than anything, I'd like to tear Trey into shreds.

Trey went too far. All he had to do was to walk away. But no.

He had to add insult to injury.

Somehow he found out that Emma is here. That's what stalkers do. They watch and they wait and then they strike.

This dog collar is a new low.

I send Noah Worthington a text.

> I apologize for contacting you so late, but I need to meet with you. It's urgent.

His response comes right back.

NOAH

> Is it something that can wait until morning? Or do we need to meet now?

This is why Noah's men are so loyal to him. He's always there for us, putting us first.

> It can wait until morning, but I have a flight at 9:00.

NOAH

> I can meet you at 6. Name the place.

"I have a meeting with Noah at 6 in the morning," I say.

"Your father is filing a restraining order," Emma says. Her voice is flat.

"If you can't reschedule your flight tomorrow," James says. "I'll take her to the police station to file charges. We'll go first thing in the morning."

"It's not necessary to take her to the police station," I say. "I'll have someone come here." I look over at Emma. "Do you have anything scheduled tomorrow? Meetings."

"Just a class in the afternoon."

"I'll get her there," James says.

"You just want to go to her class," I say.

"Busted," James says.

Nothing, not even our attempt at humor, is taking that blank look off her face.

"I have to go feed Oscar," she says, standing up. "I'll see you both in the morning."

That's a dismissal if ever I heard one.

She's not planning on spending any time with me tonight.

I watch her walk around the table, grab a bottle of water from the refrigerator, and head down the hallway toward her room. She doesn't so much as look at me.

"What are you thinking?" James asks.

"I don't know. Something's bothering her and it's not this." I lift the dog collar with one finger. Let it fall back to the table.

"This is nothing but petty childishness."

"It's mean."

James leans forward, his voice low. "Didn't you say Trey was seeing other women while they were dating?"

I scoff and sit back in my chair. "That's an understatement.

"He's being vindictive," James says. "I've known guys like him."

"How did things get resolved?"

"They got the hell beat out of them."

"Don't think I'm not tempted."

"You can't do it." James cracks his knuckles. "But I can."

I run a hand along the back of my neck. "I can't let you do that." I take a deep breath. Trey isn't worth either one of us going to jail for. "Didn't you have a date tonight?"

"Postponed."

"I don't know what I'd do without you."

"I don't think you'd make it."

I know he's just trying to make me feel better. But I also know that he's right. More right than I want to admit.

FIFTY-SEVEN

Emma

BACK IN MY ROOM, I open a can of cat food and dump it in Oscar's plate. He doesn't normally eat this late, but I'd been worried about him. Feeding him is more to make me feeling better than it is to make him feel better.

Trey had found me. Somehow he knows where I'm staying. He found out I'm not at my house. Had he been watching when Grayson and James had picked me up?

Did he have nothing better to do than to spy on me? I hadn't dated anyone else, but maybe he had. I don't have any way of knowing.

It's not like he and I were engaged. He was the one who'd humped a hostess right there where I could see him.

I *know* we're safe up here on the thirty-first floor, but what if Trey somehow found a way up here?

He could find a way if he really wanted to. He'd already paved the way by dropping off his "gift."

He called me a pet and gave me a dog collar to wear around my neck.

It's nothing more than a petty insult.

It's almost like he knows too much.

But no one can know what Grayson and I do under the cover of darkness. Especially not last night. Last night we'd been in the movie room. No windows in the movie room.

He's just taunting me. Taunting me, trying to embarrass me, because his pride had gotten dinged when I left the Speakeasy with Grayson.

He's the one who caused it. If I hadn't seen him with the hostess, with my own eyes, I'd probably be at home right now. By myself. Just me and Oscar.

I get off the floor and go into the bathroom to get ready for bed.

The first thing I do is use the magic potion to get the mascara off my eyes and the skin beneath them.

Maybe I should just stop wearing mascara.

Trey's petty gift is more annoying than anything else. It's annoying because I have more important things to think about.

Grayson's birthday is coming up. His thirtieth.

I'd seen the email spelling everything out.

He has to be engaged by the time he turns thirty and married no more than six months later.

I let my thoughts go down that path. The one that believes the email to be true. That Grayson has to be married by the time he turns thirty or soon thereafter.

Still assuming all that to be true, he'd taken me to meet his parents. To get their approval. The girl Grayson marries has to be approved by his parents.

Grayson had conveniently gotten me here living with him. Falling for him.

I stop right in the middle of buttoning my pajama top as a horrible thought occurs to me.

Maybe Trey is part of the whole thing.

Maybe Trey had played his part in making me vulnerable. In getting me here in Grayson's condo. In making things worse by sending me that dog collar and calling me Grayson's pet.

He'd set me up to bring me closer to Grayson.

Maybe Grayson didn't even know about it.

Maybe his father had paid Trey to do it.

And maybe I should take up fiction writing.

Mr. Whitaker hadn't even met me until tonight.

Just as I climb into bed, someone knocks on my door.

FIFTY-EIGHT

Grayson

I BROKE my own rule and shared a shot of whiskey with James.

Both of us needed it.

I suppose in a strange way, I have Trey to thank for being an idiot asshole. If he hadn't been so damn stupid, I wouldn't have had the opportunity to rescue Emma and get her into my life.

Now that I'm a bit more relaxed—the whiskey helped—I need to go and check on Emma.

Something was bothering her even before the dog collar

incident and I need to figure out what it is so I can fix it. I can't help thinking it has something to do with my parents.

From my standpoint, dinner with my parents had gone wonderfully. But for all I know, Emma had been frightened away. Maybe they were too nice.

Maybe she didn't want them to be that nice. Maybe she didn't want to be enveloped into my family.

I knock lightly on her door and wait.

She might be asleep already. If she is, I need to leave her be and let her sleep.

"Come in," she calls out from inside the room.

I open the door and step inside.

The room is lit from both moonlight and the glow of city lights below.

Emma, wearing her pajamas, is sitting in the middle of the bed.

"Hi," I say. "Did I wake you?"

"No. Is everything okay?"

"That's what I wanted to ask you. Can I come in?"

"Sure."

I walk across to her bed and sit down on the edge. Oscar walks over and nudges my hand until I pet him.

Emma rolls her eyes. "I don't know what's wrong with him."

"He likes me," I say. "I give really good back rubs."

"Do you now?"

"Would you like me to show you?"

"I wouldn't say no."

"Okay. Lie down. Excuse me, Oscar. I need to borrow your mom."

With a cautious glance in my direction, she lies down on her stomach.

I straddle her backside and after gathering up her hair and pushing it to the side, I begin to knead her shoulders.

"Is there something you need to talk to me about?" I ask.

"Hard to think when you're doing that."

I smile to myself. "You seemed quiet tonight. And not just when we got home and found that little present Trey left."

I moved my hands down to that area beneath her shoulder blades.

She sighs.

"Is there something you need to tell me?" she asks, her voice muffled by the blanket.

"Did my parents freak you out? Cause I can talk to them." I lift up her shirt and run my hands along her bare skin. Gently massaging her tight muscles.

"Is there something you need to tell me about your upcoming thirtieth birthday?"

My hands still on her back just for a second. Just long enough to inadvertently give her an answer.

"Why would you ask that?" Her skin is so soft. So smooth. I feel myself wanting her. Needing her.

"Are you supposed to be married by the time you're thirty?" she asks.

CHAPTER

FIFTY-NINE

Emma

THE WAY his hands missed a beat on my back gave me all the answer I need.

The email I'd seen was a real thing. Not fiction. Not my imagination.

He didn't want to answer me. I can't blame him, but he doesn't want to give me an answer.

Doesn't he know that no answer is an answer in and of itself?

Just when I think he's not going to answer, he does.

"My grandfather was a good man. A successful man. He

taught me a lot. But he became a little eccentric in his old age."

Not an answer, but I feel him working up to it. I lay quietly and let his hands work magic on my back.

"He put a provision in his will that his grandchildren... there are five of us... have to be married by the time we're thirty in order to get our inheritance. I guess he was a little old-fashioned."

"Sounds like he wanted you to be settled so you wouldn't blow the money."

"It might not be so bad," he keeps talking. "except that I didn't learn about it until Saturday. Saturday. My grandfather has been gone for five years."

"Why didn't someone tell you?"

"My father claims he hoped it would work itself out naturally."

"What does that mean?"

"It means he hoped I'd get married and the issue wouldn't be a concern."

"But you didn't get married."

"No. And he springs this on me at the last minute. So... the attorneys found a way to extend it six months if I'm engaged by my birthday."

"What are you going to do?" she asks, relaxed beneath my hands.

"I've got my own attorneys working on it. Looking for a loop hole because my father waited so long to tell me. They think they can find a way out of it."

I move my hands up to her shoulders, massaging gently but firmly.

"I don't need the money and I wouldn't worry about it except that it's my mother's father and it's important to her that her children get a share of her father's legacy."

"It's not a matter of needing it," she says.

I realize she's slipped into psychologist role. Even with my hands massaging the muscles on her back, she still slips into psychologist mode.

It runs through and through, I decide. Like me being a pilot. There's no escaping who we are at the core.

"No. It's a matter of keeping my mother happy. But I'd prefer to get out of it."

"You don't want to get married," she says.

"Someday, sure. But not because it's a provision in a will."

"That's understandable," she says softly.

A couple of minutes later I realize she's fallen asleep.

She was tired and I put her to sleep.

Moving carefully so as not to wake her, I pull the ultra-soft Italian percale sheets and the merino wool and silk blanket over her and lie down next to her, propping my head on one hand, to watch her sleep.

Sweeping her long hair, soft as silk, off her cheek, I study her red, slightly parted lips. Her black eye, no longer swollen, but instead a mottled purple now.

Even with the black eye, she is the most beautiful woman I've ever seen.

Just looking at her, lying there innocently sleeping, is making me hard.

But I'm not going to wake her up. I'm just going to let her sleep.

I am a man besotted.

CHAPTER
SIXTY

Emma

I WAKE with bright morning sunlight streaming in through the uncovered floor to ceiling windows, the sky pink with the glow of dawn.

Oscar sits next to my pillow, purring. I open my eyes and he rubs his chin against mine.

"Hungry? Already?"

I reach for my bottle of water on the nightstand and tap my phone to check the time.

It's early. Not quite seven.

I'd fallen asleep and I don't think I moved the whole night.

Sitting up, I pull Oscar into my lap and bury my head in his soft fur.

I'd fallen asleep with Grayson massaging my back, his strong hands relaxing my muscles.

Not exactly all that sexy on my part, but I'd been feeling out of sorts. Sleep was what I needed more than anything else.

I get up to feed Oscar. He hops off the bed and follows me to his little utility room across the hall. I wash his white china plate in the utility sink and open a can of cat food.

Yesterday had been difficult.

The most pressing, I suppose, is the dog collar Trey sent to me as a "gift."

Grayson alerted the concierge and the guards that work downstairs to be on the lookout for him.

Later today they'll have a restraining order in place so Trey won't be able to come near this building without getting his ass arrested.

I gently wash my face with a warm cloth. After the way he's been behaving, Trey deserves no less than to be arrested. It's what should happen.

Feeling a little better about that situation, I go into my closet and decide to pull my clothes out of my two suitcases and hang them up.

The closet is big with custom white wooden shelving. A row of white wooden hangers waiting to be used.

The other unsettling issue that came up last night is the matter of Grayson's inheritance. I'd been stunned at first and I'd actually been offended thinking he thought he was going to marry me just get his inheritance.

But Grayson had explained it well.

He doesn't even want to get married.

I sort my underwear into a drawer and fold my blue jeans arranging them on a shelf.

Before long I have all my shirts hanging on the wooden hangers. I still have clothes at my house, but with things the way things are, I don't know when I'll be going back.

I'm also not sure how I feel about that. It's something I have to think about later.

Just like thinking about how Grayson doesn't want to get married.

I hadn't come here thinking that we were in a relationship. I'd come here thinking that...

What had I been thinking?

I'd been thinking that I liked Grayson and I hadn't resisted when he'd swept me out of my house giving me a safe place to stay.

The problem is, I decide, as I idly hang up the dress I'd worn last night, it has quickly become more than that.

There's a heat between us that I can't explain. That I don't want to think too much about.

If Grayson isn't looking to get married, then maybe this is no more than just a convenient fling.

I square my shoulders. If that's what it is, then that's what it is. Nothing to be done about it.

The closet is so big, I would have to have ten times as

many clothes as I currently own, counting the ones still in the closet at my house, to come close to filling it.

As I zip up my now empty suitcases and slide them into a corner, I remind myself that it's not my closet to fill.

I'm just a visitor here.

Once things are sorted out with Trey, I'll need to move back to my little house.

It's okay. I like my little house and it's close to the university.

I'm just feeling out of sorts.

Understandably so.

I decide to wear jeans and a light blue button down shirt today, then turn on the hot water in the shower.

I'll probably be meeting with the police and who knows what else today. Things seem to be moving along a whole quicker now that I've met Grayson's family.

Grayson is already gone for his early flight and I think he was supposed to meet with his boss to talk about Trey before his flight.

I should have seen signs of Trey's narcissism earlier, but we hadn't spent enough time together for him to really let down his guard.

As I dry my hair, I make the decision to go on a dating moratorium. Then I laugh at myself.

Here I am planning to start a dating moratorium while I'm living with and sleeping with Grayson Whitaker.

Okay. He doesn't count.

I'm not counting him.

After Grayson, I'm going on a dating moratorium.

I spend some time straightening my hair, putting in some soft curls, but no makeup today.

First of all, I need my black eye fully visible and even if I didn't, I'm not even going to attempt mascara.

Now that I've taken my time getting ready, sorted through some things in my head, I walk down the wide hallway toward the kitchen to make a cup of coffee.

James is there, sitting at the marble table, glasses perched on his nose, reading a newspaper. A printed newspaper.

I stop and look at him.

"You're reading a newspaper?" I ask.

"Yeah. You want to read some of it?"

"Okay. I didn't think they still printed newspapers."

"I get tired of the Internet news." He slides the front section over to me. "Have a seat. I'll make your coffee."

"Deal." I slide out one of the heavy dining chairs and sit down.

As he fires up the fancy coffeemaker, I scan the headlines of the newspaper. Personally, I prefer to get my news online.

There's no sign of the dog collar and I don't ask what he did with it.

"What do you think about everything?" I ask, keeping my eyes on the paper.

"I assume you mean Trey," he says.

I shrug. Trey, yes. It's more than likely that James

doesn't even know about Grayson's inheritance. It's not the kind of thing a man would share with an employee.

"I don't think you'll be hearing from him again," James says, setting a big mug of steaming frothy coffee in front of me.

"I hope you're right," I say.

"I'm rarely wrong about these things," James says matter-of-factly as he sits back down and picks up the newspaper he was reading.

I smile to myself.

Oddly enough, I believe him.

SIXTY-ONE

Grayson

THE NEXT MORNING before the sun is even up, I'm sitting at a little breakfast café located about halfway between my condo and Noah's house on Memorial Avenue.

Even though rain is in the forecast, there's no sign of it yet. The skies are pink with the sun peaking over the horizon.

The café, like always, is filled with businessmen like ourselves, most of them in designer suits. Noah is in a designer suit. Even though I'm in my black pilot's uniform, it's subtle enough that unless I add my Skye Travels blazer and captain's cap, it doesn't look like a uniform.

This morning I actually put on one of my own suit jacket, the kind I wear to my own business meetings. Even though I know that Noah notices, he doesn't say anything about it.

I can't remember ever seeing a woman here other than the ones who work here. It's one of those old boys' places that women probably don't even know about.

There's no music, just the sound of bacon sizzling on the grill, plates bumping against each other, silverware clinking together, and men talking in low tones.

No telling how many important business deals are made right here in this café on mornings like this one. Probably deals made every day.

"I don't have the grounds to fire him," Noah says. "Not unless he's arrested."

"He'll be arrested if he goes near Emma again."

"Let me rephrase," he says. "I don't have the grounds to fire him. Yet."

"I understand. I mostly just need you to be aware of what's going on."

"Fortunately your father called me last night, so I got a head start thinking about it."

"He wasn't supposed to do that," I say, sitting back against the plastic booth.

Noah smiles a little. "Your father and I go way back. Don't hold it against him."

"I know he just wants to help." I just wish he wouldn't help so much.

"I'm glad he did," Noah says. "Because it gave me time to sleep on it."

"Just like my grandfather," I say.

"Smart man. Anyway. I've decided to relocate Trey."

"Relocate him." I swallow a chuckle. "Like a pesky bear?"

"Exactly like a pesky bear. I have a Lear jet out in Atlanta that I don't use very often simply because I didn't have a pilot to send out there."

"You're sending Trey." Somehow the thought of Trey being relocated to Atlanta sounds like the perfect solution.

"I can keep him flying seven days a week. He won't have time to think about anything going on over here in Houston. In fact, I'll make sure he doesn't get any flights to Houston either."

"I like the sound of that. Do you think he'll take it?"

"He won't have a choice. He might resign, but if he does, he won't work again in Houston."

I did not know that Noah Worthington had this side to him. I guess I've been lucky to not have to find out.

But one thing I do know is that if Noah Worthington says Trey will never work again in Houston, then Trey will never work again in Houston.

"I'm also going to require him to go to counseling."

"So he'll know why he's being relocated."

"He'd know anyway. No reason to beat around the bush."

"I'm sorry to put this trouble on you, Sir." I genuinely

like Noah Worthington. Even being an inordinately successful businessman, he hasn't been without his problems including a heart attack a few years back. I don't like being the one to add more stress on him.

Noah grins. "I like a challenge now and then. Besides when a man acts like Trey's acting, I delight in turning the tables."

"I owe you one," I say.

"You don't owe me a thing," Noah says. "But I can offer you some unsolicited advice. You can take it or leave it."

"Sure."

"This girl. Emma. If you like her, don't let your father keep you from marrying her."

I almost ask him if he knows about the will. But asking him would be telling him, so I clamp my mouth shut.

"What I'm saying is don't let her go just to spite your father."

"I won't," I say. "I'm just not sure I'm ready to get married."

"Take it from an old man like me. One who let the girl walk away. Not everyone gets a second chance. I was blessed to get that second chance when Savannah walked back into my life. I wouldn't take that chance again."

"I'll take that into consideration," I say. "Thank you."

"Here's your food." The waitress sets our plates of bacon and eggs and toast in front of us. "Can I get you boys anything else?"

"I'm good."

"Me too."

Efficient. We have everything worked out before our food even arrived.

I hope I can be like Noah Worthington when I grow up.

As for his advice about Emma. Like any advice coming from Noah, it's worth taking to heart.

Not that I hadn't already considered that very thing he's recommending.

Just because my father wants me to marry Emma doesn't mean I shouldn't.

CHAPTER
SIXTY-TWO

Emma

My day was what anyone would call uneventful.

I'm a little disappointed that I don't hear anything from Grayson, especially knowing that he met with their boss.

I would have liked to know what was decided, but I guess I'll hear soon enough. It's not like I don't have plenty to keep me busy.

First I spent most of the morning going over everything that happened with Trey with the female officer who came to Grayson's condo.

Then James drove me out to the university to teach my class. Although it looked like rain, the storm held off, and by the time we got to the university the dark clouds had dissipated.

I wore black rimmed glasses to disguise my bruised eye, more purple than black now, and dabbed on a bit of concealer to hide the worst of those bruises.

Class went well and it no longer bothers me that James sits in the back of my class near the door. He actually brought a notebook and took notes this time.

"Have you thought about going back to college?" I ask him on the drive home.

He looks at me in the rearview mirror. "I doubt it. I've already got a degree."

"In what?" I ask, hoping I hid my surprise. I didn't expect a chauffeur to have a college degree.

"Accounting," he says.

"Oh."

"I'm not just a chauffeur," he says with amusement. "I take care of Grayson's accounts."

That explains when I'd seen him working on something on a computer the other day.

"You're also a good friend to Grayson," I say.

"Comes with the territory."

"You don't seem like an accountant," I point out.

"What do I seem like?"

"Bodyguard," I say.

"I'll take that as a compliment." He pulls onto the freeway and weaves his way through traffic.

"As it's meant to be." I turn and look out the window.

It's been close to a week since I've driven my car. I could get used to being driven around. Not having to worry about traffic. About figuring out the best way to get from place to place depending on the time of day and the traffic patterns.

"I should have asked if you needed to go anywhere else before we go home," James says.

There's that word again. Home. It just slides off their tongues like it's the most natural thing in the world.

"I should probably go by my house," I say.

James gets in the right lane and turns on the blinker. "We'll go now," he says.

Ten minutes later, he parks next to my car in front of my house and comes around to open my door.

He stays right with me as I walk up to the front door.

I step inside and look around my little living room. The air conditioning is on, but the house still smells stale. Like no one has been here in some time, even though it hasn't even been a week.

It's not the same without Oscar there. In fact, without Oscar here it doesn't even seem like my home at all.

James closes the door. Locks it.

"Just in case," he says.

"Good idea."

"Can I do anything?"

"I'm going to clean out my refrigerator," I say, striding over and opening the refrigerator door.

I blink.

It's empty. Empty and sparkly clean.

It looks brand new.

One hand still on the door, I turn and look at James.

He looks behind me. Shrugs.

"I guess Grayson forgot to mention that he had someone clean up."

"I guess he did." I open the freezer. Nothing there either. The dishwasher is empty. Everything is spotless.

I stand in my kitchen a moment, waiting to feel something. Violated. Intruded upon.

But none of those emotions come to me.

Instead I just feel an odd sense of relief.

I walk through my house, looking for something, anything, that I want to take with me.

Since I had taken pretty much everything with me days ago, I only find two things. My favorite coffee mug. An old stained one that my father had given to me years ago after he and Mother had gone to Colorado and my wool winter coat.

With those two things in hand, I meet James back in the living room where he stands, waiting patiently.

"I'm ready," I say. "Let's go home."

My house no longer feels like my home.

If push comes to shove, I can make it feel like home again—with Oscar here, but in the meantime, Grayson's condo feels like my home.

I've fallen hook, line, and sinker.

SIXTY-THREE

Grayson

So FAR, I'd had a productive day.

It had started off with breakfast with Noah Worthington. As of tomorrow Trey is being transferred to Atlanta.

Noah is even paying to have his apartment packed up and all his things hauled out to Atlanta. Overly accommodating in my opinion, but Noah believes it's the most efficient and fastest way to get Trey out of Houston once and for all.

I'd dropped my passenger off in Dallas and made a quick turnaround putting me right back in Houston.

The rain had held off, apparently it had dissipated. The

air still smells like rain to me though and the clouds are banking.

After a smooth landing back in Houston, I drive myself in my little sports car to my attorney's office located in a house in an old part of the Heights renovated into an office.

"Come in," Andrew says. "Have a seat."

Andrew sits behind his mammoth desk, covered with stacks of files in a system that no doubt makes sense to him and probably only him.

His office smells like old leather law books with a hint of pipe smoke. Odd because he doesn't smoke, at least not that I know of.

He'd told me once that his father used to smoke a pipe in here back when it was his office. That was so long ago, maybe the smoke is simply a memory.

He pulls off his reading glasses and looks at me. Andrew is probably ten years older than me and he wears a perpetual scowl from squinting over law books for at least twenty years. I can't remember ever seeing him smile.

"Did you have time to look over everything?" I ask, getting right to the point.

Andrew is a busy man and doesn't like to waste time. I've learned over the years to not even bother with small talk.

"I did."

I sit back, unsuccessfully forcing myself to relax. I'm about as tense as I've ever been.

I had the whole flight up to Dallas and back to think

about the possibilities. It all comes down to two possibilities. Either Andrew found a way for me to get out of the will
or he didn't.

I asked him to find me a way out. I want a way out. And
yet thinking about having a way out of the will's requirement fills me with disappointment.

But when I think about him not finding a way out, I
should feel disappointment. But I don't. And when I try to
think about how that does make me feel, it's like bumping
up against a wall and I can't think about it.

"And?" I ask.

"I have good news and bad news."

"For God's sake." I run a hand through my hair.

"Which one do you want to hear first?" I swear I see the
twitch of a smile at the corner of his lips. He's doing this on
purpose to torture me.

"Just tell me. I don't care. The good news. Tell me the
good news first."

Andrew picks up a bottle of water and drinks.

"The good news is yes. I can get you out of it."

I wait for the expected relief to sweep over me.

"Sort of," he adds

Instead, all I feel is vexed.

"What do you mean sort of?"

"That's the bad news," Andrew says.

I close my eyes a moment and scratch my ear.

"Spell it out for me. Please." I can't take much more of
his torture.

"Due to the fact that your father waited for five years to tell you about the provision in the will." He pauses to take a breath. "There's a precedent. I'm assuming you don't want to know the case for the precedent."

"Is there a precedent for torturing your client in there somewhere?"

"No. You can't get out of the will's provision, but due to the precedent, you can get a five year extension. Your brothers will get a prorated extension depending on when they're told about it."

"That's insignificant," I say. My next younger brother is four years younger than me. Four years seems like nothing compared to three weeks.

Andrew's antique wooden office chair squeaks as he leans back in it.

"You don't look sufficiently elated."

"I don't feel sufficiently elated."

"I tried to find a way to make it null and void. I truly did. But it's just not there. But from what you tell me, you don't really need the money anyway."

He's misinterpreting my reaction and I'm not correcting him.

"It's not about the money and you know it."

"Yes. Yes. I know. It's about your grandfather's legacy."

"It is about my grandfather's legacy," I say. That's exactly what it's about. That and so much more. "I have to go." I stand up to leave.

"What do you want me to do? Do you want me to file the petition?"

"Don't do anything," I say, pausing a moment at the door. "Not yet."

CHAPTER
SIXTY-FOUR

Emma

It's later afternoon and I'm sitting in Grayson's favorite little sitting area reading over the next chapter in my textbook. This one on depression.

It's funny. This condo is huge and has plenty of little sitting areas, but I gravitate to this one. Maybe it's because it has a view of the vibrant Uptown area. Or maybe it's because it's small and cozy. The fireplace could have something to do with that.

Or maybe it's because Grayson told me it's his favorite. Probably a combination of all those things.

I look up when James comes to the doorway. He's holding a white dress box.

"Hi," he says.

"Hi." I put the cap on my highlighter and close my textbook, my arm marking my place.

"This is came for you," he says.

"Oh no." I feel like a rock landed in the pit of my stomach. Not again.

"No. It's from Grayson."

"What is it?" I ask, flooded with relief.

"I'm not entirely sure. But he asked that you be ready for dinner at six o'clock."

"Why?" I ask, looking at him warily.

"I'm not sure. He wants to take you to dinner."

"I see." Of course James would know because he's going to drive us.

I'm figuring these things out.

"Okay," I say, but I make no move to stand up. To take the box from him.

"Shall I tell him you'll be ready?" he asks.

It would be easy to complain that I would have liked Grayson to ask me himself, but that seems unnecessarily petty. I'm not in my normal world and things work differently.

I mark my page with my highlighter and set my textbook aside.

Check the time.

I've got less than two hours to get ready by six.

"I'll be ready," I get up and take the box from him.

He looks so relieved, I feel bad for making him nervous.

"Thank you," I say, then take the box to my room and open it up.

Inside the box is a lovely lacy silver dress. Technically, I suppose it's an evening gown.

With an A-line silhouette, long enough to pool on the floor, which it's obviously supposed to do, it has long lacy sleeves and a lacy bodice. The back is scandalously open.

I've never owned anything like it.

I'm not even surprised that it's my size. It's one of those many things that I'm getting used to.

It's silky and elegant. The tag is still on it, but the price is ripped off.

Running a hand over the soft silky material, I sigh.

I'm going to have to do my hair. And I'm going to have to wear mascara.

I should have ordered some tear proof mascara, if such a thing exists, but hopefully tonight won't be one of those nights.

I head off to the restroom to work on my makeup. To disguise what is now my purple black eye.

I have a date, an actual date with Grayson Whitaker and we're going out.

This must be some kind of celebration.

Or maybe getting dressed up and going out for dinner is just a normal night for him.

I could have asked James.

But it's actually kind of fun to just discover things as I go.

And, I realize with something of a start, I'm enjoying myself. Quite a bit.

My world was turned upside down and I'm enjoying myself.

As I slide the dress over my head and straighten the skirt, I get a text.

GRAYSON

I'm running late. James will drive you to the restaurant. I'll be waiting.

Yes. I'm enjoying myself more than I ever thought possible.

SIXTY-FIVE

Grayson

THE RESTAURANT I chose for tonight's dinner is one of Houston's finest, especially known for its seafood. Knowing that Emma's favorite food is a fried shrimp po'boy, I rule out French, Italian, and steak.

I arrive earlier than I expected to and my table has an excellent view of the front door. I'll know the moment she arrives.

I order a glass of merlot to sip on. Mostly to keep the server happy. The server, like all the servers here, walks tall and straight with confidence, wearing a formal white tuxedo.

The server recognizes me. I'm personally not a regular, but I look enough like my father, who is a regular, that I'm greeted by name. Mr. Whitaker.

It's not crowded. It's never crowded here. But the tables that aren't occupied will be soon enough. The restaurant is a frequented by successful people of both old and new money, but mostly old money.

A live three-piece orchestra, set up on the other side of the restaurant, closer to the back is playing Big Band music. Seems fitting since Emma and I first met at the Uptown Speakeasy with the same type of music playing. The main difference here is that the music drifts more in the background than being in-your-face loud.

I take a sip of the merlot and watch the door. I got a text from James fifteen minutes ago telling me that they're on their way.

According to my estimation, Emma will be walking in the door at any minute.

I'm not wrong.

James escorts her inside the restaurant, but he sees me, says something to Emma and walks away, leaving her standing there by herself.

All eyes in the restaurant, some obviously, some more subtly, turn in her direction.

As I stand up, my gaze meets hers across the restaurant and something pools deep in my bones. Something so deep and visceral it causes my breath to hitch and my knees to go weak.

She's wearing the silver dress I'd chosen and sent over for her to wear. It fits her perfectly in every way.

With the slim dress, long sleeves and high lacy bodice, the hem pooling at her feet, she looks like something between a mermaid and a princess. Maybe a mermaid princess.

She wears her hair down, swirling around her shoulders in soft curls.

Giving me a small smile, she lifts the hem of her dress enough that she doesn't trip over it, but before she can take a step, my server is there to greet her.

The server holds out an arm. She put a hand on his sleeve and allows him to escort her toward my table.

I meet them halfway.

"Thank you Isaac," I say, transferring her hand from his arm to mine.

"The pleasure is all mine," Isaac says, pulling out one of the heavy wooden chairs for her.

I hold the chair as Emma sits. As she adjusts her skirts, I sit down next to her and lean forward.

"Hi," I say.

"Hi." She swallows a bit nervously.

"Do you like your dress?"

"I love it." She shifts in her chair and lifts her hem to show me her black ankle boots. The ones she always wears. "I didn't have any shoes."

"I didn't know your size," I say, but they look adorable. Anything she wears looks adorable.

"Six and a half," she says with a little smile, then leans forward. "Just for future reference."

"Duly noted." I give her a little wink.

The waiter is back with a carafe of ice water and a glass for Emma.

"What would the lady like to drink?" he asks.

Emma looks at me, notes my glass of wine.

"Bring us a bottle of your best champagne," I tell Isaac before Emma can answer. "Is that okay?" I ask, turning to her.

"Sure."

After Isaac walks away, I put a hand over Emma's. "I'm glad you're here," I say.

Soft music from the orchestra drifts through the air and everyone else fades into the background.

Emma smiles and everything slides into place.

I'd made a lot of decisions today and in this moment, I know that they were the right ones.

SIXTY-SIX

Emma

THE RESTAURANT IS HIDDEN AWAY SOMEWHERE in River Oaks. I gave up on trying to follow James's route and just went with it. So I really have no idea where we are. I only know that I'm with Grayson.

It's one of those luxury restaurants. White table clothes. Candlelight. Waiters in white tuxedos.

Big band music drifts from a live three-piece orchestra on the other side of the restaurant. It's quite subtle. Everything is understated.

The music. The soft glow of candlelight. The scent of something on the grill. Fresh bread baking.

But none of that interests me. Not like Grayson, the man sitting next to me, looking at me with smoldering blue eyes.

He's wearing a black suit jacket, a white button-down shirt, and a dark gray tie that matches my dress.

He hadn't been home, but he'd shaved somewhere. His skin looks smooth and I long to reach out, put my fingertips on his cheek.

In fact, I think he got a haircut and he smells faintly of an expensive cologne that reminds me of dark woods, something rich and earthy, the kind of intoxicating scent that has my heart racing and something deeply primal and visceral running through my blood.

Bringing a chilled champagne bottle to our table, Isaac pops the cork and fills two crystal flutes.

Grayson raises his flute. "To new beginnings," he says.

I tap my glass to his and look at him with curiosity.

"What are we celebrating?" I ask.

"I have some good news," he says.

"Oh?" My gut clenches. What he thinks is good news might not be good news for me.

"Yes. My meeting with Noah Worthington, our boss, went quite well this morning."

"I wondered how it went." I take a sip of the bubbly wine.

"Trey is being relocated to Atlanta." He squeezes my hand.

"Relocated?"

"Moved. He'll be working out there. Living out there.

And there is already a restraining order to keep him away from you. There's a copy in the car."

"You think that will resolve things?"

"I hope. Even if he quits Skye Travels, Noah will make sure Trey never works in Houston again."

"Okay." It seems like the best solution they could have come up with. I'd researched stalkers and there's no easy way to resolve things. One website had even suggested that the person being stalked move away. So this is good. As good as can be hoped for.

"I hope this helps you feel safe," Grayson says.

"It has to, doesn't it? I'll get a security system installed at my house." I'm not sure I'll be able to sleep at night, but eventually I'll have to get used to it again.

Being on the ground, I'd discovered, is a whole lot different from living in the sky. And, I'd discovered, it feels a whole lot less safe.

Grayson doesn't say anything. He squeezes my hand again, then releases it as Isaac comes back with a tray.

"I have some crab cakes with remoulade," Isaac says, setting a plate in front of each of us. "and chargrilled shrimp."

"Did we order?" I ask after Isaac walks off.

"They don't really have a menu," Grayson says.

"Oh." I glance around, realizing we hadn't been given menus. "How does he know what to bring us?"

"He'll ask."

"Huh." I take another sip of my champagne.

"But that's not what I wanted to talk to you about," Grayson says, straightening his tie.

"What did you want to talk to me about?"

"My grandfather's will."

CHAPTER
SIXTY-SEVEN

Grayson

WHILE TALKING WITH MY ATTORNEY, I'd had an epiphany and that epiphany had led to me having a very busy afternoon.

I'd not only gotten a shave and a haircut, but I'd gone shopping.

Not for myself.

For Emma.

Isaac is back at our table, gauging our reaction to sea bass and shrimp.

Emma obviously leans toward the shrimp. I lean toward the sea bass.

He refills our champagne flutes and discretely disappears.

"You don't have to talk to me about your grandfather's will," Emma says. "It's rather private."

"Aren't you curious?"

"Of course. But it's okay. It's really not my business."

I ignore her protests, but watch her carefully.

"My attorney has found a way around it. Sort of. Mostly."

"How does sort of mostly work?"

"Since my grandfather passed away five years ago, everything can be legally delayed for five years."

"So... you still have to get married, but you have five years to do it and you can still get your inheritance."

"Yes." I sit back and swirl my champagne.

"That must be quite a relief," she says, her brow furrowed.

"Yes. It should be."

I stab my fork into a crab cake and stuff it in my mouth.

Emma narrows her meadow green eyes at me and takes a delicate bite of chargrilled shrimp.

"Thank you for telling me," she says, trying to force a smile.

"You're welcome. James tells me you had another good class."

"He took notes," she says.

I laugh and she looks even more vexed.

We eat in silence for a few minutes.

The orchestra changes from Big Band music to a popular song from the eighties.

"The weather was perfect for flying today," I say.

"I'm glad you had a good flight."

"Let's go flying this weekend," I say.

"Flying? Where?" She puts her fork down and looks at me.

"I don't know. Anywhere. You pick the place."

"You have to give me parameters," she says.

"Okay." I grin. Anywhere in the states."

She nods. "That helps. A little." She peers at me a moment. "I think maybe you should surprise me."

"I forgot," I say. "that you like surprises."

She shrugs. "Good ones. I like good surprises."

"I'll keep that in mind," I say impishly.

She narrows her eyes at me again.

"You seem happy about something," she says.

"I am happy," I say. "I'm having a nice a dinner with a beautiful young lady. What more could a man ask for?"

"I can't think of anything," she says, still looking vexed at me.

Somehow the more vexed she looks, the happier it makes me.

SIXTY-EIGHT

Emma

THE FOOD IS DELIGHTFUL. The music is delightful.

But I have too many things to think about to really enjoy myself.

And Grayson is acting almost giddy.

I suppose he deserves to be giddy if anyone does.

He's just gotten a reprieve from a forced marriage. A marriage to get his grandfather's inheritance.

As I eat my delicious fried shrimp in silence, I muse that I, too, should be feeling relieved and maybe even giddy.

The problem with Trey has been solved. He is being relocated to Atlanta. Relocated like one of those bears in

Yellowstone that starts digging into human garbage cans or walking into town. I don't really trust Trey not to find his way back to Houston, but hopefully Noah is right about not having time to worry about anything here. And he won't be able to get a job flying anywhere in Houston either.

Maybe I'd secretly hoped for a more severe punishment. Trey was an idiot and a cad, but I still maintain that the black eye was an accident.

I should be happy.

I can go home now. Oscar and I can return to the little house that I'd bought myself. We can go back to our ordinary life.

And yet deep down I know that even though I can return to my ordinary life, I will never see things the same way again.

Too much has changed for me.

I'd spent a week, nearly, being chauffeured around town. Living on the thirty-first floor of a luxury high rise building. And right I'm dining at a restaurant so exclusive it doesn't even have menus.

But it isn't just that.

Those were just the things on the surface.

Digging a little deeper, I come to the real reason I'm feeling disconcerted.

Grayson.

I'd fallen for Grayson. Somewhere along the way, I'd fallen for him.

Maybe it was that first night at the Uptown Speakeasy when he'd rescued me from a date with Trey gone bad.

And now that everything is resolved, it just makes sense that I not live with him anymore.

We'd both known it was a temporary arrangement.

Just because it makes me feel morose knowing I have to leave him. He and I hadn't exactly been dating. We hadn't known each other long enough for me to move in with him.

"Penny for your thoughts," he says as the waiter takes away our empty plates.

"Nothing. I was just thinking about all the things I have to do in order to return... home."

"How do you like living at the Arabella?"

I blow out a breath. "That's not a fair question. I like it. A lot. But I'm a college professor. College professors don't live at the Arabella."

"They can, you know."

I run a hand down the silky dress I'm wearing. "This dress probably cost several month's salary for me."

He doesn't answer that one way or another.

"Remember I told you my attorney found a way to postpone the stipulation in my grandfather's will about getting married by the time I'm thirty?"

"Of course."

"I realized that just because I don't have to get married doesn't mean I don't want to."

"I guess you can do whatever you want to do." I keep

my gaze on the bubbling champagne in my glass, reminding myself at the last possible moment to breath.

"Exactly."

When I realize he's watching me, I look up and meet his gaze.

He's wearing that amused expression again.

Annoyed with him for some reason I can't quite explain, I glance away.

"Emma?"

I draw my gaze back to his.

As I turn back, he slides out of his chair and gets onto one knee in front of me. My hands are in his.

"Emma," he says. "Will you marry me?"

"Grayson. You can't be—"

But he is serious. I know it when he holds up a diamond solitaire ring.

"I know we haven't known each other long," he says. "but I've admired you from a distance for months. I memorized your features from a photograph. I think I fell in love with you through that photograph."

"Is that even possible?" I ask, but my voice is barely audible. I'm not even sure he heard me.

"Anything is possible."

I glance around, noting that we have an audience. He was doing this in front of an audience.

I meet his smoldering gaze again. Look into those blue eyes that I've fallen in love with.

"Just say yes," he says.

"Yes."

As he slides the ring on my finger, I realize that tears are falling down my cheeks.

People are clapping. I hardly even notice them. Grayson is all I'm aware of.

"I'm always crying around you," I say, wiping at my eyes.

He's sitting in his chair again, but he's sitting closer now and no one is paying us any attention any longer.

He takes a handkerchief out of his pocket and dabs at the tears. "I came prepared," he says.

I give him a searing look. He just smiles.

"My little raccoon."

I laugh a little.

"I told you I like raccoons."

He leans close and kisses me.

Something about that kiss loosens the tension in my heart and I realize that this is really happening. Grayson and I are really getting married. I never have to leave him again.

"Let's go home," he says. "Let's go home and tell Oscar."

"Yes," I say, smiling now. "Let's go home."

CHAPTER
SIXTY-NINE

Emma

"How should we celebrate our engagement?" Grayson asks as we step off the elevator and James heads out for the night.

"What do you mean?" I ask. "Like a party?"

"I'm sure there will be plenty of parties, but that's not what I meant."

He takes off his jacket and drops it over the nearest sofa before taking a step toward me.

Something in his eyes makes me feel like I've suddenly become his prey.

I take a step back.

"What did you mean?" I ask. "If not a party."

"I meant tonight. Just us."

He takes two steps forward and I take three backwards.

"I have a feeling you already have something in mind."

"I might." He grins.

I bump up against a wall, my back pressing against it.

"You've very perceptive sometimes."

"Sometimes?"

"Yes. Well. There are some things we don't talk about."

He means things like Trey.

"Surely you aren't going to hold those things against me forever," I say.

"I don't even know what things you're talking about."

"Very smooth," I say. "You're very charming sometimes."

"Sometimes?"

I grin at this little dance we have going.

He reaches me in two long strides and picks me up, one hand beneath my knees and the other beneath my shoulders.

I laugh and wrap my arms around his shoulders.

"You're being very Richard Gere on me," I say.

"Don't girls like that?" he asks.

"It's quite swoony."

He carries me back to my bedroom and gently lays me on the bed, then he stands there and looks at me.

The train rumbles by below and a siren wails in the

distance indicating that somewhere someone else's world is not so good right now.

But mine? Mine is perfect.

Except maybe that he's just standing there looking at me.

"What?" I ask.

"You're just so beautiful." His smoldering blue eyes snap to mine and hold, making my breath hitch.

Reaching up, I tug on his tie, bringing him down onto the bed with me.

His weight settles over me and he gazes at me, his deep blue eyes radiating with love and something deeper. A promise. A promise of forever.

My pulse quickens, my heart fluttering like it did the very first time he kissed me, and he leans toward me, his breath teasing my lips, but not touching.

"You're mine," he murmurs, his voice rough but tender. "Forever."

"Forever," I whisper back. The word resonates like a vow between us, more powerful than the diamond sparkling on my finger.

Then finally after what seems like tortuously forever, he kisses me, slow and sweet, and my whole body sighs as my fingers unbutton his shirt, one by one, taking my time until I push it aside to feel the heat of his skin. With every touch, every slide of my fingers over his bare skin, I feel myself surrendering to him. Not just my body, but my heart. My soul.

His lips trail down my neck, leaving a path of heat and I arch up toward him. "Emma," he murmurs, gently touching his hands on either side of my face.

"I love you," he says, his voice deep with emotion.

"I love you too." My eyes fill with moisture at the depth of just how deeply I feel those words, that connections. I thread my fingers through his hair, pulling him closer.

He smiles against my neck, kissing me at the nape of my neck. His hands sliding up my sides, and there's gentleness in the way he touches me, making me feel cherished.

He moves slowly, taking his time, and I moan softly when he cups my breast, his thumb brushing over the sensitive peak. My body responds instinctively to him, my hips lifting to meet the slow grind of his.

"Emma," he says, his forehead pressed to mine. I open my eyes to see everything in his. Everything a woman could ever dream of. Love. Desire. His fierce protectiveness that has always made me feel safe.

"I don't want anything to ever come between us," he says softly. "Ever."

A rush of emotion swells in my heart. "It won't."

He slowly unzips my dress and slides it off my shoulders, his touch gentle, careful. I feel beautiful in his gaze, in a way I never have before.

He nudges my knees apart and enters me with slow, deliberate tenderness that has me gasping his name. My fingers dig into his shoulders, holding on as he fills me completely, body and soul.

Our rhythm is gentle at first, an unhurried promise of love and forever. The pleasure builds quickly, the friction adding a natural urgency, until we're moving together in an unspoken language that we write with every touch. Every breath.

His kisses me with a slowness, as though he's got nothing else he'd rather be doing. As though forever stretches out in front of us.

His tongue ravages my mouth with a thoroughness that echoes the way his body ravages mine.

"I can't believe you're mine," he says, his voice catching. I can feel the sincerity of his words in every thrust, in every breath that mingles with mine.

"I always have been." And I hadn't even realized it.

Release comes slowly, then suddenly, like an ocean wave crashing against the shore, taking us back out to sea. My breath hitches, we both groan, and my nails dig into his back as I cling to him like my life depends on it.

Consumed by overwhelming heat and pleasure, passion and love, I can cry out his name, not sure I can survive much more. He presses his cheek to mine, his breath warm against my ear, our bodies in sync. I hold onto him as the world explodes around me.

I whimper as the shock waves rush through my body, wanting to hold onto this feeling.

Gasping and trembling together, he holds me close, rolling aside so as not to crush me, but keeping me pressed against him, I feel it in my soul.

We have more than just passion. We have us. We have unbreakable and forever.

He shifts back to look at me, a small smile of satisfaction on his lips, and brushes a strand of hair away from my face.

"I love you," he says again. It's not just a promise. It's a vow.

"Forever," I murmur, my eyes drifting closed, my heart content.

CHAPTER

SEVENTY

Grayson

THE NEXT MORNING I stand in the kitchen I rarely use scrambling eggs in a pan I rarely use. I have bacon frying on a griddle on another burner, something else I rarely use.

I have music streaming through a Bluetooth speaker from my phone. My new favorite playlist. 1920s music. It puts me in a good mood and I hum along.

Grab two pieces of toast as they slide up out of the toaster and pop two more pieces in. Add some butter to the toast and drop them both on the griddle, buttered side down.

While the bread heats, I wipe my hands on a towel, then take a sip of the hot latte I made with my coffee maker.

"Are you cooking?"

I look over my shoulder at Emma standing there.

The sight of her sends all the blood pooling below my waist.

Barefoot, she's wearing my white button-down shirt, the hem reaching halfway down her thighs. Nothing but that and the sparkling diamond engagement ring on her finger.

Her hair flows around her shoulders looking all the world like she'd just had a passionate night in bed. Which she had.

I know. I was there.

"Every now and then I take a whim," I say with a little grin.

"Smells good."

I glance down at her attire and she tugs at the hem as though she just remembered she'd come out here in nothing but my shirt.

"Have you seen Oscar?" she asks. "I woke up and he wasn't there."

"Not lately."

"Can I check your room? You've got the morning sun."

"You can do anything you want in my room," I say.

"I'll remember you said that." She gives me a sassy look and takes off down the hallway toward my bedroom. I watch her walk away with appreciation for her cute little ass beneath my shirt.

I'm so caught up in how sexy she looks, I forget about the toast now burning on the griddle.

"Son of a…" I scoop up the two pieces of burned toast and toss them in the trash. I'm not mad. I'm too damn happy to be mad about a couple of slices of burned toast.

I get out some more bread and start over on the toast.

Whistling to myself, I stir the eggs and flip the bacon.

"Did you find him?" I ask as she comes padding back toward the kitchen.

"He sleeping on your bed. In the sunshine."

"I do have a good sunrise." I scoop fluffy eggs onto a piece of toast, add some slices of bacon. "Have a seat. You get my famous egg and bacon sandwich."

"I'm not dressed," she says, noting my slacks and tucked in polo shirt.

"You look dressed perfectly for breakfast," I say. "James isn't here, so you don't have to worry about that."

She hesitates a moment, then shrugs and pulls out one of the heavy dining chairs and sits down.

I set the plate in front of her. "Milady," I say with a little bow.

"Be careful," she says. "I might get used to this."

"If you do, my purpose in life will be complete." I pour two glasses of fresh squeezed orange juice and set them on the table.

She rolls her eyes, but takes a bite of bacon while she

waits for me to put together my sandwich and sit beside her.

"Did you sleep well?" I ask.

She looks at me sideways, a little smile playing on her lips.

"Never better."

"Good. Me too."

"You should market these things," she said.

"I reserve them only for special occasions."

"Is that so? Do you have a lot of these *special occasions?*"

"Let's see. The last time I made breakfast was last summer when my three-year-old niece was visiting."

She grins.

"So no. I do not make breakfast often. But I am willing to consider changing that."

"Just name your price."

I decide to let that go. For now at least. Several things come to mind.

"So."

"Sounds like a serious topic," she says.

I give her a quick grin. "When do I get to meet your grandmother?"

The blood drains from her face.

"I don't know if you want to do that."

"If we're going to be married, I think maybe I should at least meet your family. Since your parents live in Portugal, I'll have to wait a bit to meet them."

She sips her orange juice. "Maybe we should just fly to Portugal," she says hopefully.

I finish off my sandwich. "If I didn't know better, I'd think you didn't want me to meet your grandmother."

"It's not my grandmother so much. She lives with her sister. Aunt Franny." She takes a deep breath. "Aunt Franny has a touch of dementia." She taps her temple. "And a little blue parakeet named Enzo."

"Aunt Franny sounds delightful. Do I get to meet her, too?"

"Of course," Emma grumbles. "Why not?" She folds her napkin and places it next to her plate. She still looks a little pale. "But don't say I didn't warn you."

"Should we invite them here?"

"Oh God no." She looks toward the ceiling, then back at me. "As much as I hate to suggest it, we're better off going to their house."

"Sounds like fun." I glance at my watch. "Want to go this morning? We can take lunch with us."

"Can't we just fly to Portugal first? And you can meet Grandmom and Aunt Franny at the wedding. Or even better after the wedding."

I laugh. "You do know that the more you protest, the more I can't wait to meet them."

"Okay," she says with an exaggerated sigh. "But I have to call first. Make sure Aunt Franny is having a decent day."

"Of course. I don't want to intrude."

"Right." She narrows her eyes at me. "It was a

wonderful breakfast," she says, leaning over to kiss me as she stands up. "But I'm going to shower before I call my grandmother. She's probably not up yet."

"Take your time," I say. "I'm just going to clean up a bit in here." Which means I'll put everything in the sink.

The cleaning service will be in any time and they'll make sure everything is back in order.

As I head to my home office, I wonder if my father is going to insist on trying to approve of Emma's family. In case he does, I need to know what to be prepared for.

Not that it will matter. I've already made my decision.

And Emma has the ring to prove it.

CHAPTER

SEVENTY-ONE

Emma

"It's an old neighborhood," Grayson says as he turns onto Grandmom's street.

"They're old," I say. "But it's home."

"It's nice. I like how the old trees arch over the road, making a canopy of shade."

Grayson pulls into their driveway and parks the SUV.

I wait while he comes around to grab the takeout behind my seat and open my door.

I try not to think about how out of place his luxury SUV is in the neighborhood or how out of place he and I look.

One of Grandmom's neighbors, wearing baggy pants

and a t-shirt, is out walking her dog. Another older neighbor is outside clipping his hedges.

Grayson is wearing his usual black trousers and white shirt—not the shirt I'd been wearing this morning when I'd walked around the condo looking for Oscar.

I'm wearing jeans and a burgundy button-down silky shirt. One of the shirts I normally reserve for wearing to work. And, of course, my ankle boots.

As we walk toward the front porch, I try not to think about the marked differences between my grandmother's old cottage in one of Houston's old neighborhoods and Grayson's high rise condo floor. Literally the floor. He owns the whole floor.

Grandmom answers the door. She's wearing khaki slacks and a green t-shirt. I think she's even wearing some makeup.

"Come in," she says with a welcoming smile. "You must be Emma's new beau."

I glance at Grayson as we step inside. They must have done some cleaning after I called. The house smells like lemons and everything is picked up and put in its place.

It's actually a little impressive. Even the mismatched furniture doesn't look so bad with everything picked up.

"Franny will be right out," she says. "You can bring that right over and put it down on the table."

We follow Grandmom to the dining table just off the kitchen. The table looks out over the backyard.

The backyard doesn't look so bad from in here. It's not

obvious that there are random vegetables growing in random places. It just looks like it needs to be mowed. And landscaped. It definitely needs to be landscaped, but Aunt Franny would have a fit if anyone tried to mess with her vegetables.

I glance over to see Enzo sitting in his cage just as he should be.

"Is this Enzo?" Grayson asks, walking right over to the parakeet.

"Yes," Grandmom says. "Do you like parakeets?"

"I like all animals," he says, looking at Enzo. Enzo preens and looks back at him.

I bite my knuckle to keep from laughing. Having Grayson here at my grandmother's house is surreal. I'm still having a hard time believing that he's actually here and the ring feels heavy on my hand. Heavy and sure.

"Here's Franny," Grandmom says. "Franny, meet Emma's new beau."

Aunt Franny comes out wearing a bright blue muumuu.

"It's so nice to meet you," she says, going up and grasping Grayson's hands. "I see you've met Enzo."

"I have. Enzo is a lovely parakeet."

"Grayson like animals," Grandmom tells Aunt Franny.

"I certainly hope so. He wouldn't be a good man if he didn't."

"I warned you," I whisper leaning close to Grayson.

Grayson just squeezes my hand. "We brought hamburgers. I understand they're one of your favorites."

"You're so very kind," Grandmom says. "But I could have made some lunch."

"That's not necessary," Grayson says. "We didn't want you to go to any trouble. We actually have an announcement to make."

Both Grandmom and Aunt Franny turn and focus on us —really focus on us—for the first time.

Grayson holds up my left hand, so they can see the sparkling diamond.

"We're getting married," he says proudly.

A moment of stunned silence is followed by both Grandmom and Aunt Franny talking at once.

"Why didn't you tell us already?"

"When is the wedding?"

"Do your parents know?"

Once they finally take a breath, I answer.

"We just got engaged last night," I say. "We don't know and no. My parents don't know yet. So you're the first."

They both continue to chatter while Grayson and I pull the food out of the bag and put it on paper plates we'd brought with us. He insisted that we not give my grandmother and her sister any extra work.

"Are you sure you still want to marry me?" I lean over and ask him about halfway through lunch.

"More than ever," he says with a little grin.

I think maybe something's wrong with him, but still. I'm relieved that he hasn't run out already. My grandmother and her sister have taken right to him and he seems surprisingly comfortable with them. Not the least bit concerned that they might both be a little bit crazy.

SEVENTY-TWO

Grayson

"Do you know anything about her family?" my father asks.

The next day I'm sitting across from my father's big wooden desk in his home office. He's leaning back in his oversized black leather office chair which not surprisingly suits him perfectly.

My father is a large man, tall but with a broad, stocky build. My brothers and I have his facial features, but we take after our mother when it comes to being tall and lean.

"Does it really matter at this point?" I ask. "I've already proposed to her and she accepted."

Father chews on an unlit cigar.

"She's a nice girl. I like her."

I narrow my eyes at my father. That's quite a compliment coming from him.

"Her grandmother's sister is a bit eccentric," I admit. "Her grandmother is good people. I haven't met her parents. They live in Portugal."

"It sounds like you need to make a trip to Portugal."

"That's not part of the inheritance requirement."

"I thought you weren't doing it for the inheritance."

'I'm not, Father. What are you trying to say?"

Father sets his cigar in a little wooden cigar box on his desk. "You could ask her father for her hand. Goes a long way in the long run."

My father is slick. I have to give him that. He wants me to meet Emma's parents not for her, but for him.

"Maybe. But only if it's something Emma wants. Meeting her parents won't change anything."

"Okay," Father says. "Don't say I didn't caution you about it."

"You met her. You and Mother like her. I'm going to marry her with or without the inheritance. I'm in love with her."

"Alright," Father says. "Good enough. We need to talk about telling your brothers."

"I was hoping you would tell them."

Father nods, running a hand along the smooth wood of

the desk that had belonged to his father and his father before him.

"I'll call a family meeting."

"Good idea." I bite my tongue to keep from telling him that's exactly what he should have done five years ago.

"Are you prepared to announce your engagement on your birthday party?"

"I don't want a party."

"Your mother already sent the invitations."

Good God. Does it never end?

"And then what?" I ask.

"Then you start planning the wedding."

Planning a wedding means people in our business. So many people.

"That sounds like hell on earth," I grumble.

An idea sparks something deep in the back of my mind.

Sometimes the most sensible things are right there in front of a person. So close they can easily be overlooked.

"Anything else?" I ask. "Do I need to sign any papers or anything?"

"Don't be ridiculous."

I give my father a look that tells him I know that's exactly the kind of thing he'd do if given half a chance.

"I'll have the attorneys put together something."

"I'm not signing a prenup," I tell him.

"It's one of the will's requirements." Father says with a smug expression.

"I have to go now. I think I hear Mother calling me."

Actually I've met the quota for the week of spending time with my father.

Besides, I have things to plan of my own.

My father gave me a brilliant idea and he doesn't even know it.

SEVENTY-THREE

Emma

"I THOUGHT YOU LIKE SURPRISES," Grayson reminds me two days later.

"I do," I say. "but not when they require putting Oscar in a carrier."

Oscar sits between us on the backseat of his SUV with James driving in the front.

And not when we are so clearly driving to the airport.

"I'm not letting anyone take Oscar and put him in one of those cargo holds."

"No one is going to take Oscar. I promise."

"Oscar might not like flying." *I don't like flying.*

"I think you might be projecting."

"Are you being the psychologist now?" I sound far less vexed than I feel.

He just grins at me.

"You will like it," he promises. "And Oscar won't mind."

I sit back against the buttery leather seat, one hand in Grayson's.

He gently rubs the back of my hand with his thumb.

I can feel the excitement humming off of him.

He'd had me pack an overnight bag for me which basically means a full suitcase and although he didn't know I knew, he'd brought a backpack with a bag of Oscar's food and several cans of wet food.

We're going somewhere. An overnight trip.

He won't tell me where. I blame myself for that. I'd told him I like surprises.

But now I'm rethinking that.

Maybe I like simple surprises. Like new restaurants. Or flowers.

Maybe I don't like big surprises like overnight trips.

"You trust me?" he asks.

I look over at him with half closed eyes.

"Pretty much."

"Sassy girl. But you have nothing to worry about."

"I'm not worried." Much.

When James pulls into a private parking lot at the airport, I'm not the least bit surprised.

A strong breeze flutters my hair and my skirt as we walk

out onto the runway. The scent of jet fuel is strong and hints of excitement. That along with the sound of jets landing and taking off in the background.

Fifteen minutes later we're climbing the narrow steps into a private jet. A Phenom.

The fastest boarding I've ever experienced.

James helps with the luggage, then heads back to the car.

"Doesn't seem right making him stay here," I say.

Grayson looks at me with a raised eyebrow.

"Something I need to know about?"

"He's been very kind and it's your fault for making him go everywhere with me."

"Only when I'm not around," he says, then rubs his chin. "He's not bad looking though."

I just smile at him. "I'll let you know if I have any wayward ideas."

Then we're standing inside the jet.

"Where do we sit?" I ask.

"I'm hoping you'll sit up front in the copilot's seat."

I follow him into the cockpit and look at all the computer and dials and levers with awe.

"You know what all these things do?" I ask, sitting down, carefully putting Oscar, still in his little carrier at my feet.

"Let's hope so," he sits down and puts on his captain's cap.

My heart stutters at how handsome he is.

It doesn't matter where he's taking me. If he wanted to fly me to the moon, I'd go with him. Probably.

"What do you think about the airplane?" he asks.

Chatter from the control tower comes through the headsets, but Grayson doesn't seem to be concerned about it.

"I don't know much about airplanes." I pick up the harness and fiddle with it. "I don't even know how to put this on."

"I can help you with that."

He leans close and deftly secures my four-point harness.

Leaning close, his breath brushes against my skin and my stomach tightens.

"How's that?" he asks, his breath against my ear.

"It's 'um." He kisses me on the ear, then makes a trail of kisses across my cheek until he reaches the corner of my lips.

"It's okay?"

"It's a bit restraining," I say, wanting to get closer to him, but can't.

"I know where to get some handcuffs if you find that you like being... restrained."

"You're just full of ideas today, aren't you. Again. I'll let you know."

Then he moves his lips to mine ever so slowly, making me quiver inside with anticipation.

I lean forward and he cups my face with his hands. My eyes flutter closed as he plants his lips on mine.

As he effectively devours my lips, I tangle my fingers in his soft short hair.

"Prepare to taxi." The controller's voice comes through loud and clear almost as though they know that we aren't ready to taxi or anything else for that matter related to flying.

"Anyway," Grayson says, releasing me and picking up our conversation as though he hadn't just turned my world upside down. "I was asking because I'm thinking about buying it."

"Buying what?" I ask, my eyes feeling a little glazed and I still taste his lips on mine.

"This airplane."

"It's for sale?"

"Well. Okay. Not this particular airplane. But one like it. A new one. I haven't decided yet. It costs a lot less to get a used one."

"Like cars," I say. I take it as a good sign that he's talking about things like making major purchases with me.

We taxi out onto the runway and Grayson spends the next few moments checking the computer and conversing with the control tower in a language all their own that I don't understand.

He hands me the second headset.

"Makes it easier to talk," he says.

I put on the headset, but I don't really listen to anything they're saying.

Instead I watch Grayson.

He's in his element here. He obviously knows what he's doing.

Completely and utterly in control.

He's every bit the handsome pilot.

Sitting here next to him in the cockpit, I fall a little bit more in love with him.

So much so that quite honestly it's painful.

He sees me looking at him and grins.

I look away, feeling my cheeks heat, and clear my throat.

"Are you going to tell me where we're going?" I ask.

Instead of answering me, he takes the airplane into the air.

I feel the moment the airplane leaves the ground. The moment we're weightless.

It's just the two of us now. No one else. Well. Just Oscar.

We head straight up, leaving the ground far below.

"Portugal," he says.

"Portugal?" I look out the window as though expecting to see a GPS, then back to him. "But...?"

"Your parents are waiting for us."

"You talked to my parents?" I swallow the lump in my throat. "How did you manage to keep that a secret from me for so long?"

"It wasn't hard to keep for a couple of days. Anyway,

they're very excited about the wedding. Your mother is looking into flowers and assured me there's a little shop nearby that will have a dress for you."

"A dress?"

"A wedding dress," he says with complete nonchalance. "We'll do some more shopping, too."

When I don't answer, he keeps talking. "We worked it all out. Your father will walk you down the aisle. Your sister will be your maid of honor."

He really does have everything all worked out. I don't think I could have done better if I'd tried.

"Grayson?"

"But if you don't want to get married in Portugal, I can turn this plane around right now and go home. Or we can spend the weekend in New York. Or Mackinac Island. Just you, me, and Oscar. My mother is excited about *helping* you put together a huge wedding for us. I'm pretty sure you won't have to do a thing except show up."

As we pass through a fluffy white cloud, I unzip Oscar's carrier and pull him into my lap.

His eyes are big and he grabs hold of my shirt with his claws at first. But then he puts his front paws on the side window and looks down at the world passing below. At the trees and houses, highways, and rivers.

"Oscar," I say. "We're going to Portugal. We're going to see Grandma and Grandpa and your aunt."

I look over at Grayson under my lashes.

"And we're going to get married."

Everything is right with my world.

I'm with my handsome fiancé who happens to be a pilot.

He made arrangements for us to get married in Portugal where my family is living.

And most important of all, he'd made sure I brought my cat.

He has protected me and taken care of me since the moment we met.

And every moment I spend with him I fall a little more in love.

Something tells me this is something that will never change as long as we live.

What we have is something deeper than any vows we can make.

What we have is a forever vow of the heart.

EPILOGUE

Emma

Oscar sits, looking quite proud of his achievement, on top of a stack of banker's boxes—six high—looking for all the world like he belongs here. His tail twitches as he gazes toward the cars moving like ants on the streets far below.

"Oscar," I say. "How did you get up there?" He nonchalantly licks at one of his front paws. "Never mind. I don't think I want to know."

When Grayson and James had swept me away from my house three weeks ago, I'd brought pretty much all my essentials.

I hadn't realized just how much stuff, not necessarily essential, that I owned.

But now it's all here. Everything. Neatly boxed and labeled. I hadn't had to pack the boxes. I would have been okay with packing my own stuff, but Grayson insisted on hiring someone. I can honestly say it was the easiest move I've ever made. I had no idea how much easier it was to have a moving company pack everything up than to do it myself.

Now that it's all stacked in our bedroom—the bedroom I now share with Grayson—I have to unpack it.

Yes. The moving company would have unpacked everything and put it up where it belongs, but I insisted that I do it myself. I like the process of deciding where to put things. I'm also getting rid of a lot of things I no longer use.

Turns out I own things that have no place in the thirty-first floor condo where I now officially live with Grayson.

Like my queen bed comforter and sheets. Grayson has king beds in all the bedrooms. So the queen bedding... donation box.

My tableware. Donation box.

I'm letting the furniture go with the sale of the house, but the little things I wanted to take my time and decide. It takes a lot of mental energy.

My books—I'm keeping all them—have a place in the little home office Grayson created for me just off the bedroom. It's a private space and it's all mine. A place where

I can sit on the chaise lounge and read or sit in the office chair and work at the desk. All the while surrounded by books on one side and floor-to-ceiling windows on the other.

My arms loaded with workout clothes, I walk into my closet, almost as big as my bedroom in my old house and dump them on the counter. Yes. A counter in the closet. Grayson comes up behind me, sweeps my hair aside, and kisses me on the neck.

"There you are," he says.

"Hi." I lean back into his arms.

"Are you sure you don't want some help unpacking?"

"What? You'll help me?"

"I will do anything you ask me to do."

"Anything?"

"Anything." His breath tickles my ear wickedly.

"Are you sure?" I turn in his arms and raise my chin for a kiss.

"I'm sure." He twines his fingers in my hair and cups the back of my head with his hand as his lips press against mine.

"Happy birthday," I murmur against his lips. "I have something for you later."

"I have everything I need right here." He kisses me on the forehead and pulls me close against him.

"Me, too."

"I never gave much thought to turning thirty, but my grandfather gave it a whole new meaning."

"I'm thinking maybe your grandfather was a wise man who could foretell the future."

"That sounds very mystical for a scientist." He fingers make soothing little circles on my back.

"Psychology is an art, too, you know." My voice is muffled against his shoulder.

"Hmm." He tilts my head up until my gaze locks onto his smoldering blue eyes. "I actually think you're right."

"Do you now?"

"I think my grandfather is watching over us. Somehow guiding fate in the right direction."

As grounded as Grayson and I both are, I think he's right.

I think he and are somehow fated to be together.

As if time circled itself around us, wrapping us together.

"My grandfather once said love is the only thing worth protecting," he whispers, his voice tight with emotion.

Goosebumps run along my arms.

Because somehow, even across time and silence, his grandfather knew—this moment was always meant to play out just like this.

Two souls. One heartbeat.

A love formed out of fate, sealed with a vow—to protect, to cherish, and to never let go.

THE END.

Keep reading for a preview of *Vow to Redeem*...

BESTSELLING AUTHOR OF VOWS OF INHERITANCE
KELLA KALEIGH
He needed a bride
He chose the one who broke him..
VOW to REDEEM

VOW TO REDEEM
PREVIEW

Chapter 1
Sloane Monroe

ALL WORK *and no play makes Sloane a dull girl.*

I tap my manicured red painted nails on my phone and swipe out of my best friend's text message.

Michelle is right.

I do need to get out more. To follow my own advice.

Swiveling around in my office chair, I gaze out into the midst of downtown Houston. Bumper to bumper traffic. The daily mass exodus of downtown.

Something I do not regret giving up.

All I have to do after work is walk down the hallway to

the elevator, step out onto the street and walk two blocks to my apartment building.

Up another elevator and down another hallway. That's it. Home.

No fighting traffic. No getting stuck on the freeway for hours just to get home only to turn around and do it all again the next day.

With my western facing view, I can just see a hint of the setting sun between the high rise buildings.

The glow of sunset splashes an array of reds and oranges across the sky. Nature's art that will last no more than a few minutes. Fleeting, like most things, especially things of beauty.

Just another reminder that I should at least meet Michelle for drinks. Michelle needs no reason to celebrate. She is the epitome of a girl enjoying her life.

But my computer screen behind me chimes, reminding me of my next appointment.

Unlike my friend Michelle, my day doesn't end at five o'clock. I have clients who get off work at five and I have to be available to see them then.

My next client is a new patient. Chase White. A bland enough name, but the name Chase brings back a flood of memories.

I knew a Chase once.

Lowering my reading glasses, I press my fingers against the bridge of my nose.

Chase and I never should have met.

Both from Houston, we'd met in Princeton, New Jersey, of all places.

He'd been captain of the Polo Club at Princeton University. I'd been a doctoral intern at Princeton's psychiatric hospital when he and I first met.

Between my accelerated studies and his tendency to play more than study, we had somehow been the same age when we'd met at Princeton.

I swivel around again, turning my back to the window and log into the computer program to learn more about THIS Chase who has appointment with me in... I glance at the time... approximately twenty minutes.

The more I learn about THIS Chase, the fewer preconceived ideas I will have about him.

The less I will think of him as the charming playboy I'd met during my year at Princeton.

Unfortunately, his referral comes with no notes. No information other than his name.

I type a message to the office assistant, asking for more information, then delete it.

I'm the only person on the floor. Everyone else is out there fighting traffic to get home. Or, like Michelle, already at the bar having an afterwork drink.

It's okay. I'll treat THIS Chase as a walk-in.

With no notes to review, I take a minute to straighten my desk.

Adjust the name plaque on the corner of my desk, lest

anyone mistake me for anyone other than Dr. Sloane Monroe, Licensed Psychologist. I refill my business card holder. And close my laptop computer.

I don't take notes during sessions. Not even during intakes.

The most valuable skill I learned during my internship was how to hold information in my head.

I'll write notes after the session, of course, because if it is isn't written, it didn't happen—the second most important thing I'd learned.

I put a fresh bottle of unopened water on the little round wooden table next to the client's chair and make sure I have plenty of water in my bottle.

With fifteen minutes left before my session starts, I head to the restroom, my high heels falling softly on the plush carpet as I walk down the hallway. The hallways always smell like vanilla. Maybe it's something they clean the carpet with.

The office assistant leaves fresh flowers on the counter of the staff restroom, changing them out every couple of days. Today's flowers are daffodils. Bright yellow flowers that smell like sweet spring air and fresh green fields, their scent delicate but unmistakable. A reminder that spring is here.

Since my life is no longer demarcated by semesters, it's a much needed reminder. My days and weeks tend to blur together.

Another reminder about how time flies.

Maybe I'll meet Michelle for that drink after all.

I examine my face in the mirror.

Maybe I'm biased, but I don't think I look like I'm almost thirty. Maybe it's the cream I use religiously every night. Or maybe it's because I don't go out in the blistering hot Houston sun.

Or... maybe it's because I don't go out and party. The irony of it all. What's the point in looking youthful when I spend all my time working? My patients don't care what I look like. Not really. I make myself presentable. But they would do just as well with a psychologist who looks sixty as they do with one who looks twenty-something.

In fact, sometimes, I think I would have more credibility if I perhaps looked a little bit older.

I leave the restroom and head back to my office.

Even though I work later for a reason—a very good reason, I don't really care for being on the floor by myself.

It's just too quiet. It's always quiet. But at least during the day I know that there are other people behind the closed doors.

I find comfort in knowing that I'm not up here alone.

But that's during the day. Tonight. It's just me.

Technically it isn't all that much different except that the lights are all off under the doors.

Just knowing it's just me makes the floor feel different. More uncomfortable. It's safe with the guard downstairs, but still... it's different.

Before I even reach my office, I know that I didn't make it back before my new client showed up.

I can sense someone in my office. That happens when it's so quiet I can practically hear someone breathing.

Stopping in my doorway, I see who must be Chase White standing at the window with his back to me.

He leans against the glass, propped on one elbow. A cocky, confident stance.

Although I hadn't made a sound, he must have sensed me in the doorway. He looks up, catching my reflection in the glass.

Looking back at him, I blink.

I'd primed my brain to expect Chase Whitaker.

So that's exactly who I see.

My brain effectively erases the five years that separate now from the last time I'd seen Chase Whitaker.

But I shake it off, putting on my most professional expression, and take a step forward.

"Hello," I say. "You must be Chase. I'm…"

He turns around and looks at me with an amused expression. "Dr. Sloane Monroe." He holds up my name plaque.

"Well," I say, struggling to regain control of my fluttering heartbeat, glancing at the name plaque in his hands. "You have the advantage."

He sets the name plaque back on my desk. "You wound me. I was certain you'd remember me."

"I remember you," I say, keeping my hands lightly

clasped together in front of me. "But someone has you in the system as Chase White."

"Someone gave me an alias," he says with a little shrug.

I need to sit down. My knees are feeling a little weak at finding Chase Whitaker standing in my office.

I deliberately walk over to sit in one of the two comfortable armchairs facing each other. Most people would have angled the chairs away from the window, but I think having the traffic to focus on helps people open up. It gives them something to focus on other than me and whatever painting I might have hanging on the wall behind me.

I see the traffic as something of a neutral focal point. Granted, it takes some people a couple of sessions to get accustomed to being on the nineteenth floor.

"What makes you need an alias?" I ask, leaning forward, my elbows on my thighs.

Chase drops into the chair across from me, stretches out his long legs, and adjusts his designer tie. Dark gray that matches his black designer suit.

"I don't think I need an alias. My father made the appointment."

He looks me over, his smoldering blue eyes taking me in from head to toe. His gaze sweeps from the long hair I have pulled back and secured with a clip at the back of my head, down my short black blazer, my black pencil skirt, to my heels.

"You haven't changed much," he says.

"Is that supposed to be a compliment?" I ask. I'm not fishing. I swear I'm not. But since hearing it out loud, it sounds like fishing, I don't give him time to answer. "So your father thinks you need therapy."

"Something like that. He thinks I need to learn how to control my image."

"What does that have to do with me?" I ask, my brows furrowed. "I'm not a publicist."

"But you're a psychologist and you're supposed to be the best. I'm guessing you're the only Princeton educated psychologist he could find in Houston."

"I see." I don't bother to tell him that my degree is actually from the University of Houston. Chase would know that. His father would know it, too, if he bothered to check.

Maybe his father doesn't remember the girl his son dated in college.

Or maybe he does.

"You know I can't work with you," I say.

"No... Why not?"

I make a tsking sound. "Did I not teach you anything?"

"I was probably too distracted to listen." He grins rakishly.

"You're not helping your case," I say with a little frown.

He grins. That devastatingly handsome grin that charms every woman he meets. When I'd met him six years ago, I'd had no immunity.

But now I have immunity.

Now that devastatingly handsome grin has no effect on me.

It might be nice if my racing pulse got the message.

And maybe my dry mouth.

Might be helpful if my scattered thoughts, too, realized that I'm long over him.

VOW TO REDEEM

PREVIEW

Chapter 2
Chase Whitaker

I'D LIED to Sloane's face.

I'd told her she hadn't changed much.

Truth was she had changed much.

She's more polished now. More elegant. And more sure of herself.

She's in her element here.

When I'd known her at Princeton, she'd been an intern. Still getting her feet wet. I heard she'd stayed an extra year to do a post-doc residency or something like that.

But I'd come home.

That was when all hell broke loose back here in Houston.

My older brother, Grayson, had gotten married shortly thereafter. He swears it wasn't related, but I still don't know if I believe him. Doesn't matter though. He's happy as a lark.

Grayson has always been the good one. He'd followed the rules. Played by the book.

The only thing my parents, mostly my father, hadn't particularly approved of was Grayson's love of flying.

Grayson has his own jet now.

Funny how our parents can put their disapproval aside when they want to go somewhere.

But Grayson doesn't hold it against them. He's loyal to his family. To a fault.

Me? I can't seem to stay out of trouble.

I was okay until I came back from Princeton. That's when the trouble started.

Seems like everything I do ends up on someone's feed. And it's never the good things I do. It's always something I'd rather not have advertised.

The last episode, the one that got me here, was when I'd been spotted coming out of a hotel with two very attractive women. I'd kissed one of them, then the other. It should have been harmless enough, but, of course, someone had caught it on video and the whole thing had gone viral.

Okay. Yes. They were sisters. And. Yes. I might have fucked them both.

But it was all consensual and harmless.

At the time, it seemed like a good idea. And yet sitting here with Sloane... not so much.

I honestly hope I don't have to explain what happened with the sisters.

I don't want to see disappointment on her face.

I'd seen disappointment there before.

That disappointment had been the end of us.

The truth of the matter is... Sloane makes me want to be a better person.

"So. Chase." Sloane straightens and clasps her hand together in her lap. Her legs are crossed at the ankles and turned slightly to the side. I don't think she even has any idea that she's sitting like a perfectly proper lady.

I know for a fact that she never went to finishing school. Not like my sister. My sister is at finishing school right now.

Being composed and elegant just comes naturally to Sloane.

"Dr. Monroe?" I keep my gaze on her eyes. Sparkling green eyes that seem to see straight into my soul.

"Why don't you tell me in your words why you're here for therapy."

"My father—"

She holds up a finger. "You. Not your father. Why do YOU think you're here?"

It really is because of my father. He worries about the family image. Rightly so, but I don't want to tell Sloane that. Back to the last straw that got me here. The two sisters.

But I have to tell her something.

Something plausible.

It would have been helpful if I'd known that I was coming to see Sloane and not some stodgy old coot. I could have had my story thought out and ready.

I run a hand through my short hair and start again.

"It's come to my attention." I pause, waiting for her to hold up another finger, but she just lifts an eyebrow. "that as I near my thirtieth birthday, it's time I think about settling down."

"Why?" she asks. I don't hear any judgment there. Nothing about how that sounds absolutely nothing like the Chase Whitaker she knew before.

I shift in my seat. There's something about the way she looks at me that is unnerving. It's like she can see me. The real me beneath my charming persona.

"Because I don't want to be that pitiful single man in his thirties." Damn. That's something I've never put into words. Not even to myself. And yet truer words have never been spoken.

She smiles at me with a little smile that makes me think she already knew the answer before she even asked me. Not that she could know. How could she know when I didn't even know myself?

I've only been in her office for five minutes and already

she has me realizing things I hadn't even known were in there.

It's unnerving and unsettling.

I've seen stodgy old psychologists a couple of times. Comes with the territory of being the unruly son in a rich, prestigious family.

Go figure that it would take Sloane, the girl I'd never gotten over, to get me to see past my own bullshit. To see that as much as I might fight against getting married, there's something buried deep inside me that actually does want to get married or at the least doesn't want to not get married.

Those might be two different things. Might not be.

There's another reason, too, that I'm here. There real reason. And that real reason is something I REALLY can't tell her about.

The matter of the inheritance that will make me a billionaire.

VOW TO REDEEM

PREVIEW

Chapter 3
Sloane

"SHOULD I be telling you these things if you can't work with me?" Chase asks.

Chase has my complete focus as any client would.

But Chase has my attention on a visceral level. Even at the three feet or so apart that we're sitting, I can smell his cologne. Sandalwood and old leather. Even after all these years, my body recognizes his scent.

Just because I'm over him doesn't mean I can't appreciate the way he smells. The way he looks at me with those smoldering blue eyes.

Doesn't mean I can't appreciate his strong clean shaven jaw and the obviously expensive haircut. The way his suit fits him perfectly as though it was made for him and it probably was.

I pick up the bottle of water I keep on the little table next to my chair and take a swallow to lubricate my dry throat.

"That's actually a very good question."

He sits back. Waits for me to explain the answer to that very good question. But instead of gazing at the traffic below, he watches me with blue eyes that don't miss anything.

"In order to refer you, I have to know more so I can refer you to the most suitable person." A more bullshit answer has never been uttered. I would do well to just pretend I had immediately recognized him, which I had, and set up a referral.

"Right." He straightens in his chair and adjusts his tie, loosening it just a little. "That makes sense."

In the few minutes he and I had been talking, I'd almost forgotten that I couldn't work with him. That fact had slipped just into the recesses of my brain, probably due to the heady scent of his cologne that brought back memories I thought were filed away only surfacing in the occasional middle of the night dream. Usually a dream that involves an overheated libido.

"What kind of person are you thinking you'd refer me to?" he asks, obviously not realizing just how befuddled he has me.

"I'm not sure you need counseling," I say. "Have you tried dating apps?"

He smiles a little in a way that tells me there's something he isn't telling me. But there's always something. No one spills their guts on the first session.

Even if it's not a real session.

"Finding someone to date isn't the problem," he says.

"I see."

"Do you follow Houston's social media?" He leans forward, watching me carefully as though he's looking past my psychologist façade to see what lies beneath. To see the real me beneath.

"What do you mean? Like society pages?"

"Something like that, but not the newspaper. Social media."

"No. I don't care to accidentally run across one of my clients." It's a good excuse to help me avoid social media, something I have a natural aversion to.

A flash of relief crosses his face. I know relief when I see it.

"That's probably good," he says, then quickly adds. "I'm sure clients want to keep things private."

"I'm sure." I tap my fingers together as I consider. "Are you telling me that you're having trouble narrowing down your women? Having trouble choosing the one you want to marry?"

"I don't think I said that." He looks uncomfortable. Decidedly so. That usually means I've touched on something nearing the truth.

I unclasp my hands and rest them on either side of me, pressing my fingers against the buttery soft leather of my chair.

"Then help me understand."

"Alright," he says, glancing away, finally, toward the traffic below. "But not here. Let's not talk here."

"Where do you suggest we talk?" I feel like I'm standing at the top of a slippery slope.

One wrong step and I'll slide right to the bottom, landing squarely on my ass.

Already I've been talking to Chase, someone I know personally, in my office, under the guise of a therapy session. It's a breach of ethics. Even if his father made the appointment. Even if he is an adult.

But since he can't be my client, perhaps it is best for us to get out of the office if we're going to continue to talk.

"There must be a place around here to get a drink. Someplace quiet."

"There are a few places," I say, noting that the sun has dropped over the horizon, leaving just a lingering splash of color across the horizon.

Chase stands up. Holds out a hand. "Let's go."

I put my hand in his, uncross my feet, and stand up.

He's not a client. He's not a client. He's not a client.

I'm not breaking any ethical rules.

He's a referral. I can refer him to one of my colleagues down the hallway.

As soon as I recognized him, I knew he would be a referral. Sure we talked some. But it would have been rude and inhumane to do otherwise.

He takes my hand in his and laces his fingers with mine in that way he'd always done since he first time I'd met him.

I might have backed away from the slippery slope of ethics, but I'd turned right around only to find myself on the precipice of another slippery slope. This one just as dangerous in a completely different way.

This one is the slippery slope of Chase Whitaker.

I'd been down this slide before. The ride had been fun, but the crash landing at the bottom had been unforgettably painful.

"I just need to get my things," I say, sliding my hand out of his.

"Take your time."

He faces the window again, slipping his hands in his pockets.

The Princeton graduate, the captain of the Princeton Polo Club, is a businessman now. Whatever he does, I have no doubt he's successful.

What I doubt, however, is that the reason he gave me for coming into my office today. I don't think Chase Whitaker has even a shadow of difficulty finding a woman to date or marry or whatever it is he's looking for.

But since I'm not going to be his psychologist, I don't need to know the real reason. Whatever reason he has, it's no concern of mine.

Unless, of course, he decides to tell me as a friend. Outside the confines of this office. Whatever he tells me has to be outside of this office.

I've worked too hard and too long to risk losing my license over an ethics complaint.

I'd met Chase's father once. If ever there was a man to strike fear in a person's heart, it was Mr. Whitaker.

If he makes the connection between who I am and who he thought he was sending his son to see for help, God help us all.

I turn off my computer, grab my little crossbody purse, and I'm ready to go.

"Ready," I say.

Chase turns and smiles at me.

I am in so much trouble.

Chase has been my weakness since the moment I met him.

Apparently that little detail has not changed.

Just looking at him. Seeing the way he looks at me as though he hasn't bothered to look at another woman since me—something I would stake my life on not being true—has me feeling weak in the knees.

Very unsettling. Considering what Chase Whitaker had done before he'd left Princeton.

He'd left and I'd stayed another year to do my post-doc

work, but not a day had passed that I hadn't regretted staying in Princeton another year.

The very air had been haunted by memories that he and I had shared.

He had quite simply broken my heart.

VOW TO REDEEM

Chapter 4
Chase

SLOAN HAD ALWAYS BEEN the epitome of the perfect woman.

I'd met her at Princeton. I'd been the captain of the polo team and she had been an intern. From the day I met her until I got back to Houston nearly a year later, I had been completely faithful to her. In fact, I think that was the only year since then that I hadn't had a revolving door of women in my life.

The funny thing about all that was that I had never taken Sloan to bed. We'd kissed and made out. We'd kissed and made out a lot, but I'd put her on something of a pedestal.

And now in the five years since, I'd developed a reputation for being a playboy. Such a playboy, in fact, that my father is worried that I'll have trouble being taken seriously in the business world.

As a venture capitalist, I'd had no problems so far.

Nonetheless, I could see his point.

And the stakes are getting higher by the moment.

In just three months, I'll be turning thirty.

Thirty is something of an important age for the Whitaker family children. Some would say even a magical age.

The whole thing had been set in motion by my grandfather.

I'd been too young to know him very well, but my impression of him was that he was a wily fellow.

A wily fellow because he'd stipulated in his will that his grandchildren had to be married by the time they're thirty in order to inherit their share of his billions.

I was doing okay for myself. I had a few millions of my own, but my grandfather's inheritance was an important part of my family's legacy. It was especially important to my mother that her five children have their share of my grandfather's wealth.

It wasn't just money either. The money came with responsibilities.

As it should.

And that was where my playboy reputation really became a problem.

It wasn't like I wanted a bad reputation. It just sort of happened.

Women came on to me and I was a sucker for them.

After Sloane, no other woman had gotten near my heart.

But Sloane had. Sloane had my heart.

But that was before I messed it up.

And once I messed it up, it was like I lost myself.

There's now a concrete vault around my heart that no one can get through.

It seemed there was only one key to that vault and Sloane held it.

Unfortunately, Sloane has no idea.

And after what happened in Princeton, I can almost guarantee that she wants nothing to do with my heart. Not even if she's the one who holds the key.

I link my fingers with hers as we step onto the elevator and ride down to the first floor.

She keeps her face blank and her eyes on the elevator numbers as they tick downward.

Even though she's not looking at me, she's not pulling her hand away either. I take that as a good sign.

As we step off the elevator and walk toward the street, I promise myself that this time around I'm not going to mess things up and I'm not going to let her avoid me either. The details, of course, required to make that happen have yet to be determined.

I have no plan. Since I hadn't known I was going to see her today, or even if I was going to ever see her again, I was flying by the seat of my pants.

And with Sloane, flying by the seat of the pants can be a dangerous game.

Dr. Sloane Monroe is the kind of woman who can see right through the bullshit.

I follow her lead as we step out onto the sidewalk and turn right.

Downtown Houston smells like coastal air mixed with the usual exhaust fumes prevalent in any city.

The chirp of the metro train blends with the sound of a city bus and the roar of cars as they zip past.

I have an office not far from here. Probably why my father had made this appointment for me. How he'd managed to make an appointment with Sloane without knowing he was making an appointment with Sloane was baffling. The only thing I could figure was he'd made an appointment with the agency and Sloane had been assigned.

The odds were too astronomically unlikely for me to even begin to compute.

My grandmother would have called it fate.

Me? I called it serendipity.

Perhaps, though, my grandmother was right. Perhaps it was fate's way of giving me a chance to redeem myself.

Keep Reading Vow to Redeem...

CONTEMPORARY

Vows of Inheritance Series

(Reading Order)

Vow to Protect

Vow to Redeem

(ALPINE FALLS)

Stranded in Alpine Falls

Belonging in Alpine Falls

The Spirit of Christmas in Alpine Falls

Christmas Wishes in Alpine Falls

Secrets and Second Chances

Honeymoon with a Stranger

Finding True North in Alpine Falls

A Ghost of Christmas Magic in Alpine Falls

(SILVER PINES)

The Way Back to You

Back to Where We Began

When We Were Us

(ONCE UPON FOREVER)

My Forever Guy

Our Forever Love

Forever Vows

Finding Forever

Accidentally Forever

(TRUE NORTH)

Borrowed Until Monday

Still Mine

The Moon and the Stars at Christmas

Perfectly Mismatched

On the Way to Forever

A Merry Little Christmas

On the Way Home to Christmas

It was Always You

(UNBREAK MY HEART)

Begin Again

Love Again

Falling Again

(FOR THE LOVE OF THE FLIGHT)

Just Stay

Just Chance

Just Believe

Just Us

Just Once

Just Happened

Just Maybe

Just Pretend

Just Because

(MAGNETIC NORTH)

Second Chance Kisses

Second Chance Secrets

First Time Charm

Three Broken Rules

Second Chance Destiny

Unexpected Vows

(FALLING FOR CHRISTMAS)

The Heart of Christmas

The Magic of Christmas

In a One Horse Open Sleigh

A Secret Royal Christmas

An Old Fashioned Christmas

(CITY SKYLINE BILLIONAIRES)

Billionaire's Unexpected Landing

Billionaire's Accidental Girlfriend

Billionaire's Fallen Angel

Billionaire's Secret Crush

Billionaire's Barefoot Bride

(TRULY, MADLY, DEEPLY)

The Lady in the Red Dress

On the Edge of Chance

Sealed with a Kiss

Kiss Me at Midnight

The Heart Knows

(STOLEN ECHOES)

When Cupid's Arrow Strikes

Chasing Fireflies

A Chance Encounter

(EDGE OF THE HORIZON)

The Forever Equation

Pretend Boyfriend

All our Tomorrows

Kissing for Keeps

Out of the Blue

The Princess and the Playboy

(RED LIPSTICK KISSES)

Red Lipstick Kisses and Small Town Wishes

Stolen Dances and Big City Chances

Chance Connections and Upside Down Plans

(INTO THE MIST)

Written in the Wind

Scripted in the Stars

Destined in the Twilight

Promised in the Mist

Trapped in the Melody

(DRAGON'S BLOOD)

Dragon's Blood

Lavender Blue

Champagne Silver

Twilight Frost

Mountbatten Pink

(WHEN HEARTSTRINGS BECKON)

Rescued in Time

Meet me in 1879

(WHEN HEARTSTRINGS ECHO)

Messages Across Time

Falling Through to Forever

Once Upon a Winter's Spell

(BECKONED)

Before the Storm

Twist of Fate

When the Stars Align

Once Upon a Christmas

Once in a Blue Moon

A Wish Upon a Star

(BEGUILED)

When Lightning Strikes

Storm of Time

Midnight Storm

When the Moon Falls

Stormborn Angel

(SPELLED)

Time Tempest

The Heart Remembers

A Moment in Time

Moonlight Shadows

HISTORICAL

(TAPESTRY OF BLUE AND GRAY)

Shadows Beneath Magnolia Blooms

Secrets Among Southern Roses

(IT HAPPENED BY ACCIDENT)

Accidentally Alluring

Accidentally Married

(SOUTHERN BELLE CIVIL WAR)

Beyond Enemy Lines

Love Always

Hearts Under Siege

Hearts Under Fire

Away Down South in Dixie

The Reluctant Bride

Stay with Me

Jasmine Kisses

Magnolia Kisses

Gardenia Kisses

(THE QUINNS)

Wait for Me

Take Me Home

Keep Me Safe

FATED MATES

Riley's Mate

Aiden's Mate

Brayden's Mate

STANDALONE SUSPENSE

Lost and Found

All I Want for Christmas

Serenity

Courting Alley Cat

All of the books in each Series are standalone and can be read out of order. However, some books have characters from the previous stories in them.